"Go back

"No. I'm not going anywhere, Charlie, not until you tell me why you're doing this. You spent all the early days flirting with me, coming on to me, gazing at me as if I were, I don't know, a goddess or something. Then we made love, and ever since, you've acted as if you wish you'd never met me."

"Jenny...." He stared at her for a long time, in anguish over her pain. "I'm supposed to be supervising you, Jen. That's why I'm here. To watch you every minute and prevent you from breaking the rules of the quiz show. But how do I enforce the rules if I'm so much in love with you that I can't see straight?"

"Look, Charlie," she whispered, "I don't want to sleep with you in order to compromise you. I just want to because it feels better than anything ever has before. And because I need you, Charlie. I need you to get me through the night."

He drew his breath in sharply, then slowly, reverently, eased the robe off her shoulders....

ABOUT THE AUTHOR

"Unlike Jenny, the heroine of *Ask Me Anything*, I never had much interest in motorcycles," says Margot Dalton. "Not until I got married, that is, and my husband introduced me to the charms of the biking world." Margot's husband, a twenty-year veteran of the RCMP, always owns at least one bike. "And sometimes," he admits, "I have as many as four." Margot and her husband live in British Columbia's beautiful Okanagan Valley, surrounded by fruit trees and motorcycles.

Books by Margot Dalton

HARLEQUIN SUPERROMANCE
401–UNDER PRAIRIE SKIES
425–SAGEBRUSH AND SUNSHINE
431–MAGIC AND MOONBEAMS

Ask Me Anything

MARGOT DALTON

Harlequin Books

TORONTO • NEW YORK • LONDON
AMSTERDAM • PARIS • SYDNEY • HAMBURG
STOCKHOLM • ATHENS • TOKYO • MILAN

Published May 1991

ISBN 0-373-70451-8

ASK ME ANYTHING

PROLOGUE

THE LIMOUSINE GLIDED silently through the deserted city streets, sending up dull sprays of water as it rounded each intersection. The rain fell steadily in a fine, light drizzle, and the clouds hung close to the rooftops, gray and brooding, hiding the mountains and the broad vista of ocean.

The chauffeur, a sturdy man in his middle years, impeccably neat in his navy blue cap and uniform, guided the big car easily through sparse traffic, heading north into the city center. He glanced briefly into the rearview mirror, checking the lane to his left, and caught sight of the lone occupant in the back seat of the car.

He examined her cautiously as she sat gazing out the side window, unaware of his scrutiny. Her face was partly in profile, and she was lovely. She had the pale ivory skin, fine straight nose and full red lips that hinted at some warm, sunny Mediterranean ancestry, possibly Greek or Italian. Her hair was a long, shining, springing mass of midnight black, falling straight down her back, and her face was a pure, sweet oval. She turned to look ahead at the freeway, still oblivious to his gaze upon her, and he was stunned by her beauty.

It wasn't, he thought, just the obvious things—the hair and skin and those lovely sparkling black eyes under level dark brows. There was something else about this girl, something hard to describe. He concentrated on his driving, maneuvering the gleaming black limousine past a taxi double-parked in the driving lane, and cast another quick, surreptitious glance at the woman in the back of his car.

She was very young, just in her early twenties, he estimated, but she had a calm silence in her manner, a sort of quiet self-containment that, in an older person, would probably be referred to as dignity. She wore jeans and a white turtleneck sweater, and a long, heavy black cloth coat. The coat, he had noted earlier with his shrewd, trained eyes, was a good quality fabric, but it was smooth and shiny from years of wear, and a long rip at the corner of one pocket had been carefully mended with neat, tiny stitches.

In her lap she gripped a battered old leather handbag, its straps worn almost through in a couple of places. Her hands were slender and firm, the nails clipped short in a no-nonsense manner and free of polish. She leaned back against the rich, buttery leather of the car interior, closed her eyes and drew in a deep breath.

The chauffeur paused for a traffic light, then eased slowly back out into the driving lane. He stole another glance at the girl in the back seat and was startled to see her wide, brilliant black eyes meeting his gaze directly in the wide mirror.

My God, he thought, *but she's a beautiful girl.*

Strangely, though, it wasn't her beauty that made the strongest impression on him. He'd been driving this car for a long time, and he'd seen many beautiful women, glamorous women, people whose faces were known all over the world.

What struck him about this particular woman was the look in her eyes.

Her expression, as she met his gaze briefly, was a strange combination of courage and terror—a look of gallantry that was almost defiance, coupled with a kind of shy, fearful pleading. Her eyes flickered, and the look was gone, replaced once more with a shuttered stillness. She turned away, and again he saw only her silent, lovely profile, half-hidden by the cascade of dark hair.

The poor kid, he thought. *She's scared to death, but nobody's going to know it, not if she can help it.*

None of this was his business. He just drove the car. He never spoke to his passengers, and he did his best to be a machine, a robot, an invisible man in his dark uniform. Usually it was easy; the occasional inside glimpses he got of the lives of the rich and famous made him glad to be uninvolved and aloof.

But today, for some reason, it was different. He had a crazy urge to turn the car around, head back to the airport, bundle her onto a plane and send her home, back to wherever she'd come from, back where she'd be safe.

He shook his gray head sadly.

You don't stand a chance, kid, he told her silently. *They'll eat you alive out here.*

But he said nothing. It was raining harder now, and he fixed his eyes impassively on the road ahead of him, his broad, rugged face set in firm lines.

The dark-haired girl curled up on the rich leather seat and gazed silently out at the drops of rain that spattered against the windows and trickled slowly down the glass.

CHAPTER ONE

THE FOUR MEN who sat around the gleaming oak table were all well groomed and well dressed, men who exuded the aura of quiet authority that came from money and power. They seemed to belong in this rich, paneled board-room with its thick, plush carpet, its quiet, tasteful ap-pointments of gray and burgundy, its touches of brass and leather and polished wood.

Three of them sat in silence, their eyes fixed on the fourth, a slender, silver-haired man in his fifties, who was speaking.

He concluded his address, looked around at the other three and paused, waiting for a reaction. There was none. He stared down at the leather-covered clipboard in front of him, doodled something absently with a slim gold fountain pen and then looked up.

"We're going to match them," he said. "We'll offer half a million dollars. *If* the woman goes all the way, of course," he added.

One of the men pursed his lips in a slow, soundless whistle, but the room remained so silent that the ticking of the brass wall clock was clearly audible.

"Any objections?" the gray-haired man asked crisply. "Fred?"

A freckled, heavyset man, the one who had emitted the soundless whistle, looked at his superior with cautious, troubled eyes.

"It's a lot of money, Jerry. And our advertising program for the year is way over budget already. Are you sure we can . . . ?"

"It's nothing. *Nothing.*" The other man made an abrupt gesture of dismissal, moving his hand in a quick slash above the table.

The others watched him silently.

"You don't build a company like ours by being cautious," he continued, his voice vibrating with conviction, his eyes almost hypnotic as he stared at the other men. "They all thought we were crazy, everyone in the industry, to dream of challenging Harley-Davidson with another American-built motorcycle, let alone trying to compete with the Japanese producers. They laughed at us. But look at the sales figures for Forbes Motorcycles now. Look at our phenomenal growth. I submit, gentlemen, that it takes courage to do what we've done. And *now* is not the time to start getting cautious."

He looked around, his eyes level and challenging. The room was quiet.

Finally one of the other men cleared his throat. "If we do it the way you want, Jerry, somebody's going to have to go out there."

"I was getting to that." The president of the firm wrote something else on his notepad. "Who shall we send?"

"Well, we can't send a flunky. At this level, for what you want to accomplish for company image, it should be someone senior."

"Exactly. One of the younger executives, I thought."

Fred grinned. "Then it's Charlie," he said. "It's Charlie's turn."

The president looked dismayed. "*Charlie?* Are you sure?"

Fred nodded. "Dave went to Detroit for the Auto Show, and Hugh was in Tokyo just a couple of weeks ago for the introduction of Honda's new line. Charlie's due."

Jerry Forbes frowned thoughtfully, toying with his elegant gold pen. "I don't like sending Charlie," he said finally. "The product supply contracts for the Midwest are up for renewal soon. I'd prefer to have Charlie here."

All the other men nodded in understanding. Charlie was just that kind of man. When something important was going on, people felt more comfortable if he was around.

"Two weeks aren't going to make any difference to the supply contracts," Fred pointed out. "And at the outside, this can't take more than two weeks." He was silent for a moment. "More likely two *days*," he added with a grin. "I give the woman two days, three at the outside. We might as well send Charlie."

The men around the table nodded agreement, and the president made another notation. He looked up at the beefy, freckled man across from him.

"You tell Charlie, would you, please, Fred?" he requested his senior vice president.

"Me?" Fred asked in comical dismay. "Can't somebody else tell him?"

The other man regarded him steadily, and Fred shifted uneasily in his chair. "It's just…see…Charlie isn't going to like this," he explained lamely.

"Tell him, Fred," Forbes said gently, but with an unmistakable steely edge to his voice. "Just go on down there right now and tell him, and I'll have Dolores make his travel arrangements. He'll have to leave on Sunday."

Fred nodded and got to his feet with obvious reluctance. The other two men exchanged amused glances and grinned at each other as their colleague trudged out of the room and started down the wide, carpeted hallway.

Fred wandered slowly along the corridor, brooding about how Charlie was going to take this news. He knew that Charlie wouldn't get mad—he'd never even heard Charlie raise his voice, come to think of it. But still, there was something about him when he didn't like something...

He ran his hand nervously around inside his collar, tugging against the necktie at his throat.

Charlie had a disconcerting way of drawing you into conversations, getting you hanging on every word and then leaving you wondering afterward if maybe he'd just been pulling your leg all along. It always made Fred nervous, and he determined, just this once, to retain control of the conversation.

He turned a corner and paused in front of a heavy oak door, set with a brass plate that read, Charles Mitchell, Director of Product Supply. The door was closed, and a hand-lettered sheet was taped to the nameplate, reading, Don't Knock. Go Away.

Fred ignored the sign, knocked lightly on the door, opened it and peered cautiously inside. "Charlie? Hey, Charlie, you in there?"

"Hi, Fred," a muffled voice said from behind the door. "I see they still haven't taught you to read."

Fred closed the door behind him and looked at Charlie's back. The younger man was wearing gray sweatpants and a black singlet, and he was suspended from a high bar fixed in the archway leading to the lounge and washroom, doing chin-ups. Fred stared at him, startled by the way Charlie looked without a shirt.

Charlie wasn't a big man, maybe even a shade under medium height, and he was compact and quick-moving so that in a suit and tie he looked smaller and slighter than he really was. But now in the thin singlet the heavy cords of muscle in his back and upper arms were knotted and gleaming, and they rippled slowly as he tensed his body and raised himself, straining with effort, to lift his chin over the bar. Fred looked enviously at the taut, youthful body, wondering how old Charlie was.

About thirty, he decided. Charlie had started almost ten years ago, just out of college . . .

"Eight," Charlie muttered, panting. "Nine . . . what do you want, Fred?"

"That's okay, Charlie," the older man said, seating himself in a big leather armchair by the desk. "You go ahead and finish. I'll just wait."

Charlie did another dozen chin-ups while Fred looked around at the office. Papers spilled over the desk and across the computer table, and file folders were stacked on the floor, on shelves, on a worktable behind the desk. An exercise bike stood in one corner, and a set of weights was stacked in another. One wall was covered with shelves filled with tiny, beautifully detailed replicas of motorcycles, and parts of a real motorcycle were scattered on a pad of newspaper covering the floor near the archway. Fred saw a set of handlebars and a pair of front forks, partially dismantled, surrounded by oily rags that sent a faint, greasy odor drifting across the room.

"This place is a real pigpen, Charlie," he complained. "Why don't you get one of the staff to clean up in here?"

"Because," Charlie said, letting himself drop lightly off the bar and turning to face his visitor, "I like it this way. I know where everything is. I can find any file I want in twenty seconds."

He picked up a towel and scrubbed his sweaty face and shoulders, rubbing the towel vigorously through his hair while Fred sat and watched. Charlie had thick, sandy hair which, when he remembered, he kept neatly trimmed. But sometimes, like now, he forgot about it and let it go until it grew over his collar and around his ears in little shining curls. His eyes were a very bright blue in his tanned face, and his square, sculpted features always glinted with some inner amusement, as if he were enjoying a private joke.

"But why," Fred persisted, still gazing around at the cluttered office, "do you need all this junk? What are those bike parts doing in here?"

Charlie seated himself on the exercise bicycle, swinging one sneakered foot, smiling at his colleague. "There's been a lot of customer complaints about that model, about the front suspension and wear in the forks, and the boys in the shop can't find any obvious design flaw to account for it. I figured I'd take a set of forks apart myself and have a look at the whole thing, see if I can find out what's causing it." He was silent for a moment, still looking intently at the other man. "C'mon, Fred," he said finally, "you didn't wander in here to discuss my housekeeping. What's on your mind?"

Fred shifted uneasily in the chair, nervous under that bright blue gaze. He took a deep breath. "We just had a meeting with the Man," he said.

"I heard he was back from Hawaii," Charlie said, leaning over to tug at a shoelace. "Did he get a good tan?"

"I doubt that he was out in the sun at all. I think he was in offices the whole time, doing deals."

Charlie laughed, and Fred went on, encouraged. "Hey, Charlie, what do you know about *Ask Me Anything?*"

Charlie looked up and grinned. "I know that it's a rash statement for *you* to make, Fred."

"No, I mean the TV show."

Charlie shrugged. "I don't know. I never watch television."

Fred was sidetracked briefly by an urgent temptation to ask Charlie what he did do in his free time. Nobody knew, really. Charlie was a hard worker on the job; probably, if the truth were told, the single most valuable man in the company. But he was a bachelor and an intensely private man, and nobody had any real idea of what he did for fun or hobbies. He was cheerful and sociable around the office, but he had an amazing ability to keep the two halves of his life separate. He seldom socialized with his colleagues, and he didn't talk about his private life.

There were all sorts of office rumors, of course—that Charlie bred tropical fish, that he was a keenly competitive downhill skier, that he acted in amateur theatricals, that he was a dedicated fan of the Cubs—but nobody really knew.

Sternly Fred resisted the urge to pry, knowing from past experience that Charlie would just wind up teasing him and, in the end, he wouldn't know any more about the man than he did now.

"This TV program," he said, "is called *Ask Me Anything*. It's a game show. It's the most highly rated show on TV. They run it during supper time, and more people watch it than watch the news."

"You're kidding." Charlie glanced up at him, his eyes dancing with amusement. "Fred, are you going somewhere with all of this? Is there a point here?"

Fred took another deep breath and plunged ahead. "This show is a quiz thing—general knowledge, sort of. The way they run it, they have four contestants who go through a preliminary round of general questions and get points for their answers. Then, whoever gets a certain number of points, gets into the final part of the show."

He glanced up at Charlie, who looked back at him solemnly. "I'm with you, Fred," he said gently. "I grasp it completely so far. Go on."

"Okay. The guys who get to the final, they gotta have specialized knowledge in a specific field, see? They're tested in advance to make sure they're really smart, and they can't even get on the show unless they score really high."

"In what? General knowledge or their specific area?"

"Both. And then the ones in the final, they get just one question in their special field, and if they get it right, they get to come back the next night and try again."

"Fred," Charlie said patiently, "I think I'm still waiting for you to get to the point."

"I'm trying," Fred complained. "This is kind of complicated, Charlie, okay?"

"Okay. So each guy gets asked one question, and if he gets it right—"

"If he gets it right, he gets a thousand dollars."

"Wow," Charlie said dryly. "Big spenders, aren't they?" He picked up a gray sweatshirt from the back of a nearby chair and tugged it over his head.

"The *first* night it's a thousand," Fred said. "And then every night after that they double it. Like, he has a choice, see? He has to gamble. He can take what he's won so far or go for another question, and the questions get harder every night. If he's wrong, he doesn't get anything. Loses everything he's made. If he's right, they double his winnings."

Charlie glanced at the big man, suddenly interested. "For how long?"

"Two weeks. Ten nights."

"Wow!" Charlie said again, genuinely impressed for once. "That means if he goes all the way, he's looking at a shade over half a *million* the last night! All or nothing."

Fred stared. That was the unsettling thing about Charlie. The man was a genius. If you asked almost anybody off the top of their head what a thousand dollars doubled ten times was, they'd probably guess fifty or eighty thousand. But Charlie knew instantly, without pausing, exactly what the total was. It made a man nervous, dealing with somebody like Charlie.

"Yeah," he said, "that's how much it is. Now, Charlie, the hotshot boys down in Advertising, they like to play all the angles. You know that. And they've had a notice out to this program for a long time, letting them know that if somebody ever came along whose special field was motorcycles, then we'd like to know about it and maybe get some play off it."

"A light," Charlie observed, "is beginning to dawn." He fixed Fred once more with that disconcerting blue gaze. "And now somebody's come along whose field is motorcycles. Right, Fred?"

"Right. They let Jerry know last week, called him while he was in Hawaii. They have somebody starting Monday who scored higher than anyone ever has before on the general knowledge tests and who's a world-class expert on bikes. Somebody they figure has a real good shot at going all the way."

"Hey, that's great," Charlie said with enthusiasm. "I wish I could meet this guy."

Fred hesitated, studying his right shoe with close attention. "You're going to, Charlie," he said finally.

"Beg your pardon?"

"The Man wants to get into this, Charlie. He wants to put up a prize, donated by Forbes, to match the quiz show's money if the...if this contestant goes all the way."

Charlie stared, dumbfounded. "He's putting up a *half a million?*"

"It's advertising, Charlie. A spot on that show costs over three thousand dollars a second. And we'll get play on it for two whole weeks. Everybody in the country will be watching. We don't have to pay unless the contestant goes all the way, and if that happens, everybody in the *world* will be talking about it. Jerry's really high on this."

Charlie nodded thoughtfully. "He's right, you know. It's one hell of a promotional idea. And I get to go out and present the check?" he asked. "In L.A.?" he added hopefully.

Fred squirmed nervously in the chair. "Well...not exactly."

Charlie glanced at him, suddenly alert. "What do you mean, *not exactly,* Fred?"

"Well, it's not exactly in L.A. I mean, the show is based there, but this is part of their Canadian tour, and the contestant is from Calgary, I think. They're taping in Vancouver."

"Okay," Charlie said, still looking carefully at his visitor. "So it's in Vancouver. That's a nice place when it isn't raining. And I go out there and present the check if this guy wins the bundle. Right, Fred?"

"Not exactly," Fred said again, wishing fervently he were somewhere far, far away.

Charlie waited, silent and intent.

"See," Fred went on miserably, "Jerry's really concerned about this. It's the biggest promotion we've ever had, and he wants to be absolutely certain, when our name's going to be linked to it, that it doesn't blow up in our faces. Like a scandal or somebody saying afterward that the show's rigged or something, you know?"

"Well, of course. For that kind of money I can understand his concern."

"Yeah, well, all the contestants sign this deposition stating they're being quizzed for their knowledge *as of the beginning of the show*. Like, they're not supposed to study or do research or anything while the contest's running. But apparently the show doesn't monitor it, and everybody just signs this thing and then ignores it. They spend all of their time between shows in the library and stuff, studying their heads off."

"But *our* guy," Charlie said in a flat tone, "isn't going to be allowed to cheat."

"The Man is really firm on this, Charlie. If we're putting up half a mill, then all the rules are going to be followed right to the letter."

"So how do you supervise the guy for two weeks? Move in with him?" Charlie asked sarcastically.

Fred was silent, giving close and careful scrutiny to his left shoe this time.

Charlie stared at his co-worker's bent head. "Another light," he said slowly, "is beginning to dawn. A horrible light. Fred, tell me it isn't true. Tell me I don't have to move in with this poor sap for *two weeks* and frisk him before he goes into the bathroom to make sure he's not sneaking banned materials in there with him."

"Charlie . . ."

"Damn it!"

"Charlie, it won't be so bad. At the very most it's two weeks, and Vancouver's a nice city."

"Two weeks," Charlie said bitterly. He looked at the other man. "Fred, I love motorcycles. I'm a motorcycle man. Bikes are my life. I'm not a baby-sitter or a...a watchdog. How can they do this to me?"

"It's your turn," Fred said lamely. "Dave went to Detroit and—"

"Hughie went to Tokyo, and what's *my* little treat? I get to go to Vancouver and sit around for two weeks making sure some poor guy doesn't peek at the library books!" He smashed his fist against the padded seat of the exercise bike, and stared darkly at the opposite wall.

Fred watched him in cautious silence.

"No way out, hey, Fred? The Man is serious about this?"

"'Fraid so, Charlie. Dolores will make your travel arrangements, and you'll have to leave on Sunday."

"Hell."

"I guess," Fred began, heaving himself to his feet, "that I'd better be—"

"What's his name?" Charlie asked suddenly, vaulting off the bike and starting toward the shower.

"Whose?"

"The quiz show guy. The contestant."

Fred hesitated awkwardly in the doorway.

"His name, Fred," Charlie prompted. "Do you know it?"

"It's...it's Jennifer D'Angelo."

Charlie's mouth dropped open and he stared, stunned. "A woman? This world-class motorcycle expert is a *woman?*"

"I'm afraid she is, Charlie."

"And *I* have to stay with her for two weeks? Why don't they send somebody else? Another woman?"

"Who? One of the secretaries? When there's half a million dollars and the company's name on the line? No way, Charlie. Jerry wants it to be an executive. He wants it to be you." Fred hesitated. "I'm sure they'll be discreet," he said soothingly. "They'll provide you with a suite or something, so you won't be . . ."

Charlie gazed gloomily off into space. "I'm a bachelor, Fred. I've never been married."

"I know that."

"You know why I've never been married?"

"I guess," Fred said cautiously, "you've never met a woman you liked—that way, I mean."

"Hell, no," Charlie said wearily. "I like 'em all. I like every woman I meet, almost. But, Fred, I've *never* met one I liked well enough to stay with day and night for two weeks!"

Fred shifted nervously on his feet, longing to escape. Charlie turned back to look at him again. "Do you know anything about this woman? What kind of woman is a world-class expert on bikes?"

"All I know is that she got record-breaking scores on their preliminary tests—in both general and specialized knowledge." He hesitated and his eyes gleamed suddenly. Now that the hard part was over he was beginning to enjoy Charlie's discomfiture. "But I'll bet," he added wickedly, "that she weighs three hundred pounds, wears leather to bed and has an eagle tattooed on each shoulder."

Fred ducked, laughing, as Charlie flung the wadded towel at the door. Then he turned and hurried off down the hallway.

As CHARLIE HAD EXPECTED, it was raining in Vancouver, a thin, relentless spring rain that chilled him to the bone. He parked his rental car near the television studio and sprinted for the wide entry doors, showing his pass and making his way through a pushing, hysterical mass of people in the lobby, all trying to get rush seats for the show.

The previous evening Charlie had dined with the show's producer, who had been almost beside himself with delight over Forbes's incredible offer. Charlie could still see him over the bouillabaisse and saddle of lamb, counting up the ratings figures, mentally rubbing his hands together in glee.

"Anything you want, pal," he'd said with a confiding grin. "Cars, a suite, entertainment—you just say the word. We're all yours."

Charlie, who disliked being called "pal," particularly by men wearing toupees, had replied politely that what he really wanted was to go back to Chicago.

Now, edging his way through the masses of onlookers in the studio to his reserved seat in the front row, he wanted to go home more than ever. He had yet to lay eyes on Jennifer D'Angelo, but he wasn't looking forward to it.

Fred's description still lingered unpleasantly in his mind. Fred wasn't a particularly imaginative man, but Charlie had the uncomfortable feeling that, in this case, he might have been painfully close to the truth.

Charlie settled into his seat and looked around. The set was typical for this sort of thing—just four stands for the contestants, a little podium for the emcee, and a huge scoreboard, topped by a massive, glittering neon sign reading, *Ask Me Anything*. The show attributed part of its enormous popularity to the fact that it was "almost live." They didn't, like many of the game shows, tape fifteen segments at once and run them for the next three weeks. Each day's show was taped singly in the afternoon and run just a couple of hours later.

The whole thing, from Charlie's observations, was a slick, classy, high-budget operation, but that didn't make him feel any better about his part in it. He watched as the cameramen moved into position with a sort of orderly chaos that was fascinating to observe. Boom mikes descended eerily from upper regions, spotlights raked the set, and a camera rolled slowly across the stage on silent wheels.

Stillness fell, the house lights dimmed and the suspense grew. A loud drumroll sounded from the effects room, and a blinking sign near the stage commanded the audience to applaud. The sign was totally unnecessary. As a side curtain parted and the contestants walked onstage, the din was almost deafening.

Charlie got caught up in the excitement in spite of himself. Leaning tensely forward in his seat, he studied the small group of hopefuls. They moved close together in a tight little knot, as if drawing comfort from one another, and hesitated, seeming reluctant to separate and take their places at their respective stands. There were two women that he could see. One was a comfortable, housewifely type with short graying hair, and Charlie dismissed her immediately. Another woman stood beside a tall bald man with a hawk nose, and Charlie studied her, his spirits falling. She wasn't three hundred, but she'd certainly tip the scales at well over two, and she wore an electric-orange tent dress and lace-up sandals. Her hair was peroxide blond, hanging down her back in a style about twenty years too young for her. Charlie examined her gloomily.

"Damn it to hell," he muttered aloud, and the woman in the seat beside him turned to stare at him with surprised annoyance.

The fourth contestant, who had been hidden behind the hawk-nosed man and the hefty blonde, now moved out and walked quietly across the set to take her place. Charlie watched her with warm, startled admiration.

She was, he thought, absolutely beautiful. She wore a soft, high-necked, long-sleeved knit dress of pale pink. The style was obviously intended to be reserved, but nothing could look *really* demure on a body that fantastic. The soft fabric clung to her long, slender legs, her taut, flat stomach and her high, shapely breasts. Her flowing, rich black hair was brushed back simply from her face and held at her neck with a wide silver clip. She moved with the graceful, self-contained walk of a model or an athlete, ignoring the sudden bursts of wolf whistles and shouts from the audience. She seemed completely composed, but Charlie, studying her intently, saw the delicate flush on the lovely pale oval of her face and the slight trembling of her slender hands as she took her place and turned to face the audience, her head high, her brilliant, dark eyes challenging.

God, what a woman, he thought with admiration that bordered on awe. Scared to death, but still ready to look you right in the eye and dare you to try to get to her.

He was so fascinated by her beauty that it took him a moment to register when the emcee arrived and the contestants' names flashed into view on the front of each stand. He stared, stunned and disbelieving, at the name Jennifer that blazed forth in front of the dark-haired girl.

But that means . . . is this girl . . . can she be . . . ?

Frantically he swiveled to examine the other nameplates. The housewifely type was Sarah, the man was Earl and the big blonde was Amy.

"Well, I'll be damned," Charlie muttered again, and the woman beside him cast him a nervous glance and edged to the other side of her seat.

Charlie was oblivious to her, to everything, in fact, but the gorgeous girl in pink, the loveliest girl he'd ever seen, a girl who was a world-class expert on motorcycles and who was setting out to convert her knowledge into a cool million dollars in cash.

A girl, he remembered suddenly, with whom he was to live day and night around the clock for the next two weeks.

"Oh, *God!*" he moaned, and clapped his hand to his forehead.

The woman in the seat beside him clutched her handbag in shaking fingers, her eyes dark with panic, and looked urgently around for an usher.

CHAPTER TWO

JENNY STOOD TENSELY behind her little stand, already baking in the glare of the spotlights, dismayed by the trembling of her hands. She held them at her sides and clenched them, still staring blindly out at the masses of people crowding the studio auditorium.

Panic rose within her, an urgent, paralyzing terror that numbed her mind. All the months of study, all the thousands of carefully memorized bits of information, seemed to have been wiped completely away. She could hardly remember her own name.

She wanted to turn and run, to flee this bright stage and all those staring, expectant faces, to run out of the building and out of this city and be swallowed up in some kind, vast, empty wilderness. To her horror, tears pricked behind her eyelids, and she knew if she started crying, she'd never be able to stop.

She tried to compose herself by remembering the practice rounds and telling herself that this was really just the same thing, except that now a few people were watching, that was all. They had run through two practice rounds before the audience was admitted, just to give them the feel of the question board and the response buzzers.

But the questions then had been things like "how many months are there in the year?" and "on what day does Christmas fall?" to make sure no answers to possible actual questions were given or implied. They had been fun, the practice rounds, with the contestants teasing and joking with one another and the host.

But this wasn't practice, Jenny realized, taking a deep, shuddering breath. This was the real thing. And everything that mattered to her, everything in the whole world that mattered to all the people she loved, depended on how she conducted herself.

Mama, she thought. Oh, *Mama.*

Her mother's thin, aristocratic face flashed into Jenny's mind. She saw the dark eyes filled with love and understanding, and the sweet features, hollowed and sculpted by suffering, that still conveyed such depths of compassion.

Help me, Mama, Jenny pleaded silently. *I'm doing this for you, Mama. For you, and Papa, and Steve and Sheila and the baby.*

The thought of her family restored a measure of equilibrium. Her heart still thundered in her chest, and her breathing was quick and ragged, but she felt herself beginning to calm down a little as the host strode onto the stage amid another thunderous burst of applause.

His name was Jay Allen and his face was almost as well-known as the President's. People everywhere recognized his clean-cut, handsome features, his smooth blond hair and tall, erect figure. He was suave and smiling, with a kind of easy boyish charm that made him perfect for this job.

He greeted the audience, outlined the rules of the game briefly and then said a few words to each contestant. When it was Jenny's turn, she murmured something almost inaudible about being a bank teller and how her hobbies were reading and hiking.

"And, of course, motorcycles," Jay Allen said. "After all, folks, doesn't this girl just look like your typical motorcycle expert?" He turned to grin at the audience, which laughed appreciatively.

"Yes," Jenny said, a little more firmly, "and motorcycles."

The crowd roared again, and Jenny felt, irrationally, that there was something hostile about their laughter. She felt ridiculous, like a figure of fun. Again she had the urge to turn and stumble off the stage, away from the glare of the spotlights and all these hundreds of sharp, avid eyes.

Blindly she stared out into the auditorium, and her gaze fell by chance on a man sitting in the front row. He was staring at her like everybody else, but he wasn't laughing. He sat tensely, leaning forward a little, his eyes fixed intently on her. He was handsome and athletic-looking, wearing a soft tweed jacket over an open-necked shirt and gray dress slacks. His face was nice, tanned and clean-cut, with an alert, cheerful look, and he seemed to be concentrating every ounce of his attention on Jenny.

It was almost as if he sensed her distress and was sending her waves of encouragement. Like somebody fighting to keep from drowning, she fixed her eyes on the man's face. He apparently realized that she was looking directly down at him, because he gave her a nod and a small thumbs-up sign.

Jenny was too nervous to acknowledge his message, but it helped her enormously, this warmly human gesture coming from the crowd of strangers. She took a deep breath, rested her hand on her response buzzer and turned to face Jay Allen.

The game was planned with painstaking care to give everybody an equal opportunity in the general knowledge round. First, Jay furnished each contestant with a pencil and a blank pad of paper. They could use the paper to do rapid calculations and to make notes and memos for themselves during the commercial breaks. They were allowed, as well, to take these notes away with them after each show, but not, of course, to bring them back the next day. .

The categories in the general knowledge round weren't revealed. The contestants took turns calling a number at random, from one to five, and the number introduced a hidden category. After that, five questions would be asked in the category, and then the next contestant selected a different number, moving them to a new category.

There was no money to be won in the preliminary round, although a number of the questions, indicated by a bell and a flashing light, had prizes attached to them—sets of luggage, camp stoves, small stereo systems. The prizes, though, were of little consequence. What mattered were the points. Each question had a point value assigned to it, and each contestant who accumulated enough points during the initial round advanced into the final part of the show—a question in his field of specialty, and a shot at the really big money.

After her initial panic subsided, Jenny moved easily through the opening round, answering almost automatically. Steve and Sheila had drilled her so intensely for so many months that it seemed there was no question she couldn't answer.

Her main problem, she found, was in adjusting to the pacing of the show and the speedy responses of her competitors. She had to be really fast on the response buzzer, to ring in first, and she was occasionally plagued by hesitation. It was a delicate balance, Jenny found, between confidence and recklessness. On the one hand, if you weren't fast, you lost the chance to respond. But if you were too fast and rang in without actually being confident of the answer, you were apt to get it wrong.

And mistakes, she knew, were costly. With each incorrect response the point value of the question was doubled and then deducted from that contestant's total.

Jenny ran the first two categories, world geography and science trivia, allowing only three responses out of the ten to go to any of the others. But she faltered badly in French cuisine, a category that went entirely to Amy, whose special field was the culinary arts.

Jenny made a note to herself during the first commercial break to devote her study time at the library that evening almost exclusively to food and cooking terms. It was clearly a weak area for her.

She frowned in concentration and jotted rapidly on her pad, making note of other things she'd thought of during the first question round—things she wasn't clear on and wanted to look up later.

Then she rested, rubbing at the back of her neck, which still felt stiff and tense, and frowned down at the pad in front of her. She was thinking about the paper she'd signed that afternoon before beginning the first show.

On it she had certified all the usual things—that she was eligible to be a contestant, that she wasn't related to any of the show's writers or producers and that she agreed to abide by all the rules and regulations. That was all routine, and she'd expected it.

What bothered her was the clearly stipulated rule that "contestants will be quizzed on their general and specific knowledge as of their *initial* appearance on *Ask Me Anything.* During the course of their appearance on the show, contestants will not study, research or otherwise enhance their knowledge of any topic, either related to the general knowledge portion of the show or to their field of specialized knowledge."

They had never, in any of their cramming and planning during the months since she'd received her notice of acceptance, heard anything about this rule. And the other contestants, when she'd asked them about it, had merely laughed.

Provided his or her daily point total in the preliminary round was over a certain minimum, each contestant could risk another specialty question or choose to retire with his or her winnings. Amy was back for her third time, and Earl for his second, while Sarah, like Jenny, was just starting that day.

"Hell, sweetie," Amy had said earlier over coffee in the visitors' lounge, grinning at Jenny and giving one of her huge, booming laughs, "I spent the whole goddamn *weekend* down at the big library on Burrard Street. I woulda taken a sleeping bag down there if they'd let me. And," she added wickedly, "I saw a guy down there about twenty times who looked an awful lot like ol' Earl here, too. You know that?"

Earl grinned, his cheeks creasing cheerfully on both sides of his sharp, jutting nose, and said nothing.

"But," Jenny began in confusion, "this thing we signed. It says we're not supposed to."

"It's just the game everybody plays these days," Amy said comfortably. "It's called Cover Your Flank, honey, and these boys play it better than anybody. If there's ever any complaints from a sponsor or a losing contestant that somebody was cheating, loading up on his subject or wiring himself for sound or being prompted from the audience or using self-hypnosis—whatever crazy thing might happen—then the show's protected. The poor contestant's signed this deposition, so he's the one who gets it in the neck, and the producer, well, he's still lily-white. It's show business, dear."

"But," Jenny persisted, "once you've signed it, how can you ignore it? Aren't you scared that if you win, they'll take all the money away, saying you broke the rules?"

"Hardly." Amy chuckled. "Jennifer, child, they've been running this show for almost four years. Everybody in the world watches it. And everybody who's on it signs that paper and then ignores it, and not a word's ever been said, not even once. I'm going with the odds, babe. I'm studying—every damn second I've got."

Remembering, now, Jenny shook her head with a little troubled frown, still doodling absently on her notepad. *So am I,* she decided. *I'm going with the odds, too. I have to.*

There were tremendous advantages to studying during the course of the show. Each round pointed up weaknesses and gave a clear indication of areas that needed more concentration. It was insanity to obey the rule. If nobody else did, you virtually denied yourself any possibility of winning.

And winning was what mattered. More than anything in the world.

Jenny set her mouth in a firm, determined line, squared her shoulders, took a deep breath and faced Jay Allen as the lights flared and the cameras began to roll for the second half of the preliminary round.

When it was over, Jenny was in the lead by an uncomfortably narrow margin and was more than ever determined to spend every free moment she had buried in reference books. Amy, though she finished in second place, had scored high enough to qualify for a specialty question and return the next day if she chose to, and she was a formidable opponent. Earl and Sarah were both gone, so there would be two new contestants tomorrow.

Jay Allen announced Jenny as the day's winner to the accompaniment of another thunderous drumroll and shouts of approval from the audience. The stage manager signaled, the effects room played the show's cheerful theme song, and a camera lens zoomed in tight on Jenny's face, then slowly faded to the commercial messages.

During the break, the two losing contestants murmured words of congratulations and then departed quietly from the set, leaving Jenny and Amy alone behind their stands. Jenny clenched her hands, her heart hammering so loudly that she was sure it was audible back in the third row, and suffered, wondering how she could ever have been so insane as to think she knew enough about motorcycles to be standing up here in front of all these people, waiting for a question.

Almost involuntarily she let her glance wander to the young man in the front row, who still watched her with a look of lively admiration. When their eyes met, he grinned, a warm, cheerful, boyish smile that reminded her of her brother Steve.

Jenny smiled back, and the audience stirred and murmured, craning their heads to see the person she was smiling at. It was the first time during the entire show that her tense, businesslike concentration had lapsed even for a moment.

But she stiffened and turned her head as the spotlights came up and Jay Allen strode leisurely back onto the stage. He gave Jenny one of his famous smiles, then turned to face the audience.

"You all know how this works," he told them comfortably, "and I'm not going to bore you with the details of..." He went on, amid indulgent laughter, to recite exactly how the show worked, how Jenny and Amy, if they continued to score high enough in the preliminary rounds each day, would be given one question each session in their fields of specialty, with the prize money doubling for each correct answer and the question getting harder. He reminded them of the risks involved—if either woman chose at the end of the day to come back for the next show rather than retiring with her winnings, then she placed herself doubly at risk. She had to win the preliminary round *and* answer her specialty question correctly the next day, or she'd lose everything she'd made.

"But, folks, our new contestant's position is just a *little* different for a couple of reasons. First, she is without doubt the most gorgeous motorcycle expert we've ever had on the show." He turned, on a wave of laughter from the audience, and gave Jenny a quick, private glance of frankly sexual appraisal. Her cheeks flamed with anger and embarrassment, and her vivid dark eyes flashed dangerously.

Seeing her reaction, he gave her a slow, lazy, confident grin that irritated her even more, and then turned back to the audience.

"And secondly," he went on, "this is the first contestant who's ever been offered a generous prize by a sponsor in addition to the quiz show prize, if she should last all the way through her category."

Jenny stared at him, puzzled and confused.

What was he talking about? What sponsor? What prize?

He continued smoothly, reading from a little card in the palm of his right hand. "Maybe you haven't heard a lot about Forbes Motorcycles, folks, but I can guarantee that you're going to learn a whole lot more about this company during the next two weeks. Forbes Motorcycles," he went on, "is an American motorcycle manufacturer, based in Chicago, that's set out to challenge the Japanese giants, and it's doing very well. *Very* well, as you're about to hear. Because, ladies and gentlemen, Forbes is interested in this particular contestant, and they've offered to match the money awarded by *Ask Me Anything* if Jennifer here should go all the way to the top in her category.''

He paused for a moment to let this sink in, then said, ''Folks, they're offering to match our grand prize. On her final night on the show, if Jennifer answers her final question correctly, then *Ask Me Anything* and Forbes Motorcycles will *each* pay Jennifer five hundred and twelve thousand dollars. That will set her total winnings at *over one million dollars!*''

There was a gasp from the audience, and then a rising tide of excited comment, but Jenny was unaware of it. She stared at the suave host, her eyes wide with disbelief, her slender body quivering.

Oh, no, she thought. *This is too much. I could hardly deal with the pressure before. How am I supposed to stand this?*

But she had to. There was no other choice. She was committed now, and there was no turning back.

She waited in an agony of tension while Amy, as the second-place finisher, was given the first specialty question. Amy stood calmly and impassively, her broad face unreadable, staring at Jay Allen, who asked, ''What is the primary ingredient of Peruvian Seviche and how is it prepared?''

Jenny drew her breath in sharply and glanced quickly at Amy, who frowned in concentration.

''The main ingredient is striped bass,'' the big woman said finally. ''It's marinated in lime juice for twelve hours and then garnished with grapefruit and other seasonings.''

''Correct!'' Jay Allen sang out, beaming at Amy. ''That brings your winning total, Amy, to four thousand dollars, and if you choose to come back tomorrow, you'll be going for eight thousand!''

Amy nodded again, smiled placidly for the cameras and left her podium, pausing to give Jenny's arm a comforting squeeze as she walked offstage. Jenny looked after her plump new friend wistfully, squared her shoulders and turned to face the show's host.

"Now then, Jennifer," Jay Allen began, "are you ready for *your* first question in the field of motorcycles?"

"Yes," Jenny said quietly. "I'm ready."

"All right. I have the question here, compiled by our expert research panel. I'll read you the question and you'll have thirty seconds to give your answer. You may use the notepad for calculations if you wish, and I have to insist on total silence from the audience, *please,* while the contestant considers her answer. Jennifer?"

Jenny nodded, waiting tensely.

"What was the make, model and year of the first mass-produced rotary-engine motorcycle?"

Jenny's mind whirled as a spinning kaleidoscope of bikes turned, separated and merged in sparkling patterns inside her head.

Her brain went numb, and she stared out at the audience in blind panic. Instinctively she sought the face of her unknown friend down in the front row and looked at him. His handsome features, formerly so cheerful and open, were dark with indignation. He scowled at Jay Allen, and Jenny could see exactly what he was thinking.

He's furious, she thought. *He thinks it's too hard a question for the first day, and he wants to go up there to the control room and punch the "expert research panel" right in the nose.*

She almost giggled, picturing this. There was something enormously comforting about the thought of his support. She looked at his clean-cut, tanned face, so outraged on her behalf, and she felt warmed and protected.

Her mind settled and relaxed, and facts began to file into position, lining neatly up in front of her. She looked up once more at the question, which was displayed on the huge twelve-foot screen that formed the other wall of the set.

Then she turned to face Jay Allen. "The Suzuki RE 5," she said quietly. "Model year 1975."

"Jennifer D'Angelo, that response is—" he paused for dramatic effect "—absolutely *correct!*"

The audience shouted and applauded, and Jenny collapsed inwardly, almost sick with relief. As the host came over to congratulate her and give some details to the viewing audience about the next day's show, Jenny took one last peek at the young man in the front row.

He was gazing up at her with an expression of awe and amazement and a kind of startled, boyish delight. Jenny laughed aloud at the look on his face, but by that time Jay Allen was shaking her hand, giving it a meaningful extra squeeze, obviously thinking that the glow on her lovely face was just for him.

The theme music started, the audience stirred and began to move, and the closing credits rolled up on the monitors. Jenny freed her hand, murmured something and escaped gratefully backstage, making her way to the visitors' lounge.

There were about a dozen people in the lounge—television technicians, guests and dignitaries, all smoking, talking loudly and sipping coffee. Amy was there, nursing a cup of coffee and taking long, grateful drags on her cigarette. Her big body in its vivid orange dress seemed to fill half the room. She looked up and beamed as Jenny entered, then blew an enthusiastic cloud of smoke into the air. "Way to go, kid! You're one smart cookie, you are."

Jenny smiled. She had only known Amy since lunchtime, but they now shared an experience that most people would never, ever have, and it made her feel as if they'd been friends for years.

"Have some coffee," Amy said. "It's only slightly more ghastly than it was before the show. Whew!" she added, mopping at her damp forehead. "It's always such a *relief* when the goddamn thing's over!"

Jenny got a cup of coffee from the table in the corner and came over to sit across the little table from Amy.

The big blond woman smiled at her. "You're scary, Jenny-girl," she observed cheerfully. "Really scary. I'm going to have to work some to give *you* a run for the money. I can see I'm going to have to hustle down to the library tonight and spend about six hours reviewing my world geography if I'm going to beat you tomorrow."

"Well," Jenny said with an answering grin, "I guess I'll see you there, then. *I'm* going to be down there studying up on international cuisine!"

Amy laughed, and Jenny's face sobered as she thoughtfully stirred sugar into the thick dark, coffee. "They're such...such hard questions, Amy. Aren't you scared? Don't you just want to give up and take your winnings so far and not risk any more?"

"Hell, kid, what's life without risk? This is just a kick, you know. A real blast."

Jenny looked up with troubled eyes at Amy's garish makeup and her kind, shrewd eyes.

"I look at it this way," the other woman went on. "I never had any money when I started. I was flat broke. So I've got nothing to lose really. Besides, just getting on this show is a tremendous boost to anybody. It's incredible the publicity you get. This is my third day, and just because my specialty field is cuisine I've already had two offers to do dining columns for major newspapers."

Jenny stared. "You're kidding. Since *Thursday?*"

"You bet. This is big-time, Jenny. Millions of people watch this show."

"I don't like to think about it," Jenny said with a little shudder. "I like to think it's just like a…a game at a party or something, you know, and pretend the cameras and everything aren't even there."

"Well, you'll find out. As you go on and everybody in the world starts recognizing your face, you'll find them pretty hard to ignore."

"I wish it were all over," Jenny said gloomily. "I wish I were done and I could just go home."

Amy reached out a plump hand, laden with heavy, ornate rings, and patted the girl's slender arm. "Hang in there, kid," she murmured. "You'll make it. Hey," she added brightly, "how does a gorgeous dame like you happen to be an expert on motorcycles, anyhow?"

"I'm not sure," Jenny said, sipping her coffee and smiling back at the big woman. "I guess, partly, it was just like everything else in my life. I was trying to keep up with my brother Steve. I've spent my whole life doing that."

Amy watched her with bright interest, and Jenny paused, looking thoughtfully out the window, and then continued. "Steve was my only playmate when we were little. He was two years older, and we lived on a tiny farm outside Calgary, so we didn't have any other kids to play with, just each other. And Steve wouldn't play with me unless I could pull my own weight, so I turned into a real tomboy."

Jenny laughed, remembering. Amy laughed with her, and Jenny was grateful for the other woman's tact. Amy was obviously making an attempt to help Jenny relax, to get her mind off the next day's show and the fabulous prize offered by Forbes and all that was at stake.

"I learned to pole a raft and catch frogs and hit a ball really well—all that stuff. And when Steve got into motorcycles, it just seemed natural for me to get interested in them, too, so he wouldn't get ahead of me. And then I took an automotive course in high school and found it really interesting. And when Steve and I were about sixteen and eighteen, we bought our first bike, in partnership, and I just fell in love with it."

She smiled, drained her coffee cup with a little grimace and looked up at Amy. "It was so incredibly fascinating. That little motor with all its tiny, beautiful components— a little carburetor and a miniature battery no bigger than a pound of butter—all machined and designed to operate so efficiently. And it was just wonderful when I got my license and learned to ride it out on the highways and the back roads, smelling the trees and the hay meadows, with nothing between me and the world, just total, magic freedom—like riding on a flying carpet."

She paused, her eyes shining with remembered pleasure, gave an embarrassed laugh and went to get another cup of coffee from the urn on a nearby table, taking Amy's cup with her to fill, as well.

"So you were a farm girl?" Amy asked, swiveling in her chair to watch.

"Well...not exactly. It wasn't really a farm—just an acreage. My parents came here from Italy when they were just newly married," Jenny explained over her shoulder, "and my father always worked in the city. He's an audio-visual technician. He sells and services cameras, stereo equipment, that sort of thing."

Amy nodded. "My ex-husband did that," she said. "When he worked at all, the bastard," she added gloomily.

Jenny laughed. "But his job has always been secondary to Papa. His home and family are everything. On this little acreage he and Mama have done their best to create a tiny Italian villa. They keep bees and grow fruit trees and onions and tomatoes and peppers—even grapes. Papa has a grape arbor."

"Grapes?" Amy asked in disbelief. "In *Calgary?*"

"You'd be surprised," Jenny said, coming back to the table with the two brimming cups carefully balanced in her hands. "Some years they freeze, but lots of times he has a really good harvest and makes wonderful white table wine. Papa makes all kinds of wine."

Amy smiled at her and took the cup of coffee from her, ladling generous amounts of sugar and cream into it.

She was such a warm and interested listener that Jenny, who was suffering badly from tension and homesickness, wanted to go on, to tell Amy all about her mother's illness, Steve's wife's pregnancy and the misfortunes that had plagued her family in recent years, all of which had resulted in her being on the game show, trying to win a vast sum of money.

But she decided against confiding in Amy, mainly because it seemed selfish to talk about herself so much and not express any interest in Amy's life.

So, instead, she smiled brightly at the big woman and asked, "How about you, Amy? Where did you grow up and how did you get so smart?"

Amy let loose with her warm, rich laugh. "Kid, I was *born* smart!"

Jenny laughed with her and then looked across at her, startled by the look that had suddenly appeared on Amy's face. The jovial woman was staring at the door, her eyes wide, her brightly painted lips formed into a circle of intense admiration.

"Get this, Jenny-girl," she muttered out of the side of her mouth, still staring at the door. "Get a load of *that* cutie over there in the doorway with the big brass!"

Jenny swiveled in her chair and looked over her shoulder, following Amy's gaze, and then smiled and flushed with pleased surprise. A man was leaning casually in the doorway, scanning the room with intense, searching eyes, and Jenny recognized him instantly as her unknown friend from the front row of the audience. He carried a fine leather briefcase and had a topcoat slung easily over one shoulder, but apart from those details he wasn't at all like the other executive types in the room. There was something about him—a poised, alert look on his tanned face and a contained, athletic grace to his body even as he stood casually in the doorway—that set him apart from other men.

At this distance Jenny could see what she hadn't been able to discern earlier: his eyes were a bright, sapphire-blue and his sandy hair curled slightly over the collar of his crisp white dress shirt.

Jay Allen and Walker Thompson, the show's genial, dapper producer, were with him, and the three men chatted briefly in the doorway, looking over at Amy and Jennifer. Then the two game show executives were gathered in by a noisy group of well-dressed women on the other side of the room while the younger man lingered in the doorway.

"I ask you," Amy muttered again, "is that not a *gorgeous* sight? Look at the man's eyes! And his shoulders! Yummy!"

Jenny smiled in agreement and then turned aside awkwardly as the man straightened, waved a casual refusal to join Jay Allen's glamorous group and started across the room toward Jennifer and Amy.

"So what do you think?" Amy asked in a stage whisper. "Do you think he's succumbed to my fatal charms, or could he, by some fantastic stretch of the imagination, be interested in you instead?"

"Don't, Amy," Jenny whispered urgently, looking at the table with downcast eyes and flaming cheeks. "He'll hear you!"

Amy chuckled, and then the man was beside them, standing at the end of the table, so close that Jenny could smell the fresh, pleasant scent of him . . . of rain and fine tweed, of expensive shaving lotion and clean, healthy male.

"Hi," he said, greeting Amy first and smiling at her. Jenny peeped up, appreciating the way his eyes crinkled and his white teeth flashed in his tanned face as he grinned. "You did a great job," he went on, still addressing Amy. "I was really impressed."

"Thanks," Amy said. "But," she added generously, "I don't stand much of a chance with Jenny here as my competition. She's a killer, this kid. Mind like a steel trap."

The bright blue gaze moved to rest on Jenny, and she shifted awkwardly in her chair. "Not really," she protested. "I just have a good memory, that's all."

The man extended a bronzed hand, and Jenny reached out automatically to shake it. "I'm Charlie Mitchell. From Forbes. I'm here to check out your tattoos."

Jenny stared up at him in confusion, while Amy threw her head back and roared with laughter.

"In that case," the big woman said, "you two will want some privacy. And I have to do a little shopping and then get on down to the library and start hitting the books." She heaved herself to her feet, gathered up her enormous handbag and briefcase and turned to go. "Nice meeting you," she said to Charlie. "See you later, Jenny."

"I'll be down at the library right away," Jenny promised. "I was too nervous to eat before the show, so I'm going to have something now and then start studying. I'll probably see you there around six, okay?"

"Okay," Amy said, and departed, moving out of the room with stately, swaying dignity.

Charlie seated himself at the table, watching Amy's broad orange back as she disappeared. Thoughtfully he toyed with a stir stick discarded near his elbow, then glanced up at Jenny and smiled.

"Would you...like a cup of coffee?" she offered shyly. "There's some in the urn over there, but it's not very good. It's awful, actually."

He shook his head. "No thanks. I'll have some later with a meal." He hesitated. "Nobody at the show told you anything about me?" he asked finally.

"I didn't know a thing about it, the prize, I mean, until Jay Allen announced it during the show. I was just, just so..." Jenny floundered, searching for words to express her emotions.

"I can imagine," Charlie said dryly. "You *do* know something about Forbes Motorcycles, though, don't you?"

"Well, certainly," Jenny said. "Everybody in the bike world knows about Forbes. They're beautiful machines, and it's so nice to see another American manufacturer giving the Japanese a run for their money."

Charlie grinned at her, and she smiled back, more than ever attracted by his humorous, boyish expression and his clean-cut, handsome face.

"As a matter of fact," Jenny went on, encouraged by his warmth, "that's one of the things we plan to do with the money if I win here. My brother Steve and I, we'd like to open a Forbes dealership in Calgary and run it ourselves."

Charlie glanced up in surprise and nodded with thoughtful approval. "It's a good idea. You'd likely do really well. The Canadian market is just starting to take off, and there aren't many franchises open yet. It's a good time to jump in there."

"That's what we thought."

There was a brief, awkward silence. It almost seemed, Jenny thought, that he wanted to tell her something but didn't know how to begin. To help him, she asked, "What do you do with the company exactly?"

"A little of everything. Design, marketing, supply, service—kind of an all-purpose executive."

"Oh," Jenny said, impressed. "But you're so young!"

Charlie laughed and then sobered, avoiding her eyes. "Jennifer..." he began, "May I call you Jennifer?"

"Call me Jenny. Everybody does."

"Good. And I'm Charlie." He hesitated and took a deep breath. "Jenny, I'd better explain to you why I'm here."

She looked at him, puzzled. "I assumed you were just here to announce the prize and to present it if I win."

He gave her a rueful grin. "I wish it were that simple. When I agreed to come out here on this damn assignment, you see, I didn't know you were going to be so—" He caught himself, then continued. "Jenny, this is a big promotion for our company. Massive, in fact. And the president of Forbes is really concerned about it. He wants to make sure everything, absolutely *everything,* is open and aboveboard and according to the rules."

"Well, of course," Jenny said. "But he's safe here, isn't he? I mean, this show has a really good reputation. We checked it out carefully for a long time before I applied to be a contestant."

"Yes, it has a good reputation. But my boss wants to make sure *all* the rules are followed."

Jenny glanced up at him sharply, and her eyes widened. "You mean . . ." she began slowly.

He nodded, meeting her glance with a direct, troubled look. "Right, Jenny. No studying during the course of the show. No library."

Jenny was still staring at him, her eyes dark with horror. "But that's not fair!" she burst out. "Everybody does it! All the rest of them are studying. I won't stand a chance if I don't!"

"Sure you will. I heard you today. You have so much general knowledge that they can hardly stump you on anything."

"But I don't! There are all kinds of categories where I need to—" She hesitated and looked at him again. "How are they going to enforce this? How are you going to know whether I'm studying or not when I'm not here?"

"Because, Jenny," he said softly, "I'm going to be with you."

"With me?" she asked blankly. "That's crazy. How can you be with me every minute of the day and night?"

He met her gaze silently, and she stared at him in stunned silence. "Oh, my God," she said in a flat, toneless voice.

"I've had a meeting with the show executives, and the producer has booked a nice suite for us in the hotel you're staying at," Charlie said calmly. "In fact, he's already had your things moved up there. We'll go out for a terrific dinner now. Then we'll catch a movie or something. And then we'll just head on over there and make sure you get tucked in and have a good sleep so that you're all fresh and rested for tomorrow."

"But I can't!" Jenny said in despair. "Don't you understand? If I don't study, I can't win! I *have* to go to the library!"

"No, you don't, Jenny. You just have to stay calm, relax and enjoy yourself."

"Enjoy myself!" she said bitterly. "Sure, great. I'll bet I can really enjoy myself, knowing that it's costing me and my family half a million dollars."

"Come on," he said calmly, ignoring her anger. He pushed his chair aside, got to his feet and reached politely for her elbow. "Vancouver's famous for its food. Let's go and find something great to eat."

Jenny sat stubbornly at the table, staring at her clenched hands, drowning in helpless misery. Finally she took a deep breath, squared her shoulders and reached for her handbag.

The only thing to do, she decided, was to go along with him and wait for a chance to give him the slip.

She got to her feet, ignoring his outstretched hand, and walked gracefully out of the room in front of him, her head high, her black eyes flashing fire.

CHAPTER THREE

IN THE VESTIBULE outside the visitors' lounge, Charlie held Jenny's coat for her, chatting amiably and ignoring her chilly silence. As they turned to leave, a small figure materialized beside them, exuding enthusiasm.

Charlie introduced the man as Walker Thompson, the producer of *Ask Me Anything,* who gazed up at Jenny with something close to adoration and wrung her hand warmly.

"Isn't she wonderful?" he asked Charlie. "Such stage presence, such composure, such mystery. And those bones!"

Charlie nodded in agreement. "The bones," he agreed gravely, "are especially impressive, I think."

Jenny glared at him, and he gave her a cherubic smile in return.

Almost too angry to speak, Jenny turned to the producer. "Look, Mr. Thompson, I take it you know about this man and the situation I'm in?"

Walker Thompson nodded. "Mr. Mitchell's people have been in constant communication with us. And Mr. Mitchell himself has been most cooperative. *Most* cooperative."

"Oh, I'm sure of it," Jenny said bitterly. "But none of this is fair, Mr. Thompson. How can a requirement be made of me that isn't made of any other contestant?"

"I assume you're referring to the rule against studying during the course of your appearance on the program?"

"Of course I am," Jenny said, indicating Charlie with a wave of her hand. "After all, that's why he's here, isn't it?"

"And you object to his presence, Miss D'Angelo?"

Jenny took a deep breath and tried to keep herself from smacking the little man's plump pink face with her handbag. "Of course I object to it. Why should I have to follow a rule that nobody else does?"

Thompson gazed at her with a sudden steely edge to his expression, and Jenny understood, all at once, what inner qualities had carried this plump, pink, innocent-looking little man to a position of such enormous power in the television world.

"Miss D'Angelo, the rule *does* apply to everybody. All contestants sign the same deposition, and all of them are bound by the same agreement."

"But they don't follow it!" Jenny said. "They all just go ahead and—"

Charlie laid a gentle, warning hand on her arm. But she shook it off impatiently, still staring angrily at the producer.

"I see," Thompson said softly. "They're breaking the rule, are they? All you have to do, then, Miss D'Angelo, is to name any contestants who are breaking any rules of the show, and they'll be immediately disqualified and stripped of all their winnings."

Jenny stared at him in horror, thinking of Amy, warm and generous and full of happiness, already on her way to the library.

"Why should *I* have to report them?" Jenny asked. "Why can't your people monitor it when it's your own rule?"

"Oh, come, Miss D'Angelo. We can hardly budget for the expense of keeping a twenty-four-hour watch on our contestants. Although a sponsor like Forbes, who chooses to do so..." He nodded at Charlie with a bland smile, and Charlie inclined his head politely.

"Any interested sponsor is certainly free to take on the duties of surveillance. For our part, we assume our contestants are responsible adults who will honor their own signed agreement. If they don't, and we're made aware of it, disciplinary action will be taken immediately."

Jenny stared at him in silence, slowly realizing the hopelessness of her position.

He returned her gaze calmly. "To resume, Miss D'Angelo. *Are* you aware of any particular contestant who is violating our rules?"

Jenny hesitated, then looked directly at him, her dark eyes blazing. "If I were, Mr. Thompson," she said quietly, "I certainly wouldn't tell you."

"Very well, then. It's your choice, isn't it?" He paused and then turned to Charlie. "If you require some free time at any point, Mr. Mitchell, I personally would be pleased to spend an evening with Miss D'Angelo, and Jay Allen has asked me to express a similar interest on his behalf."

Jenny flushed with outrage and gave Charlie a glance that was halfway between pleading and fury.

Charlie avoided her eyes and looked solemnly at the pompous little man in front of them. "That's very kind of you both, Mr. Thompson," he murmured. "If Jennifer becomes too unhappy with my constant presence, perhaps we'll take you up on your generous offer."

He smiled amiably, took Jenny's elbow and guided her out of the studio, sprinting across the rain-washed street to their waiting car.

Once in the car, Jenny sat silently in the front seat beside him, staring at the hypnotic sweep of the windshield wipers and trying not to cry with frustration.

Charlie glanced quickly across at her. "I guess it's all a little hard to take, isn't it?" he asked with sympathy.

"I'm an independent person," Jenny responded tonelessly. "I'm used to looking after myself and being in charge of my own life. And all of a sudden I feel like a...an object, I guess. A racehorse or something that can be hauled around, supervised, passed from hand to hand. I just hate it."

"Look," Charlie said, "I was just kidding, you know. I wouldn't really make you spend an evening with one of those stuffed shirts if you didn't want to."

Jenny remained silent and stared out the window at the city streets, dim and sparkly with early-evening lights gleaming on the wet pavement. Charlie cast her one more glance, encountering only her still, distant profile. Finally he turned away and concentrated on his driving, maneuvering the big rental car expertly through the downtown streets and humming along with the radio.

At the hotel they walked in silence through the plush lobby and into the brass-paneled elevator. Charlie pressed the button, and Jenny started involuntarily. "Twenty-eight?" she asked. "We're on the twenty-eighth floor?"

"All the nice suites are higher up," Charlie said comfortably. "Why? Are you afraid of heights?"

"Certainly not," Jenny said with dignity. "I just like to be on the lower floors because...because thirty floors is a long way down if there's a fire or something."

"You are scared," Charlie said with a grin.

"I am not!" she said furiously. "I just happen to believe that if God had meant for me to be thirty floors up in the air, he'd have given me wings, that's all."

Charlie laughed, and the door opened to admit a plump, elegant woman in a silver mink, far too warm for the day, carrying a small white poodle that was beautifully coiffed and wore a plaid ribbon around its neck.

The poodle squirmed restlessly in the grasp of his owner and emitted alarming little choking sounds.

"Higgins just *detests* elevators," the woman confided. "I do hope he isn't going to be sick."

Jenny's face paled, but Charlie eyed the little dog with professional detachment. He leaned over to place two strong brown fingers on Higgins's bony, tufted head and listened intently to the rasping bark. Finally he straightened, his face grave.

"It's the rapid change in air pressure," he told the woman solemnly. "Very traumatic to the semicircular canals in the inner ear. It would be much better for Higgins to use the stairs."

She stared at Charlie in horror. "But it's…we're on the twenty-first floor! That's twelve more flights!"

"Oh, well," Charlie said casually, "it's your decision. Poor Higgins," he added.

Hastily their companion pushed the button to halt the elevator and bundled Higgins out into the hallway, setting him down and grasping his jeweled leash.

"Come, darling," she murmured, "Mummy wouldn't want his itsy little precious ears to suffer now, would she? We'll just use the stairs the rest of the way, won't we, sweetums?"

Charlie and Jenny stood in the doorway of the elevator and watched as the two of them set off down the hall toward the stairs, Higgins trotting gaily, his owner already puffing in her heavy fur.

"Can you believe she actually said that?" Charlie asked finally. "'Itsy little precious ears'? Can you believe that people actually talk that way in real life?"

"You're really awful, you know that?" Jenny murmured, trying hard to maintain a severe expression.

"Using the stairs will be good for her," Charlie said, closing the door and starting the car on its slow upward journey. "She could stand some exercise. Besides, you didn't want Higgins throwing up on your shoes, did you?"

Jenny looked at him curiously. "Did you mean that, about the semicircular canals? I mean, did you know what you were talking about?"

"Of course," Charlie said cheerfully. "You're not the only person in the world with a whole bunch of exotic information, you know."

Jenny was saved from responding by their arrival at their floor. She stepped out into the corridor, looking around curiously at the lavish fittings and appointments. She had thought that the guest hotel patronized by the quiz show was incredibly luxurious and that her previous room on the fifth floor was the nicest she'd ever seen. But up here it was a different world altogether, a rarefied atmosphere of luxury and elegance that took her breath away.

Silently she followed Charlie into their suite and then paused, gazing in awe. Their rooms were beautifully decorated in dusty pastels, with brass accents and subtle abstract paintings. One whole wall of the sitting room was glass, overlooking a dizzying view of the sprawling West Coast city with the ocean beyond.

"That's my room over there," Charlie was saying, "and this one's yours. You should check right away and make sure all your things got moved up here properly and if—"

"What about the bathroom?" Jenny interrupted. "I mean, this is kind of embarrassing, you know? I don't even know you, and we're expected to share a bathroom?"

"Not entirely. There's a half bath in each room, and a full bath to service the suite. So we just need to schedule our shower times so that they don't conflict, that's all. Now, after we come back from jogging—"

"Jogging!" Jenny interrupted. "Who's going jogging?"

"We are, Jenny," he said calmly. "Every morning at six o'clock we're going for a two-mile run."

"Over my dead body."

"Jenny," Charlie said patiently, "you really have to adapt to this situation. You have to face the facts. You and I are going to be spending every minute together for as long as you're on this show, which for your sake, and my company's sake, we hope will be two whole weeks. So we're going to have to adjust to each other's habits. Now, if there's anything you really want to do on a daily basis, we'll do it. But I jog two miles every morning at six o'clock and, as a result, so will you."

Jenny glared at him but said nothing.

"What's the matter? Can't you run? You look reasonably athletic."

"You're damn right I can run!" Jenny exploded. "I'll bet I can run *you* right into the ground! I just don't happen to be insane enough to want to run *anywhere* at six o'clock in the morning, that's all."

"Jenny, Jenny," Charlie said, "it's beautiful outside at six in the morning. A gorgeous time of day and a time that almost everybody misses. You're going to love it. I'm certain you're going to love it."

"The only thing I'm certain of," Jenny said grimly, pausing in the doorway of her own room, "is that I'm growing to hate this situation more with every passing minute."

She went inside, refraining with considerable strength of character from slamming the door. Charlie gazed at the closed door with a bemused expression and then wandered over to look out the window at the broad gray vista of English Bay.

"I THOUGHT you were hungry," Charlie said, glancing across the table at Jenny's plate, still almost untouched.

"So did I," Jenny said briefly. "I guess I was wrong."

Charlie looked at her thoughtfully. He'd made a number of unsuccessful attempts during the course of the meal to draw her out and get her to talk about herself, her family, her home life, her reasons for coming on the show, her fascinating knowledge of motorcycles—anything to draw a spark of warmth and humanity out of her. But she either ignored his questions altogether or answered in unrevealing monosyllables.

He watched her for a moment longer, but she kept her dark head bent and poked at the congealed mass on her plate. "Pity," he said finally, attacking his chocolate mousse with enthusiasm. "It was a great filet. Melted in my mouth."

Jenny looked around the elegant dining room that was tucked into a corner of the main floor of their hotel. Expensive hunting prints glowed in lighted alcoves, while plants, antiques and old calf-bound books were artfully displayed on tiered wooden shelves here and there. Soft classical music rippled discreetly in the background, and tall leather-upholstered booths enclosed quiet couples and foursomes, all of them looking prosperous and comfortable.

Charlie, too, appeared completely at ease in this setting, but Jenny was painfully aware that she had never in her life been in such an elegant and expensive place. The big hand-lettered menus didn't even have prices on them; the unspoken implication was that if you had to ask, you couldn't afford it.

"Who's paying for all this?" she asked abruptly.

"All what?" he asked, looking up at her.

"This." She waved her hand at the plush surroundings. "And the suite, and the car, and everything."

Charlie shrugged. "Credit cards," he said briefly. "I just submit my expenses, and it'll be taken care of. I guess Forbes and the game show will work something out. Anyhow, it's not our concern."

"Must be nice," Jenny said with a touch of bitterness.

"What do you mean?"

"Oh, you know, just to buy what you like and have somebody else look after it. Where I come from," she went on, "you watch your pennies because you know you're going to have to pay the bills yourself. Nobody pays them for you."

He gave her a quick glance. "And you think I don't know what it's like to pay my own way?"

"Look, I really don't care," Jenny said wearily. "I have no desire to hear your life story. Right now I just wish you were far away."

"Jenny, listen . . ."

She pushed her plate of food aside with a quick, impatient gesture and looked up at him. "Charlie, I've been thinking. Couldn't I just refuse the prize from Forbes? I mean, it was never part of our planning, anyhow. Couldn't I just say I wasn't interested and that I was satisfied to take my chances with the quiz show winnings, and then you'd go away and leave me free to do what I want to, what everyone else is doing?"

He shook his head emphatically. "Not a chance, Jenny."

"Why not?"

"Well, think about it. How would it look? When somebody turns down half a million in prize money, there has to be a reason. And when the reason becomes known, how does the show look? If you turned down the prize, they'd just quietly disqualify you and you'd lose everything, anyhow."

She stared down at the table and pleated her heavy linen napkin between her fingers.

Charlie watched her, his open, handsome features troubled and unhappy. "Listen, Jenny, you have to believe I'm really sorry about this. I hate it. For what it's worth, *I* wish I were somewhere far away, too."

"Then why can't you help me?" She gazed across at him with sudden, impassioned pleading, her delicate cheeks flushed, her huge, dark eyes fixed on his. "Why can't you just look the other way a little? How could it possibly hurt anybody if I go to the library and study, when everyone else on the show is doing the same thing and everybody knows they are?"

He studied her lovely, passionate face for a moment in thoughtful silence, and their glances met and held. Charlie looked away first, nodding politely as the waiter filled their coffee cups. "I guess," he said finally, "that you just have to understand something about me, Jenny. I'm a little different from most people. I just can't cheat. I'm pathologically honest."

He laughed awkwardly while Jenny watched him with silent intensity. "Like," he went on, "I could never live with myself if I lied on my tax return, for instance. And if a cashier gave me change for a twenty instead of a ten, I'd walk five miles through a blizzard to give the extra money back to her. And if I use any office supplies for myself, like company stationery or envelopes or anything, I keep track of what I take and put the money back into the petty cash fund."

Jenny stared at him in disbelief.

"This is my job," he went on earnestly. "I said I'd come out here and make sure you follow all the rules. I told my boss I'd do that, and now I regret the promise, but that's still what I have to do. No matter what. It's just . . . it's the way I'm made, Jenny."

She shook her head slowly. "Oh, great," she muttered. "Just great. The only honest man in America, and *I* have to get stuck with him."

Charlie laughed aloud, even though he was uncomfortably aware that she wasn't really joking. "Well," he said with an attempt at heartiness, "I guess we're finished eating. What would you like to do for the evening?"

"I'd like to go to the library," she said promptly, "and study international cuisine."

"Jenny, Jenny," he said sadly, "I can see you're going to be a real problem for me."

She stared back at him in silent rebellion.

He sipped his coffee. "I guess, since you have no preferences and we seem to be joined at the hip, you'll just have to come shopping with me. I wanted to go downtown and look at some of the little shops down there."

"What for?"

"I need a breeding cage and some plant cover for my Siamese bettas."

"Your *what?*"

"My bettas. Siamese fighting fish."

"Oh," Jenny said. "When you talked about a cage, I thought maybe you kept tigers or something."

Charlie grinned cheerfully. "I'm eccentric, but not *that* eccentric."

Jenny looked gloomily around the room. Finally she pulled herself together with a visible effort and glanced over at him. "Why do they need a cage?"

Charlie smiled in pleased surprise. This question was the first attempt at normal conversation she had made during the entire evening and, small progress though it was, he was encouraged by it. "They're tropical fish. Beautiful fish with long, flowing tails and really bright colors. Back home in my apartment I have six of them in separate aquariums, and I want to establish some breeding pairs. But it isn't easy."

"Why not?" Jenny asked, sipping her coffee.

"Well, because they have to *like* each other before they'll mate. That's why you need the cage. If you want a male and female to breed, then you have to put them in the same aquarium but protect one of them in a transparent breeding cage until you see how they're going to get along. Otherwise, if one of them feels threatened or unhappy with the arrangement, it could easily kill the other one."

"I know the feeling," Jenny said dryly, and Charlie laughed so heartily that a couple dining nearby turned and smiled at them. "What happens if they do breed?" she asked after a moment's silence.

He arched one eyebrow and grinned wickedly, his teeth flashing white against his tan.

Jenny blushed. "I mean," she said awkwardly, "do they lay eggs, or bear live young, or what?"

"It's really interesting, actually," he told her. "When they're ready to breed, the male blows a nest of bubbles out of his mouth and the female lays the eggs. He fertilizes them and then catches them one by one in his mouth and carries them up to put them in the nest. And afterward he takes full charge of the nest and of the little fish when they hatch.''

Jenny stared at him, clearly fascinated. Her dark eyes shone, and her creamy oval face glowed with interest as his words created a picture of another world, of a pair of lovely, graceful fish, tending their silken, transparent bubble nest.

''Will there be some of them—what do you call them?''

''Siamese bettas.''

''Will they have some in the shops we're going to? I'd love to see them.''

Charlie looked at her vivid face and her dark, shining eyes, and his body stirred and surged with a sudden, urgent longing.

Watch it, Charlie, he told himself sternly. *You can't afford to feel this way, not right now. You can't develop that kind of feeling for this girl, or it's going to be awfully hard to do your job.*

But when he looked at that beautiful face, and the slender, firm body with its graceful curves, ripe with promise beneath the soft knit dress, he wondered how long he was going to be able to control his reactions.

''I'm sure they'll have some,'' he said, his voice carefully noncommittal. ''Bettas are fairly common aquarium fish.''

Jenny nodded, gathered up her handbag and coat and pushed her chair back.

''Where are you going?'' he asked.

''To the ladies' room,'' she said.

''Wait a minute, okay? I'll just get the bill and then I can—''

"You can what? Come with me?" She sank into the chair again and gave him a level, challenging look. "Don't I even get to go to the bathroom alone, Charlie?"

"Well, of course you do. It's just that..." He shifted uncomfortably in his chair. All the good feeling that had developed between them while they talked about the fish had evaporated now, like mist in the heat, and she was staring at him with open animosity.

"Just *what*, Charlie?"

"I'd like to wait for you in the corridor," he said finally. "Just to make sure you don't duck out the back way or something and try to give me the slip."

She flushed a deep pink, and he wasn't sure if she was genuinely angry at his accusation, or if she really had been planning to make a break for freedom and was embarrassed at having been caught out.

Maybe, he thought grimly, *all her interest in the fish was a put-on just to get my guard down.*

They stared coldly at each other, like boxers in a grudge match.

"You really want to win this game show, don't you?" he asked slowly. "What is it with you, Jenny? Do you just have a burning desire to be rich, or what?"

Jenny hesitated.

She seemed, he thought, to be on the verge of telling him something, and he waited in careful silence. She opened her mouth, was about to speak and then apparently changed her mind. A bleak look crossed her face, followed by an expression of grim resolve.

"Yes," she said wearily, "that's it. You've got me all figured out, Charlie. I just have a burning desire to be rich."

She sat, cold and silent, waiting for him to deal with the bill. Then she got up, shrugged into her coat and moved rapidly across the room to the service corridor, with Charlie close behind her.

CHAPTER FOUR

STEVE D'ANGELO STOOD at the stove in the cramped kitchen of his apartment, stirring a big saucepan filled with simmering, aromatic tomato sauce. He was darkly handsome, with the same fine, classic features as his sister Jennifer. But while Jenny's habitual expression was one of calm composure, Steve's face looked lively and alert, with a cheerful, boyish grin always hovering around the corners of his mouth, and people often mistakenly assumed he was younger than his sister rather than two years older.

He tasted the sauce, paused thoughtfully and then moved over to the fridge to get a clove of garlic, edging past the bulky form of his wife, Sheila, who stood at the counter, crumbling lettuce for a salad.

"God, you take up a lot of room," he complained, giving her an affectionate pat on the bottom as he passed.

She looked up at him, made a face and laughed. Sheila D'Angelo was, in contrast to her black-haired husband, almost strikingly fair, with pale, delicate skin, gentle blue eyes and a long, shining mass of white-blond hair that she tied in a ponytail. She was tiny and fine-boned and enormously pregnant so that, as Steve observed, she seemed to fill half their little kitchen.

He kissed her and went back to the stove to chop the garlic and add it to the sauce. Then he tasted it once more, smiled with satisfaction and prowled restlessly through the dingy little apartment to the living room. He drew the curtain aside and stared down at the street, his face brooding.

Sheila appeared beside him and touched his arm gently. "It'll be all right, Stevie," she murmured. "You'll see."

He shook his head. "I just hate telling her, sweetheart. She's going to be so upset."

"We *have* to tell her," Sheila said practically. "She's going to find out, anyway, and it's better to come from us. Here they are," she added. "I'll go get out the wine."

She hurried awkwardly back to the kitchen, and Steve watched as his father maneuvered the family station wagon into a parking spot at the curb below. Frank D'Angelo stepped out of the car, wrestled a wheelchair from the back and opened it out, then lifted a frail woman from the front seat and settled her in the padded chair.

At the sight of the thin, wasted figure in the wheelchair, hot tears pricked behind Steve's eyelids. He hurried out of the apartment and down the elevator, arriving in the lobby just as his parents entered the building.

"Papa," he said, embracing the broad, sturdy, gray-haired man pushing the chair. Then he looked down at the woman. "Hello, Mama. How are you feeling today?"

He leaned to kiss her, and she patted his cheek lovingly. Her hand, Steve thought, was so thin and light that it felt like a tiny dry leaf against his face. But her voice was still vigorous.

"Stevie," she said. "My boy, this is so nice, to have us over like this. But," she added, her dark eyes full of worry, "isn't it too hard for Sheila?"

He smiled down at her, swallowing the lump in his throat. How like Mama, he thought, to be concerned about everybody else when she thought so seldom about herself....

"It's our pleasure, Mama," he said. "We love having you."

"Well, it's nice to be here. Frank's such an old stick-in-the-mud that we never go anywhere anymore."

Frank D'Angelo patted his wife's shoulder from behind the chair, and she reached up to grasp his hand and hold it tightly. Steve stood beside them, looking down at his mother.

Irena D'Angelo was drawn and emaciated by sickness and suffering, but she was still a lovely woman and a commanding presence. Her dark eyes were enormous and brilliant with intelligence, and her aristocratic, aquiline features were as beautiful as they had ever been, though her face was thin and her skin almost transparent. Her hair was still thick and black, lightly dusted with gray, and she wore it, as she always had, in a regal coronet of braids on the top of her head.

"So what do you think?" she asked her son teasingly as he gazed down at her. "Am I presentable, or do you want to send me back home?"

"Oh, Mama . . ."

"Is Jenny here?" Irena asked as her husband wheeled her into the elevator.

Behind the chair Frank D'Angelo and his son exchanged a quick, troubled glance, and finally Steve replied. "No, Mama. Jenny's not here. Are the apple trees blooming yet? Mr. Schwartz, across the hall, he says . . ."

Skillfully Steve made small talk until they were safely inside his apartment.

"Mama!" Sheila said, coming shyly to embrace her mother-in-law.

"Sheila, sweetheart," Irena said, patting her daughter-in-law's swollen abdomen. "How are you feeling?"

"Just fine, Mama. A little tired, and it's getting hard to walk these days, but it won't be much longer."

Irena caressed Sheila's silken hair as she knelt beside the wheelchair, and smiled down at her. "Such a little thing to be carrying my grandchild. She still looks like she should be in the schoolyard, playing jump rope, doesn't she, Frank?"

Sheila greeted her father-in-law with a fond smile and, with a quick glance of complicity, helped him to settle Irena on the couch, covering her thin body with a warm knitted afghan.

"We'll watch TV for a little while and have our wine," Steve announced casually, "and then we'll eat."

"Oh, no, we won't," Irena said, poised and queenly in her place on the couch.

"Beg your pardon, Mama?"

"We won't watch TV or drink our wine," Irena said calmly. "We won't do anything at all until you tell me, all of you, just what's going on."

"Mama..."

"Don't Mama me!" Irena said with a flash of the old fire in her eyes. "I may be sick, but I'm not stupid, and I know when my family's keeping something from me! Now where's Jenny?"

Sheila came back into the room, carrying a little tray with four crystal wineglasses, and hesitated in the doorway, watching as Steve and his father exchanged another rapid glance.

Irena lay on the couch and waited. "I said," she repeated patiently, "where's Jenny? I've called her apartment a dozen times since the weekend and there's no answer. I got worried and called her at work, and they said she's on holidays. I come here for a family dinner, and she's not here, and you and your father—" she fixed Steve with a relentless stare "—are skulking around and acting like criminals. Now *where is she?*"

Steve cast an anguished glance at his mother, walked across the little room and switched on the television set.

Irena watched him in puzzled silence. "Stevie," she began finally, "I asked you a question. Why are you—?"

"Wait, Mama. Just watch for a while, okay?"

She parted her lips as if to say something more and then stared, speechless with shock, as the opening credits for *Ask Me Anything* rolled up on the screen and the contestants walked onstage.

"But that's..." she began faintly. "How can she be...? Frank, that's Jenny!"

"I know, dear," Frank said gently.

"But how? When?" Irena turned her head frantically on the pillow, looking at the others, and struggled to sit upright. Sheila went and curled up on the floor beside the couch, taking the older woman's thin hand in hers and holding it gently.

"Steve," Irena said in a stronger voice, "I demand that you tell me why Jenny—"

"Please, Mama," Steve said, straining to hear the television. "Please, just watch now and we'll tell you all about it later. Just watch Jenny."

Still distraught, Irena sank back on the pillows and listened as Jay Allen introduced the contestants.

"And finally," he sang out, "our second returning champion and resident motorcycle expert now back for her third day and going for four thousand dollars in prize money—Jennifer D'Angelo!"

The crowd roared its approval, and Irena stared in disbelief. "He said her *third day!* Has Jenny been . . . ?"

"Please, Mama," Sheila murmured anxiously. "Just wait and watch and Steve and Papa will tell you everything when the show's over. That's why we invited you here tonight, so we could tell you about it.''

Irena nodded, finally regaining a little of her composure, and settled with bewildered resignation to watch the bright, strange image of her only daughter trapped in the small television screen.

The opening round proceeded, and Steve watched with taut concentration. When Jenny gave correct responses, he muttered approvingly, and when she missed, he groaned aloud.

There were two other contestants giving her problems, he noticed. One was the fat blonde, now back for her fifth day and getting more accurate with the responses all the time. The other was a new contestant who looked like trouble—a tall, confident man with horn-rimmed glasses who seemed to know everything.

At the first commercial break Jenny was trailing the new contestant and considerably short of the minimum points required to get into the final round. Steve turned aside, wrung with tension, and slammed his fist against the arm of the chair.

"I can't understand it!" he burst out angrily. "The first day she missed all those questions on cuisine, and then yesterday they had a couple of questions on the Korean War—and both topics have come up again today and she's missed them *again!* Why isn't she studying her weak areas? The plan was that she was supposed to make notes as she went along and spend her free time studying the things she..."

He felt his mother's dark eyes upon him, and his voice trailed off into silence.

"Steven," she said quietly, "if this whole thing was your idea, then I want you to know that I may never be able to forgive you."

"Mama..." he began in despair. But then the program started again, and they all riveted their attention once more on the battle raging on the little screen.

Irena's fine, lovely face was drawn with anguish as she watched Jenny. To all outward appearances, the girl looked composed and confident, though very quiet. But Irena could see, with a mother's insight, the tension in the girl's shoulders and the terrified flicker in her eyes from time to time when she was unsure of an answer.

"My baby," she murmured. "My poor darling...this is killing her."

"Don't, Mama," Sheila pleaded softly. "Please don't. Everything's going to be all right."

Only once in the opening round did Jenny show any sign of emotion at all. Near the end, when she still trailed the newcomer by a narrow margin, a different category was introduced.

"Tropical fish!" Jay Allen sang out, and Jenny threw her head up, clearly startled.

"Oh, God!" Steve moaned. "We never studied this. She doesn't know a thing about it."

But, to his amazement, Jenny dominated the category, answering with quick, steady confidence. She pulled into the lead, along with Amy, and Jay Allen read the final question.

"Name a type of tropical fish that is categorized as a 'bubble nest builder.'"

"The Siamese betta," Jenny said firmly. The camera zoomed in on her and caught the small, lopsided grin that she gave, apparently to someone in the audience before the fade to the commercial break.

Steve turned again, limp with relief. "Well, *that's* over for another day. Now she just has to answer the motorcycle question, and we can all go and eat."

"Did you know about this, too, Frank?" Irena asked her husband.

"Yes, Mama," he said quietly. "I knew."

She nodded and turned back to the show, watching as the big blond woman answered her specialty question correctly and departed, amid a solid round of applause. Jenny stood alone on the stage now, her hands clasped on the stand in front of her, waiting as Jay Allen read the final question.

"How many years elapsed," he began solemnly, "between the introduction of the first and second water-cooled production motorcycles?"

"My God, they're hard questions," Steve muttered. "And this is just the third day! I wonder what they'll be like next week."

They all watched tensely as Jenny stared into the distance, her face drawn and tight with concentration.

"Come on, Jen," Steve urged from his chair. He leaned forward, gripping the chair arms so hard that his knuckles were white. "Come *on!*" he shouted at the television set. "You *know* this, Jen!"

The room was silent as Jenny's family watched her lower her head and scribble rapidly on the notepad in front of her. Finally she looked up at the announcer. "Sixty-four years," she said in a low, clear voice.

Steve exhaled a great burst of air and sank back, exhausted.

"Absolutely correct!" Jay Allen shouted. "Now, Jennifer," he went on smoothly, "you already have the answer, and you have the four thousand dollars, and the opportunity to come back tomorrow and double it. Now, just for fun, can you tell our audience the names of those two particular motorcycles?"

Jenny looked at him quietly. "The first was an English bike called the Scott, built in 1908," she said. "And the second was the Suzuki GT 750, produced in 1972."

Jay Allen turned to face the cameras with an eloquent grin. "I ask you, folks," he said. "Is this girl something or is she something?"

Steve grinned and then laughed aloud. "Damn, but she is!" he said. "She's terrific!"

He walked across the room, switched off the set and turned to his mother, sobering instantly when he saw the expression on her face.

"I'm waiting, Steve," she said quietly.

"Mama, it wasn't all my idea," he began defensively. "It was . . . a joint project, you might say."

"He's right," Frank said. "You can't be too hard on Steve. We all worked together on this. For months," he added.

"But *why?*" Irena asked, staring at all of them, her dark eyes enormous. "Why is she doing this? Maybe it's okay for *you* to go on TV, Steve. You always liked showing off. But Jenny, my Jenny, she was always shy. The poor girl is going through hell, and for what?"

"For money," Steve said briefly.

"Since when," Irena began, her eyes flashing, "does this family need money so badly that we throw that girl to the wolves just to see what she can earn for us? Tell me! Since when?"

They were silent. Steve and Sheila looked at each other and then looked away while Frank cleared his throat awkwardly. "Since recently, Mama," he said. "Just recently."

Irena turned to look at her husband, and fear rose in her eyes. "Frank . . ." she began.

"Now, Mama," he said soothingly, "we don't want you getting all upset. That's why we haven't told you any of this. But you have to realize that . . ." He hesitated.

"That things aren't all that good," Steve said. "See, Mama, since you've been using the dialysis machine at home, and Papa's been staying home with you, you've been living on savings . . ."

"Well, obviously," Irena said crisply. "I'm not a complete idiot, Stevie. I'm certainly aware of our own situation, and I don't need you to spell it out for me. But we still have lots. Don't we, Frank? Even if you're not working?"

"We did," he said miserably. "But home dialysis is an expensive business and some of your medical expenses haven't been covered, so I've had to pay them. And then there was the stock market crash. Most of our mutual funds dropped to half their value overnight, it seemed, and since I haven't been working, quite a lot of debts have accumulated."

"A lot?" she asked sharply. "How much is 'a lot,' Frank?"

He met her eyes unhappily. "Almost forty thousand."

She stared, wide-eyed and speechless. "But, Frank . . . most of the bonds are locked in, aren't they? Where did you get that kind of money?"

"I mortgaged the property."

"My house? You mortgaged my house?"

He continued to look at her steadily. "I had to, Irena. The bills had to be paid."

She nodded. "You're right. I'm sorry, darling." She was silent for a moment. "You're not working," she said finally. "How are you making the mortgage payments?"

"We've all been helping," Steve said. "Jen and Sheila and I have all been kicking in enough out of our pay-

checks to make the payments. But it's not enough, Mama.
I mean, you and Papa have to live, and Sheila can't keep
on working much longer, and Jenny and I hardly make
enough to..."

He hesitated, and Irena looked around in terror at her
family. "Will we lose the house?" she whispered.

"Not if we can help it," Frank said grimly.

Irena sat in silence for a moment, frowning with concentration. "Why," she asked finally, "has all of this been
going on without anyone telling me about it?"

The young people looked at Frank, who hesitated awkwardly. "I just couldn't seem to find the right time, Mama.
I wanted to tell you, but then when you had the last attack
and had to go into the hospital, the doctor said not to
worry you about anything."

She nodded, still thoughtful, and then looked up. "It
won't be forever, you know," she said fiercely, still gazing
around at the others. "You know that. All of you do.
There could be a call from the hospital tomorrow that they
have a kidney for me, and then I'd get well and Frank
could go back to work."

"Mama..." Steve began.

"I'm at the top of the list," she said stubbornly. "The
doctor told me last week."

"The list doesn't mean anything!" Steve shouted in despair. "The donor has to match, Mama. It could be
months, or years, before they get a matching donor, no
matter where you are on the list!"

"So," she said finally in a flat, toneless voice, "because of me little Jenny had to go off and make a fortune
for us by selling her soul."

"Oh, Mama," Steve began in exasperation. "She's
hardly selling her soul! She's just answering a few ques-

tions, and she's going to answer a few more, and then she's going to come home with buckets of money."

He was silent, watching his mother's face carefully. "Everybody knows," he went on, "what a fantastic memory Jen's always had. I mean, it's uncanny. Photographic. You know, Mama?"

Irena smiled in spite of herself. "I know. You don't have to tell me about Jenny's memory. The girl's a genius."

"Well," Steve said judiciously, "I don't know if I'd say *that*. She's not even all that bright sometimes. I mean, she still hasn't figured out how to program her VCR, and she's had it for almost a year. But she does have that incredible memory. Once she sees or hears something, she never forgets it. And we've all taken turns for months, coaching her out of almanacs and trivia books and atlases—everything we could think of—to get her ready for the general knowledge round."

"I see," Irena said dryly. "And why motorcycles for her specialty field?"

"Well," Steve said, "partly because she does know a lot about them. You know how she's always coming down to the shop while I work on bikes, asking questions and stuff. Besides," he added, "we figured that the novelty of it—a female motorcycle expert, you know—would give her a better chance of getting picked as a contestant in the first place."

"You've really planned all this carefully, haven't you?" Irena asked slowly.

"Yes, Mama, we really have."

"And what happens next?"

"Well, next, Jenny comes home with a million dollars or so and we pay off all our bills. Then Sheila and I make the down payment on a nice house with a nursery and a big yard for the baby, and Jen and I go into business together in our own bike shop, and you get a new kidney and go with Papa on a nice long trip to Italy. How does that sound?''

Irena stared at her son's dark, animated face. "It sounds," she said quietly, "like an awful lot of pressure on my poor Jenny."

She choked briefly, then stared at the blank television screen while her husband patted her shoulder in silent concern. "Mama..."

Irena shook her head. "My poor Jenny," she whispered again. Tears filled her eyes and trickled slowly down her pale, hollowed cheeks.

JENNY LEFT THE PODIUM amid a round of applause that was even more sustained and deafening than usual. She made her way to the visitors' lounge, where Amy and Charlie were already drinking coffee and chatting sociably. Amy wore one of her customary tent dresses, a sort of mottled green this time that made her look like a giant clump of jungle foliage.

Charlie stood quickly to hold a chair for Jenny as she approached their table and gazed down at her with something close to awe. "God," he muttered, "the 1908 Scott. I'll bet there aren't a dozen people in America who could have answered that question. How do you *know* all this stuff, Jenny?"

"Oh, come on," Jenny said with a little self-deprecating wave of her hand. "How about Amy? How many people do you suppose would know that moussaka with eggplant originated in Bulgaria, not Greece?"

Amy grinned. "So I just happen to like food," she said. "As anyone can see," she added, and Jenny smiled at her.

Charlie got up to fetch a cup of coffee for Jenny, and both women watched as he stood at the little table, judiciously adding exactly the correct amounts of sugar and cream.

"I guess he knows how you like it," Amy observed.

"He should by now," Jenny said wearily. "In the past three days we must have had a hundred cups of coffee together."

Her voice was bleak, and Amy looked curiously at her and then back to Charlie, who was casually dressed in lightweight slacks and an open-necked blue polo shirt that made his eyes sparkle like sapphires in his tanned face.

"And you're *complaining?*" Amy asked in disbelief. "Jenny, I just can't figure you out. Believe me, if it was me..."

Charlie returned to the table, carrying Jenny's cup carefully, and the big woman's voice trailed off.

He looked at her suspiciously. "Talking about me again, were you, Amy?"

"I was just wondering," she said wickedly, "what the Terrible Twins are doing tonight. Taking in another opera? Wind-surfing on Burrard Inlet? Shopping for antique button hooks? Going to a dog show?"

Charlie grinned at the teasing note in her husky voice. "Go on," he said. "Make fun of me just because I happen to have varied tastes and interests. As a matter of fact, Jenny's finding this a very broadening and delightful experience, spending all her time with me. Aren't you, Jenny?"

Jenny made a wry face and sipped her coffee, not deigning to answer.

"And furthermore," Charlie went on cheerfully, "what we're doing tonight is absolutely ordinary, run-of-the-mill, wholesome American entertainment."

"What?" Jenny asked with sudden suspicion. "What are we doing?"

Charlie leaned back in his chair, arms behind his head, shoulder muscles rippling beneath the soft cotton shirt, and casually extended his legs. "We're staying home in our suite," he informed Amy solemnly, "and watching the Cubs game on TV. They're doing great this year, the Cubs are. Just two games back and a terrific pitching staff. If they can come up with a few more..." He paused and turned to Jenny, who was staring at him in horror.

"A *baseball* game?" she asked in disbelief. "I have to sit in that room for four hours, watching a *baseball* game?"

"You've got something against baseball?"

"Just that it's absolutely, without a doubt, the most boring game in the entire world. I mean," Jenny went on, "in my personal opinion, watching paint dry is far more exciting than watching baseball."

"Ah," Charlie said, unperturbed. "It's plain that you've never been taught the finer points of the game, the exquisite subtleties that make baseball a true art form. I'm going to enjoy this chance to introduce you to yet another of life's greatest pleasures."

"Oh, God," Jenny said. "Like the opera?"

"Now, Jenny," Charlie said patiently, "you were really nasty about the opera, but you have to agree that you enjoyed it when you finally allowed yourself to watch with an open mind, didn't you?"

Jenny was silent, morosely sipping her coffee.

"Didn't you?" Charlie urged.

"Well, maybe a little," Jenny agreed reluctantly. "I mean, I've never seen an opera, and I *was* impressed by all that power and passion. But," she added, "it made me so homesick, everybody singing in Italian. The lead baritone sounded exactly like Papa."

Charlie grinned and turned to Amy. "Going great, kid," he told her with enthusiasm. "You're up to sixteen thousand dollars after today."

Amy nodded gloomily in agreement.

"What now?" Charlie asked. "Are you going to take the money and run or gamble another day?"

"Oh, I'll gamble some more, I guess. But it's getting a little scary." Amy looked up at them, her plump features creased in a gallant attempt to smile. "I always figured I never had anything to lose because the money wasn't mine to start with. But when the dollars mount up, and you start thinking what you could do with all that cash, it gets harder, you know?" She paused. "And," she added darkly, "so do the damn questions."

Jenny nodded in bitter agreement and then looked more closely at her friend. "Amy," she asked, "is something wrong?"

"Why?"

"Oh, I don't know. You just seem . . . not like yourself today. A little down or something."

Amy shrugged and doodled small designs on the table with a stir stick while Charlie and Jenny watched her in concern.

"Amy?" Charlie said gently. "Anything we can help with?"

"Hell," Amy said, shaking her plump shoulders and trying to laugh, "it's not something that anybody can help with. Nobody in the world."

By now Jenny's face showed real concern as she looked across the table at the other woman. "What is it, Amy?"

"It's just . . ." Amy hesitated and then tried to laugh. "It's stupid really," she told the two younger people. "I just thought I saw someone in the studio audience today, and it shook me up a little."

"Somebody you know?" Jenny asked.

"Somebody I used to know a million years ago. Somebody from my checkered past that I haven't seen for years."

Jenny and Charlie looked at her with interest, and she shrugged.

"It probably wasn't him, anyhow," Amy went on. "I was probably just imagining it. The house lights are dim, and he was way at the back. Besides," she added, dropping her voice and looking down at the table again, "there was a time for five years or so that I thought every second guy I saw was him, and it never was. I think I was always just trying to imagine him into existence, you know?"

She glanced up, her eyes filled with unhappiness, and the other two looked at her in sympathy.

"Was he...he must have been someone who was important to you, Amy," Jenny said gently.

"Yeah, well, like I said, it was all a million years ago. And I haven't the foggiest notion where the man is or even if he's still alive. And besides, you two aren't interested in the romantic fantasies of this fat old broad."

"Amy," Charlie said, "quit putting yourself down. You're one terrific lady. You're a really impressive person. You know, if Jenny here didn't insist on monopolizing every single minute of my time..."

Jenny snorted with derision, and Charlie gave her a reproving glance.

"We'll all just ignore that unladylike response," he said with dignity. "Now, Amy, as I was saying..."

"Oh-oh," Amy muttered, gazing over Charlie's shoulder. "Here comes trouble, kids."

They turned to see Jay Allen approaching the table, his tall figure graceful and athletic in his beautifully tailored suit, his smooth cap of blond hair gleaming under the harsh overhead lights.

"Greetings, all," he said, flashing them a warm smile. "Congratulations on another successful day, Amy."

Amy nodded curtly and drank a huge gulp of coffee.

"How are you, Mr. Mitchell?"

"I'm fine," Charlie said. "How are you, Mr. Allen?"

"Call me Jay, call me Jay."

Charlie nodded and winked at Amy while the host turned his famous smile on Jenny.

"Jennifer, we are, of course, aware of your—" he paused delicately "—of your somewhat unusual situation. Now, as Walker Thompson may have indicated to you, I'm entirely willing to relieve Mr. Mitchell of his supervisory duties for the evening and allow him some free time. I thought you might like to go out for dinner, possibly take in a few clubs."

Jenny looked at her two grinning companions with a trace of panic while Jay leaned toward them confidingly.

"There are some very interesting places in this town," he murmured, "if a person knows where to go."

"I'm sure of it," Charlie said solemnly. "What do you say, Jenny? I think you should go. Sounds to me like you'd have a lot of fun."

Jenny kicked his ankle under the table and frowned at him, and he returned her look with a bland, innocent smile. Jenny glared at him for a moment longer, and then turned to look up at the other man. "It's very nice of you to offer," she said earnestly, "but I'm afraid I can't, not tonight. The Cubs are playing tonight, you see, and I *never* miss a Cubs game."

Amy choked on her coffee suddenly, Charlie laughed, and Jay Allen nodded, puzzled. "Well, then, perhaps another time."

"Perhaps," Jenny agreed, and the three of them watched soberly as he made his graceful departure, wending his way among tables of admirers.

"What a brazen wench you are, Jennifer D'Angelo," Charlie said with considerable admiration. "Just an absolutely shameless liar."

"Oh, be quiet," Jenny said, "and drink your coffee."

THE DODGERS PULLED their pitcher midway through the fifth inning, and Jenny watched in sympathy as he walked slowly off the field, glove dangling, shoulders slumped in dejection.

"The poor guy," she said to Charlie. "That's just the way I'm going to feel when I finally miss the specialty question one day and have to walk offstage in disgrace."

Charlie gave her an alert glance. She wore snug, faded jeans and a shapeless black Harley-Davidson T-shirt with an eagle on the front, and she was sitting cross-legged on the couch, embroidering with small, careful stitches. The embroidery, in a little wooden frame, was a scene of a farmyard and orchard that he had bought for her the day before when she noticed it in a shop and said it made her homesick.

"What do you mean *when* you miss the question? What kind of confidence is that?"

"Come on, Charlie. It's just a matter of time, and you know it. This kind of memorizing relies on steady input and instant recall, and I'm not allowed to refresh my memory," Jenny said matter-of-factly. "Things are already slipping away from me, and I should be down at the library, reviewing constantly. I'm going to miss one of them any day now if I'm not allowed to study. I can just feel it."

"No, you're not," Charlie said comfortably. "You know more about bikes than anybody I ever met. You're just incredible. You're going to go all the way and win a million dollars, and I get to hand you the check."

Jenny shook her head, and stared gloomily down at her work.

"How did you get to be a motorcycle expert, Jenny?" he asked. "Why won't you ever tell me anything about yourself or your family or how you happen to be here?"

Jenny ignored the question and looked back at the TV screen, where a new pitcher was arriving on the mound and taking off his warm-up jacket. "What happens now?" she asked.

"Now there's a break while he gets as many warm-up pitches, within reason, as he feels he needs, and then the game starts again."

"But..." Jenny stared in horror. "But he's in such a *mess,* Charlie, and it's not even his fault! The other pitcher did it. I mean, the bases are loaded, there's nobody out, they're down by two runs already, and *he* has to deal with it?"

Charlie nodded. "Part of the drama of baseball. All he needs is a pop fly and a double play. Then they're safely out of the inning, and he's a hero."

Jenny watched the thin, tense young relief pitcher begin his warm-up, her face still troubled.

Charlie smiled at her. "Still think this is as boring as watching paint dry?"

Jenny frowned, considering, while Charlie watched her secretly. One of the things he found especially appealing about this girl was the way she thought questions over before answering, biting her full lower lip and knitting her dark, level brows and really applying her attention to whatever you asked her.

"No," she said finally. "Actually, I'd say," she added judiciously, "that it's only as boring as watching paint being *applied*."

Charlie shouted with laughter and then settled back, pressing the mute button on the remote control as an endless array of commercials began to scroll past. "You know what I miss?" he asked.

Jenny set her embroidery aside, got up and prowled restlessly across the room to look out the window, shuddering as she always did at the dizzying height.

"No, Charlie," she said, pulling aside the drape to examine a pair of small birds out on the ledge. "What do you miss?"

"Popcorn," he replied promptly. "At home I always make a big bowl of popcorn when I watch a ball game. It just doesn't seem the same without it."

Jenny turned to look at him.

"Do you think room service would send up popcorn if we called them?" he asked wistfully.

"I doubt it, Charlie. I doubt if anybody down in the kitchen is making popcorn. They're all busy making chateaubriand and baked Alaska."

"Yeah, probably."

"Charlie..." Jenny began, and then hesitated.

"Hmm?"

"Charlie, I could go out and get you some popcorn, and then you wouldn't have to miss any of the ball game," she said earnestly. "There's a theater just a couple of blocks over, and I could run out and buy you a giant container and be back in no time."

Charlie watched her calmly. "Sure, Jenny," he said. "And then you could tell me you had trouble finding the theater and that there was a big lineup at the refreshment stand when you got there, that you had to wait forever, and that that's why you were two hours late getting back. Right?"

Her face flushed, and she turned on him in fury. "You just make me so damn *mad!* You think you're God or something, running the whole world all by yourself, and if you don't watch me every single second of every hour, I'll be—"

"Down at the newsstand," he finished calmly, "gobbling up copies of *Cycle World* just as fast as you can. Admit it, Jenny. Let's be honest with each other."

She stood by the window, her hair tumbled around her face, her eyes blazing, her cheeks pink with anger.

Charlie gazed at her, awed by her beauty. There were, he was beginning to realize, any number of Jennifers, and he had really just seen a few of them. There was the powerful, conditioned athlete who ran with him in the mornings, taking a grim pleasure in setting a pace that sometimes he actually had to struggle to maintain. There was the severe, tailored intellectual who stood with expressionless composure on the quiz show podium each afternoon. And there was this tomboy in jeans and T-shirt who lounged around their suite, chuckling at the comedians on TV and occupying herself incongruously with exquisite, meticulous needlework.

A few times Charlie had seen glimpses of another Jenny, a childlike, soaring, joyous spirit, delighting innocently in a carousel or a street musician or a bag of peanuts, fresh-roasted and fragrant and purchased from a vendor's stand.

This Jenny enchanted him and made him want to pursue her, but she always vanished, lost almost at once in the rebellion she felt over her entrapment and her resentment of Charlie's presence.

Sometimes, in spite of his best efforts at self-discipline, he found himself fantasizing yet another Jennifer, a woman, warm with passion and melting with love, her rich, curved body opening to him, her dark eyes glowing with desire. This image was enough to take his breath away and set his heart hammering painfully in his chest.

He looked at her now, drew his thoughts firmly under control and changed the subject. "What did you think about Amy and her mystery man, Jenny? Do you think somebody from her past has really turned up? Do you smell romance in the air?"

"I hope not," Jenny said flatly. "I hope Amy's too smart to get involved with somebody, if he *has* turned up, who's obviously caused her nothing but pain in the past." She hesitated, still framed by the huge, lighted expanse of window, awash with a rich sunset glow, and looked sharply over at him. "What's the matter? Why are you staring at me?"

"Because you're beautiful, Jenny," he said softly. "You're the most beautiful woman I've ever seen."

She drew back as if she'd been struck, turned pale and then whirled on her heel and walked out of the room. "I'm going to have a bath," she said over her shoulder, "and go to bed. Six o'clock comes awfully early, I find."

"Okay," Charlie said. "You want me to wake you?"

"No thanks," she said coldly. "I'll set my alarm."

"Good night, Jenny. Sleep well."

She didn't answer, and Charlie sat, his handsome face silent and distant, all the laughter stilled, gazing thoughtfully at the closed door of her room.

CHAPTER FIVE

THE NEXT MORNING Irena D'Angelo sat on the back deck of her country home, lifting her thin face to the sunlight and smiling as she watched a butterfly hovering over the raspberry plants along the fence.

"Everything is so green this year," she said to Frank, who sat beside her, sipping his morning coffee. "We've had so much rain. The garden should be just lovely."

She looked wistfully down at her hands, veined and gnarled with work. She had toiled so happily beside Frank in their garden and orchard for so many years. She had been tireless, vibrant, full of energy, building their home and raising their children. Then, with terrifying suddenness, the disease had struck, taking first one kidney and then the other, so that now she was reduced to this invalid state, dependent on regular dialysis to keep her alive, barely able to walk a few steps on her own.

Frank saw the shadow that crossed her face, and sighed. After thirty years of marriage, he knew exactly what she was thinking, but he said nothing. What, after all, was there to say?

The phone rang, and he heaved himself from his chair and went to pick up the outdoor extension they had installed because Irena preferred to spend almost all of her time out here on the deck, shaded by Frank's grape arbor, looking at the garden and flowers.

"Hello?" he said while Irena returned to watching the butterfly, now joined by another one that fluttered in the air nearby, doing a graceful aerial ballet.

She was barely aware of the conversation, only that Frank seemed to be doing a great deal of listening and very little talking. At last he hung up the receiver and stood stock-still, gazing at nothing.

"Sweet Mother of God," he muttered in Italian.

"Speak English, Frank," Irena reminded him automatically. They had resolved long ago to speak English even while alone together. They loved this rich, spacious country that had been so good to them and their children, and they wanted in every way to be part of it.

All at once something about his actions and posture caught her attention, and she turned to him in alarm. "Frank?" she said. "Frank what is it?"

Still he clutched the edge of the patio table and didn't answer.

"Frank! Tell me! What is it? Is it one of the children? Is it Sheila? The baby? Frank!"

Slowly he shook his head. "No, Mama," he said in English this time, but heavily accented, as his voice always was under the stress of strong emotion. "Not the children."

She stared at him, comprehension slowly dawning. "It's time," she whispered.

"Yes, Irena. It's time."

She trembled, gripping the arms of her wheelchair. "Frank, who was it?"

"Irena, don't..."

"Tell me, Frank. Who was it?"

"A boy, Irena. A young man killed during the night in a motorcycle accident. His parents chose to donate his organs."

"Oh, Frank..." Her face was as white as chalk, her fine, dark eyes tortured with suffering. "Frank, just a boy. Think of his poor mother."

"Irena," he said with sudden decision, "we have no time to think of that now. Later we think about the boy's mother. Now we think about you."

"When will it be, Frank? When do we go?"

"Now, dear. We pack this minute. They'll prep you when you get there and operate as soon as they can."

Still she gazed at him, unable to move. "Frank, I always thought that when this moment came it would be the happiest of my life. And now," she said, "I can't feel anything. I'm just numb."

"Numb is good," he said, trying to smile. "Numb is much better than panic-stricken. I'll pack a few things for you," he added, "and call the children."

He started into the house while Irena watched him. Suddenly she gathered herself together. "Frank!"

"Yes, Mama?"

"You can tell Steve and Sheila, Frank. But I don't want Jenny to know."

He stared at her, appalled. "Irena, this is major surgery. Of course I have to tell Jenny. We can't keep something like this from her."

Irena shook her head stubbornly. "No," she said. "Jenny has so much pressure on her right now. And I know how weak I am. I mean, it's going to be all right, Frank. I have faith in that, but all sorts of things could go wrong at first, and Jenny would be so worried that she couldn't concentrate on what she has to do. I don't want her to know until it's all over and I'm getting better."

Frank D'Angelo stared at his wife in an agony of indecision. "It doesn't seem right," he muttered, "not to tell her."

Irena returned his gaze with quiet determination and shook her head.

"But, Mama," he argued, "I thought you hated her being there. I thought you wanted her to come home."

"No, Frank. I do hate the idea of her being there, but I also know how determined she is, and how much she hates to fail at anything. I don't think she should be there. It was your idea, all of you, to send her. But now she's there, give her a chance to make a success of it, Frank. Otherwise it'll haunt her forever." Still he hesitated while Irena stared at him fiercely. "Frank," she said in slow, measured tones, her eyes blazing, "Jenny is not to know this!"

"All right, Mama. All right. I won't tell Jenny."

He vanished inside the house, and Irena sat and stared out at the sun-washed garden, her face taut with emotion. Finally, with a great effort, she composed her features and folded her thin hands gently in her lap, waiting for her husband to return.

LATER THAT SAME DAY Jenny left the set of *Ask Me Anything* after successfully answering her specialty question once more and augmenting her winning total to eight thousand dollars.

Sixteen thousand tomorrow, she thought, and thirty-two on Monday.

Her mouth tightened involuntarily. At first the dollar amounts had seemed so small that it really was just a game. But she was beginning to understand what Amy meant about the pressure that accumulated as the total mounted. Next Wednesday, for instance, if she survived that long and was awarded a specialty question, she would either lose sixty-four thousand dollars or increase her winning total to a hundred and twenty-eight thousand.

She shivered and quickened her steps. The urge to drop out, she realized, was going to become more and more difficult to resist. The longing just to be finished with this, to take her winnings and not risk any more, not live all the time with the terror of losing what she'd won and the gnawing frustration of not being able to study and review while all the facts that she had so carefully memorized were beginning, slowly but relentlessly, to slip away from her, that feeling got worse every day.

Wearily she made her way to the lounge and entered the room that seemed by now so familiar that she might have been coming here every day for half her life. She walked quietly across the crowded room, graceful and elegant in a trim charcoal suit with white pinstripes that set off her dark eyes and delicate complexion.

Conversations stilled and heads turned to follow her progress, but she was unaware of the effect her appearance had. She was conscious only of the table at the far side of the room where Charlie and Amy sat. They had been joined by Eric Morris, a new contestant and the first one since Jenny's arrival to win enough points to advance to the bonus round along with Amy and Jenny. His specialty was classical music, and Jenny felt a quick rush of sympathy for him, thinking of the horribly difficult questions he would have to answer.

Eric was a small, thin, gentle young man with colorless, watery eyes, a pale complexion and prominent front teeth that gave him an unfortunate resemblance to the rabbits Steve and Jenny had once kept behind the shed at home. He was painfully shy and onstage found it almost impossible to speak above a whisper, although his general knowledge was indeed impressive.

Just now, though, he seemed more at ease. Seating herself at the table with them, Jenny soon realized this was due to Charlie, who had taken the nervous young man in hand and drawn him into a deep, involved conversation about the life and work of Franz Liszt, a topic clearly so engrossing to Eric that he forgot to be terrified by his surroundings.

Charlie had a knack for doing this, Jenny thought. He seemed to have an uncanny ability, no matter who he encountered, to search out that person's deepest interest and then enlarge upon it with so much charm and intelligence that his companion was soon perfectly at ease. It was a gift, Jenny realized, and also an indication of the man's own kindness and concern for others.

Charlie, she thought gloomily, accepting the cup of coffee he offered and acknowledging it with an automatic smile, was actually a very nice man.

If I didn't hate him so much because of what he's doing to me, she thought sadly, *I'd probably really like him.*

"The passion in the third movement, for instance, is extraordinary," Eric was saying while Charlie nodded thoughtfully. "Don't you feel . . . ?"

Jenny smiled across the table at Amy, who was smoking moodily and gazing into the distance.

"Another day, another thirty-two thousand dollars. Congratulations, Amy."

"Sure," Amy said absently. "Same to you." She looked up at Jenny, drew herself together and tried to smile. "Sorry," she said. "My mind is a million miles away."

"I noticed," Jenny said.

"Well, listening to these two longhairs over here—" she indicated Charlie and Eric, still deep in conversation "—talking about dead guys who wrote dull music is enough to bore anybody into a stupor."

Jenny chuckled.

"Say, Jenny," Amy asked suddenly, "are you going home this weekend?"

"Not unless I miss my question tomorrow," Jenny said with a grin.

"No, I mean it. Are you and the baby-sitter just going to sit around all weekend, glaring at each other, or what?"

"Amy, I can't afford to go home when I've only got a few days left here, anyway. It costs a lot for a plane ticket to Calgary. A lot," she amended, "if you're employed as a bank teller and have a grand total of six hundred dollars in savings."

Amy stared at her. "You mean, you didn't know that they'd cover it?"

"Who'd cover what?"

"The quiz show. This damn thing we're involved with."

"Are you saying, Amy," Jenny asked slowly, "that they'd pay for my plane ticket if I wanted to go home for the weekend?"

"Well, sure. I live here in the city, so it doesn't apply to me. But you remember Earl, who was here your first day?"

Jenny nodded.

"Well, he won on Friday, so he got to come back on Monday, and he was from somewhere out east, Manitoba or some god-awful place, and they told him on Friday that if he wanted to fly home for the weekend, they'd cover it."

Jenny sipped her coffee in thoughtful silence.

"Of course," Amy added with a wicked grin, "Earl declined, because he wanted to stay here and study all weekend without distractions. But since *you're* morally opposed to studying, anyhow . . ."

Jenny made a bitter face at her companion, who chuckled and nudged Charlie beside her. "Hey, Charlie! Don't you think that's a great idea?"

"Hmm?" Charlie turned toward them. Eric, in his un-alloyed delight at having found such an attentive compan-ion, was now branching out into more exotic musical fields.

"You take, for instance, campanology or the Grego-rian chants," Eric said. "They're both prime examples, I think."

"Hey, Jenny," Charlie said, "there's one for you. Campanology. What does that mean?"

Charlie, who was enchanted by Jenny's encyclopedic knowledge and photographic memory, never missed an opportunity to test her mental stores, often firing ques-tions at her randomly, just for the fun of hearing her an-swers.

He gazed over at her now with bright interest, and Jenny looked back at him thoughtfully. His blue eyes sparkled in his alert, tanned face, and beside the pallid, fragile Eric, he looked athletic and muscular. He still needed a hair-cut, but he hadn't bothered to get one, primarily, she sus-pected, out of concern for her, because she would have been forced to wait for an hour in the barbershop under his watchful eye. But, Jenny mused, the little shining golden curls around his ears and along the nape of his neck ac-tually suited him somehow.

Realizing they were all waiting for her to say some-thing, she pulled herself together hastily. "Pardon?" she asked. "I was daydreaming."

"Campanology, Jen," Charlie repeated, "what is it?"

She stared at him, frowning in concentration, her dark, level brows drawn together as she ran through whatever mysterious storage and retrieval mechanism was em-ployed by her remarkable brain.

"I think," she said finally, "that it has something to do with bells. The study of bells and bell ringing, that sort of thing."

"My God," Eric breathed, gazing at her in awe. "That's right!"

Charlie beamed, as proud as if he had personally invented Jenny and set her in motion. "Amazing, isn't it?" he asked the others. "And to think that this brain, ladies and gentlemen, is supplied to a woman who lacks the directional skills to find her way back from the bathroom unaided."

"Charlie, it was a really *big* mall," Jenny protested. "And besides, it all looked the same, with those silly little planters and benches down every aisle."

"What's this?" Amy asked.

Charlie grinned. "I sent her to the washroom this morning at the mall just before we came over here and told her where to meet me when she was done, and the lady genius came out, took a couple of wrong turns and got totally disoriented. I finally found her wandering like a little lost girl among the salami and knackwurst in the deli section."

"Maybe she was just trying to give you the slip again," Amy pointed out while Jenny ignored them with silent dignity and concentrated on her coffee cup.

Charlie shook his head. "Not this time. She was really panicking when I found her, afraid she was going to be late and miss the show. I think," he added with a reminiscent smile, "that it's the only time the woman's ever actually been *glad* to see me."

Eric was following this conversation, clearly puzzled by what he was learning about the relationship between Jenny and Charlie.

"I thought," he ventured, "that you two were, I mean," he went on, flushing, "you're staying together at the hotel, aren't you? I assumed you were, you know."

"No, Eric," Jenny said quietly. "I mean, we *are* staying together, but we certainly aren't ... you know. Not a chance."

"Oh," he said, more puzzled than ever.

"Charlie," Amy said, "I was trying to tell you that the show will spring for the tickets if Jenny wants to go home for the weekend."

Charlie raised his eyebrows. "Really, Amy?" He turned to Jenny with enthusiasm. "You hear that, Jenny? We get to go to Calgary on the weekend, and you can see your family. She's homesick all the time," he said to the others.

Jenny was staring at him in horror. "You don't mean, you can't *possibly* mean that if I go home, you're going to insist on coming with me!"

"Well, of course I am. Come on, Jenny, what do you think? Is there any less chance of your being exposed to relevant literature at home with all your own books around you? How could I not come?"

She glared at him in fury. "Well," she said finally, "I'm certainly not going home if I have to take you with me. I'll just call them tonight instead and find out how everybody is."

"Haven't you even called home yet, Jenny?" Amy asked.

Jenny shook her head. "My mother's not very well, and she's not even supposed to know I'm here, so I've been afraid to call home. Besides, I knew that talking to my family would just upset me and hurt my concentration. But I'm getting so worried," she added, her lovely face drawn with concern. "I keep having this feeling that something's happened, something terrible."

"I think we should go," Charlie said with sudden decision, catching the bleak tone in her voice. "Let me talk to one of the girls up in the office about getting some tickets."

"Charlie," Jenny told him, "I *can't* go. Not if you're going to insist on coming along. Apart from the fact that I haven't the slightest desire to take you home with me, you have to realize that my brother Steve would kill you if he knew what you're doing to me."

By now poor Eric was totally at sea, gazing from one face to another with a sort of mystified fascination.

"I'll explain it all to you later, dear," Amy told him, reaching across the table to pat his hand. "It's absolutely hilarious," she added cheerfully. "The funniest thing I ever heard in my life."

"Thanks a lot, Amy," Jenny said. "Do *you* want him for a while? I'm generous. I'll share."

Amy was about to reply when one of the studio errand boys materialized at her side and handed her a folded note. "Mrs. Wecker?" he asked.

Amy looked up at him, suddenly tense.

"This is for you. A man in the audience said to give it to you."

Amy reached out a trembling hand and took the note. The others watched as she stared down at it, her face pale, all the laughter and teasing gone.

"Oh, my God," she whispered. "My God..."

"Amy," Jenny began, "what is it?"

But Amy was oblivious to all of them. Her hands still shaking, she unfolded the note and read the brief message. Her companions at the table waited as her broad, expressive face registered a whole gamut of emotions: shock, horror, joy, excitement, alarm, fear.

But by the time she had read the note a couple of times and smoothed it carefully with her hands, she had her face under control again. She looked up at her friends as calm and deadpan as ever. "Well, this is certainly interesting. A voice from my past, you might say."

"What is it, Amy?" Jenny asked gently, sensing the undercurrents of emotion that still surged beneath the other woman's casual exterior.

"See for yourself."

Amy passed the note over to Jenny, who looked anxiously at her friend for a moment and then down at the page while Charlie came around the table to read over her shoulder.

"Amy," the note began in a strong, dashing masculine hand, "I don't know if you've ever forgiven me, and God knows you have no reason to, but if you want to see me again, let me know by wearing your orange dress on the show tomorrow night. I'll be in the studio audience."

The note was signed simply "Sam."

Jenny looked across at Amy. "Who is he, Amy?"

"Nobody," Amy said promptly, but there was a sudden soft glow on her face that belied her words. "Just somebody I used to be married to a long time ago," she added casually.

She heaved herself to her feet and began to gather up her belongings. "Well, I'd better get going. Eric, do you want to share a cab down to the library?"

Eric accepted this offer with alacrity and then turned hesitantly to Jenny. "Don't you ... aren't you coming to the library with us? To study for tomorrow?"

Jenny was silent, her face as cold and pale as sculptured marble.

"Sorry, Eric," Charlie answered for her. "Jenny's busy tonight. We're going roller skating," he added, dropping his hand casually onto her shoulder. "Jenny loves roller skating. She's really excited about it."

"Oh," Eric said hesitantly, "I...I see. I guess." He backed away, his Adam's apple bobbing, and smiled shyly at them. Then he turned to plunge awkwardly off behind Amy, who was swaying out of the room in stately dignity, her face deeply preoccupied.

"Wow," Charlie said, turning to look down at Jenny. "What do you think of that? Somebody she used to be *married* to, she said."

Jenny stirred her coffee and sipped it thoughtfully. Charlie's hand still rested on her shoulder, and she was painfully conscious of the contact. He almost never touched her unless they were crossing a street or getting into a car, and the feeling of his hand on her shoulder was disturbing: warm and exciting somehow so that her heart seemed to beat faster.

"I don't know what to think," she said, still concerned by the intensity of her body's reaction to his touch. "And neither does she, I'd guess. Did you see her face, Charlie? Half excited, half terrified like a high school girl on her first date."

He nodded and straddled a chair next to Jenny, leaning his chin on his folded arms and gazing at her intently. "Yeah, well, I guess we'll just have to see what happens, won't we? But," he added, "I'd hate to see Amy get hurt, you know? I only met her a few days ago, but she's one of my favorite people. I think she's just terrific."

"I know what you mean."

They were both silent for a moment, thinking about Amy with her generous spirit, her ribald comments and her warm, rich laughter, and the sudden expression of terror and joy on her face when she read that brief note.

"Charlie?"

"Hmm?"

"Charlie, I *hate* roller skating."

CHARLIE FLUNG HIMSELF down into the armchair in their suite, extended his legs and let his head fall back, exhaling with pleasure. "Lord, but that was fun. Wasn't that fun, Jen?" he called over his shoulder.

Jenny looked up from the doorway to her bedroom, where she was bending and flexing her legs to ease the stiffness from them. "Yes," she said in surprise. "It *was* fun. The last time I went roller skating," she added, "was with a bunch of other twelve-year-old girls at somebody's birthday party. I had no idea it could be so—" she paused, searching for the right word "—so *civilized*."

She went to the phone, dialed and waited, her pale face drawn with tension, while Charlie watched her from the chair.

"No answer?" he asked as she hung up slowly.

"No, but that was my brother's place. His wife works in the radio room at the police station downtown, and she often has evening shifts. And when she does, Steve is just as likely to stay late at the shop, tinkering with some motorcycle that's been brought in for servicing."

"I think I'm going to like Steve," Charlie said.

"Well," Jenny said, giving him a level glance, "Steve sure isn't going to like *you* if he ever finds out what you're doing here. We spent a lot of time preparing for this, Charlie, and planning our strategies, and you've really messed it all up."

He was silent, watching her as she stood by the phone, thinking deeply.

"I'm going to call my parents," she said finally. "It's Thursday now, and I've been here almost a week. I'm sure they haven't been able to keep it from Mama this long, so I might as well call and let her know I'm all right.''

Charlie nodded agreement and watched while she dialed again. After letting the phone ring for a long time, she hung up and turned to him, her eyes wide with fear. "Charlie, they don't answer! There's nobody home!"

"Is that so unusual? People do go out sometimes, Jen."

"Not my parents. Mama is . . . she's really sick, Charlie. You don't know. She must be in the hospital again, and the doctor's been concerned for months that if she got an infection or something . . ."

Her voice was low and frantic, and her hands twisted the telephone cord nervously. Charlie got up and came over to her, putting his hands on her shoulders and drawing her close to him. "Jenny," he murmured. "Jenny, listen to me."

She struggled briefly against the firm grip of his hands and then gave up and relaxed, allowing herself to be drawn into the comforting circle of his arms.

"What's wrong with your mother, Jenny?"

"She has kidney disease. She's lost both kidneys now, and she's on dialysis, just waiting for a donor so that she can have a transplant. She's so weak. Oh, Charlie . . ."

Her voice broke, and she burrowed against his broad chest. Charlie held her gently, marveling at the slender, rounded delicacy of her body, and gazed over her head at the opposite wall.

"And that's why you're here, trying to win all this money?" he asked. "Because of your family? Because of all the medical problems and expenses?"

She nodded against his chest, and he tightened his arms around her.

"Oh, Jenny . . ."

They were silent for a moment.

"Look, Jenny," he said finally. "Your family knows where you are, right? They know the name of the hotel?"

She nodded again.

"Okay. Then you know that if there was a serious problem, they'd have notified you. You *know* that, Jenny. So quit worrying, all right? Tomorrow I'll contact the game show office first thing in the morning and get us two tickets for an evening flight. We'll leave right after the show."

"All right. Thanks, Charlie."

He patted her back comfortingly. As if suddenly aware of where she was, she drew away from him hastily, turned aside and started toward her room.

"Jenny?"

"Yes?"

"You're not going to lie awake all night worrying, are you? Because you need your rest, you know. Those specialty questions are getting harder all the time, and you've got to have your wits about you."

"No, I won't worry all night." She looked up at him, a little color beginning to come back to her cheeks. "You're right. If this was anything serious, they would have called. Mama's probably just in for tests. She has to do that sometimes—have her blood levels monitored—and Papa always stays late at the hospital with her at night so she can fall asleep. But," she added, "it'll still be nice to go home and see them for myself. I feel as if I've been gone a year."

"Good girl." He smiled at her. "Have a bath and get some sleep. I won't make you run tomorrow morning because we won't have time."

"Why?" she asked, pausing in the doorway to her room. "What are we doing in the morning?"

"We're going shopping," he said promptly. "I want to buy you a new dress."

"Like hell," she said immediately. "You're not buying me any clothes, Charlie. No way."

"We'll put it on the expense account," he said, unruffled by her sharpness. "Your audience deserves it, Jenny. I want to see you in something really fantastic. You always wear those drab executive-type things or washed-out pastels, as if you're trying to hide your looks. Not," he added, "that looks like yours can ever really be hidden."

She looked up at him, flushing, her eyes sparkling dangerously. "I didn't realize you were so critical of my wardrobe. What do *you* want me to wear?"

"Something plain and tailored," he said promptly, "but fitted and in a really vivid color that looks terrific on television. Red or royal blue or something to show off that fabulous Latin coloring."

Jenny stood with one hand on the doorknob, regarding him steadily.

"Charlie," she said finally, "you know what you're like? You're like a kid with a new toy. You act as if I'm some kind of animated, wind-up Barbie doll or something with a fabulous computer program in its head, and you can just dress it up, show it off, get it to do memory tricks." She hesitated.

He looked at her. Her black hair was loose, curling in small tendrils around her vivid face and tumbling in a glorious cascade down her back. Her dark eyes glowed, her curving lips were red and she was still flushed from the pleasant exertion of their evening of roller skating.

He swallowed suddenly and began to speak, but his voice wouldn't obey him.

"Tell me," she went on, "what are you going to do next week when I'm gone and you don't have your new toy anymore?"

"I don't know, Jenny," he said softly, meeting her eyes with a direct, searching gaze. "I honestly don't know."

She returned his look briefly and then turned aside. "Just kidding, Charlie. I'm certain," she said over her shoulder as she entered her room, "that you have lots of other toys to occupy you. You don't need me."

She vanished, closing the door behind her. Charlie wandered over and sank into the armchair again, lifting one leg over the padded arm and swinging his foot, his normally cheerful face intent and brooding.

EARLY IN THE AFTERNOON they arrived on the set of *Ask Me Anything,* entering through the staff doors into the atmosphere of barely controlled mayhem that preceded every show. Charlie excused himself and headed for the upstairs office while Jenny leaned against a camera dolly and looked around curiously.

She always wondered how a show so orderly and dignified in its presentation could emerge from such wild confusion. People raced everywhere but to no apparent purpose. Key grips, lighting men, audience prompts, contestant coaches, script girls and sound technicians scurried around, shouting and snarling at one another while the makeup people did last-minute work on Jay Allen, and tried, usually vainly, to get the contestants to submit to their ministrations.

It was absolute chaos, hopeless and insoluble, and yet when the theme sounded and the opening credits rolled up, the show was miraculously smooth and flawless.

Jenny wandered backstage to the visitors' lounge. Eric was already there, sitting at their usual table with a cup of cold coffee, reading an encyclopedia hidden behind a newspaper, and biting his nails. Amy, Jenny noticed with concern, hadn't arrived yet. Charlie came up, waved the two airplane tickets at her and helped her off with her coat, hanging it away on the rack beside the door.

Jenny stood, painfully self-conscious all at once, smoothing the fabric of her new dress over her hips. Dozens of garments had been shown to them, a vast and bewildering array of styles and colors. The dress that Charlie had finally selected was a vivid crimson with a plain jewel neckline, a wide belt and a trim, fitted skirt, shorter than she usually wore. It was real silk, incredibly soft and rich to the touch, and Jenny knew it looked wonderful. She was also uncomfortably aware that this one dress had cost almost as much as her entire wardrobe, but Charlie had entered it on the credit card as casually as if it had been a chocolate bar.

"Wow!" Dorothy, the show's harried assistant producer, paused on her way past with a bundle of scripts and gave Jenny a frank, admiring glance. "Now *that's* more like it! That dress alone will jump our ratings by ten points. Buy some more of 'em, Jenny. Bill 'em to us. You're hot stuff."

She hurried off. Jenny turned to Charlie, her face taut with embarrassment.

"Charlie," she whispered urgently, "I hate this! I hate being 'hot stuff.'"

"You can't help it, Jen," he said soothingly, taking her arm and guiding her into the lounge. "You were born that way. Besides," he said, with a grin, "she's not referring to your morals. She's just speaking of your photogenic quality."

"But I still don't like it."

"Shh. Don't fret about it. *Enjoy* being gorgeous, for God's sake. Here's Amy," he added.

Jenny fell silent, and they seated themselves at the table with Eric, watching tensely as Amy set her carryall aside and prepared to remove her bulky raincoat.

Jenny looked at her friend and felt a sharp stab of disappointment. Amy wasn't wearing orange. She was in her old green tent dress, and her expression was cold, bleak and withdrawn.

CHAPTER SIX

THE CONTESTANTS straggled out onto the stage to begin their practice rounds, a procedure that by now was merely a dull routine for Amy and Jenny. In fact, Amy normally entertained all of them during the practice round with her witty and outrageous responses to the simple test questions. Today, however, she was silent and preoccupied, barely participating at all.

Eric, Charlie noticed with a grin, seemed unable to relax even at this level and took the practice round as seriously as he did the real show. He leaned tensely on his podium, hand poised over the response buzzer, ringing in frantically to answer questions like "who had a little lamb?" and "how many days are there in June?"

With each correct response he exhaled an exhausted, triumphant breath, beamed at Amy and Jenny and bounced on his heels, waiting for the next question. The new contestant was a young trial lawyer whose specialty was American antiques, and who seemed, Charlie thought, too preoccupied with Jenny's appearance to concentrate very hard on anything else.

Pull yourself together, pal, Charlie admonished him silently. *Go for the cash, because, believe me, the girl isn't interested.*

He was called away to the telephone and ran lightly up the stairs, taking them two at a time, to answer the phone in Walker Thompson's office. The producer, Charlie saw with relief, was out, so he was spared the considerable irritation of having to speak with him.

"Charlie?" a voice said at the other end of the line. "Hey, Charlie, is that you?"

Charlie sighed. "Yes, Fred, it's me."

Any telephone conversation he ever had with Fred, anywhere in the world, invariably began with those same six words.

"What's the matter, Fred?" he asked. "Is there some problem with the Midwest contracts?"

"No, Charlie, no problem. We've set them over till you get back. The boss asked me to call and tell you to come home. Your flight's booked for tomorrow afternoon, and Dave will be flying into Vancouver in the morning to take over for you."

Charlie gripped the receiver and gazed blankly at a lurid abstract painting above Walker Thompson's desk. "What?" he asked finally. "What did you say, Fred?"

"I said," Fred began patiently, "that you can come home and—"

"Okay, okay," Charlie interrupted hastily. "I got that, Fred. I just wondered why the boss decided this, that's all."

"Well, Charlie, he knew how upset you were about having to go out there for two whole weeks during the busy season, and Dave's volunteered to take over for you, so the Man figured you'd just be happy as hell to get out of there and—"

"Hang on, Fred. Wait just a minute and let me try to get this straight. You say Dave *volunteered* to come out here? Why would he do that? He spent about an hour laughing when he heard *I* had to come. Why did he change his mind all of a sudden?"

"Hell, man, are you crazy?" Fred's voice sounded a little indignant, as it always did when he harbored a suspicion that Charlie was making fun of him. "Why do you think he changed his mind?"

Charlie drew a deep breath. "I don't know, Fred," he said carefully. "Suppose you tell me."

"Because he's *seen* her, Charlie. We all have."

"Seen who?" Charlie asked blankly.

"Jennifer, Charlie. The quiz show girl. The bike expert. God, what a doll! And Dave figures it isn't fair that you should get to..."

Charlie was silent as Fred's voice droned on. He realized with sudden amazement that they would, of course, have seen Jennifer in Chicago. Everybody on the continent would be watching her, from Juneau to Jacksonville. All at once he felt an overwhelming surge of protective sympathy for her and a consciousness of the tremendous pressure she was under.

"How did she get to know so much about bikes?" Fred was asking. "Is she on the level, or is someone in the audience feeding her the answers?"

There was a brief silence on the line.

"I guess not," Fred said in answer to his own question. "That's why you're there, right, Charlie? To make sure she isn't cheating?"

"Yes, Fred, that's why I'm here."

"Anyhow, she's really incredible. All the guys here are just nuts about her, Charlie. And she's such a gorgeous, sexy babe, isn't she, Charlie?"

"No, Fred," Charlie said sharply. "She isn't a babe. She's a person."

"Oh," Fred said, and was silent for a moment. Charlie wondered if Fred was capable of making such a fine distinction.

"What's she like, Charlie? I mean, really?"

"Really," Charlie said, "she's just a person with an incredible memory who misses her mother and gets lost in the mall and likes to collect penguins. She's nice, Fred. That's all. She's just really nice."

There was another silence on the other end as Fred struggled to align this image of Jennifer with the lovely, brilliant, desirable woman he saw on his TV screen each day.

"And," Charlie went on, "you can tell them to cancel that flight. They sent me out here, and I'm not leaving till the whole thing's over. I mean it, Fred."

"But Dave's really excited about—"

"Dave can go to hell!" Charlie exploded. Damn it, he thought, the man wore trendy clothes, had a blow-dried coiffure and bragged endlessly about his sexual exploits. The idea of Dave moving into the hotel suite with Jenny filled Charlie with a hot, searing anger that he was afraid to analyze.

"I mean it, Fred," he went on in a more controlled voice. "Tell Dave to stay where he is. I'm finishing this job myself."

"Okay, Charlie. What should I tell the Man?"

"Just what I said. And, Fred . . . ?"

"Yeah?"

"Talk to Hughie, if he's not too busy, and get him to look up the facts and figures on the Canadian franchise picture and fax them out here to me early next week if he can. Okay?"

"Why, Charlie? You thinking you might like to stay up there with the Eskimos?"

"Just do it, Fred, okay?" Charlie said wearily.

"Sure, Charlie. Whatever you say."

Charlie hung up and clattered back down the stairs to take his seat in the studio audience just as the house lights dimmed and the opening theme sounded.

SOMETHING WAS different today, Jenny thought. During the first commercial break, she relaxed her hand on the response buzzer and glanced around, feeling troubled. Maybe it was Amy's listless, detached attitude or Eric's terrible nervousness or the way the new contestant kept staring at her legs and her body in the tailored red silk dress.

At least *he* wouldn't be back on Monday, she knew. He was far too limited in the general knowledge categories to make it through to a specialty question.

But, as the show progressed, she was beginning to be afraid that Amy, as well, wasn't going to make it. At this point Amy was risking over thirty thousand dollars, and going for more than sixty thousand, but she didn't really seem to care. She often rang in late or not at all, and she was only saved, in the end, by a category on French cuisine that she could have dominated in her sleep.

The new contestant left the stage at the end of the preliminary round while the other three waited nervously through the commercial break for their specialty questions. This was usually the point where Amy joked and clowned, cracking them up so that they could barely get their faces sober again in time for the cameras to roll. But today Amy stood silent and unhappy, her head high, trying not to look out at the studio audience.

In her dignity and her obvious pain the big woman seemed, Jenny thought, almost beautiful, despite her bulk and her garish accessories. There was something noble about Amy today, something that made her look striking and impressive.

But she seems so terribly unhappy, Jenny mused, *I wish she'd look over at me and grin, just once, and say something awful the way she usually does.*

In contrast to Amy's grim detachment, Eric was so nervous that it was painful to be near him. He kept rocking on his heels, cracking his knuckles, clearing his throat and casting Jenny desperate glances of appeal.

She gave him a reassuring smile and touched his arm, feeling a wrench of sympathy when she realized how his body was quivering.

Predictably, when his question came, it sounded brutally difficult to Jenny, almost impossible.

"Give the name and the originator of the system of musical composition," Jay Allen said, "that gives the composer a total of forty-eight alternatives for any given tone row."

Eric gazed at the suave host in a blind panic and looked exactly like a rabbit caught in the glare of a car's headlights.

There was a long, long silence, broken only by an awkward cough from somewhere deep in the audience.

"Eric?" Jay Allen urged.

"The...the dodecaphonic," Eric whispered. "Pioneered by Schönberg in the 1920s."

"Correct!" the host said, and Eric sagged against his podium, almost faint with relief.

Jenny gave him a quick smile and a little pat of congratulation and watched fondly as he stumbled offstage. Then she waited tensely for Amy's question, which sounded, to her despairing ears, equally impossible.

"For a total of *sixty-four thousand dollars* in the category of international cuisine, Amy, can you describe for us the composition of Himmel und Erde?"

"It's a German dish," Amy said tonelessly. "Meaning, literally, Heaven and Earth. It's made up of fried black pudding, apple sauce, mashed potatoes and—" she hesitated briefly, frowning in concentration "—onions."

Even Jay Allen was impressed. He gave a small, impromptu leap of genuine excitement that made Jenny like him a little better, but his response was swallowed up in the massive roar of the crowd, with whom Amy was a great favorite. She seemed oblivious to it all and continued to keep her eyes carefully averted from the studio audience as she made her way, impassive and unsmiling, off the set.

Jenny watched her disappear with a worried glance and then gathered herself together and turned to face the host, composed and beautiful in her vivid crimson dress.

"Now," he said with the special, significant smile that he reserved only for Jenny, "we come to the question you've all been waiting for. Jennifer D'Angelo has now won a total of eight thousand dollars in her specialty field of motorcycles, and a correct answer today will double her winning total to sixteen thousand. But next Friday, ladies and gentlemen, Jennifer's cash total, if she continues to advance, will be over a *million dollars!*" He paused while Jenny looked at him steadily. "Are you ready for your question, Jennifer?"

"Yes," she said quietly, "I am."

"What," he asked, reading from his card, "according to the manufacturer's specifications, was the dry weight of the 1985 Honda Rebel?"

Jenny stared at him, appalled. The question was ridiculously difficult, almost as picky as asking a baseball expert how a certain batter had performed in the fifth inning of a regular season ball game four or five years ago.

The dry weight . . . the dry weight . . . Her mind whirled.

She glanced down at Charlie, who gazed back at her with outraged sympathy.

He doesn't know, either, Jenny thought. *He lives and breathes motorcycles and he couldn't answer this question.*

She closed her eyes in panic and remembered Steve grilling her mercilessly with specification sheets, mountains of them, one for every bike ever manufactured.

"Just study them, Jen. Commit them all to memory. You have no way of knowing what they're going to ask. Memorize them all, and then, if you get a spec question, don't concentrate, just let your mind wander and go with your first hunch."

"One hundred and thirty-six kilograms," she said suddenly.

Jay Allen stared at her but said nothing.

"That's, I think it's just a shade under three hundred pounds," Jenny told him with a note of desperation creeping into her voice.

"Jennifer," he said after another long pause, "that's...*correct!* You now have sixteen thousand dollars, and *we'll* see *you* on Monday!"

The abrupt easing of tension made her feel almost sick to her stomach. She turned away blindly after the credits rolled up and the lights dimmed, then wandered unsteadily backstage in the direction of the lounge.

THE OTHERS, except for the young lawyer who had already departed, were all assembled there, looking somewhat the worse for wear. Eric sipped moodily at his coffee, Amy stared off into space, and Charlie gazed with reverent concern at Jenny as she approached.

"Jenny, Jenny," he murmured, leaping to his feet to hold out a chair for her, "have I ever mentioned that you're incredible? Have I told you lately how wonderful you are? The *dry weight* of a six-year-old bike! God!''

He hugged her warmly as she came up beside him. At his unexpected touch Jenny's heart began to pound and her cheeks flamed. For a moment she could feel the iron firmness of his muscular body and the strength of his arms. She could smell the elusive, spicy fragrance of his after-shave. Suddenly her body felt weak and hollow, aching with an inexplicable longing. But she pushed the feelings resolutely aside, drew away from him and sat down, hiding her trembling hands in her lap.

Eric, who looked as subdued as a squashed bug, glanced up at the others with mute appeal. ''Where do they find the sadists who make up these specialty questions?'' he asked plaintively.

''They keep them in a tiny room with no windows and a million reference books, feed them nothing but stale potato chips, make them listen to heavy metal music around the clock and flog them twice a day,'' Charlie said cheerfully. ''It tends to make them a little nasty.''

Eric nodded gloomily. ''I'm scared,'' he announced. ''I want to quit.''

''Oh, Eric,'' Jenny began. ''You've got to...''

But her voice trailed off, and all of them watched in tense silence as the studio boy approached Amy with another folded note.

''Oh, geez,'' Amy muttered under her breath. ''Not again. Please, please, not again.''

She held her breath and opened the note. Slowly a flush mounted on her cheeks and, after a long moment, she looked up at her friends with tears shining in her eyes and a wry smile tugging at the corners of her mouth.

"What a man," she murmured. "What an absolutely, incredibly presumptuous, outrageous, awful little..." Her voice trailed off.

Jenny took the note from Amy's plump, outstretched hand, smoothed it and held it for Charlie to read beside her.

"Okay, Amy," it said in the same bold handwriting, "you always were hard to get, girl. One more chance. If you don't wear the orange dress on Monday, I swear I'll go away and never bother you again." As before, the name at the bottom was just "Sam."

Charlie grinned and looked over at Amy. "Well, you've got to admire the guy's style. I like it. Not pushy but real persistent."

Amy stared at him coldly. "You said it, pal. And just about fifteen years too late."

Eric excused himself, too nervous to sit still any longer, and left to spend a lonely weekend immersed in reference books at the downtown library.

His companions watched him go, exchanged eloquent glances and refilled their coffee cups. Then Jenny turned to Amy. "Tell us about Sam, Amy," she said softly.

"He was my husband," Amy said briefly. "I married him when I was in my second year of college. He was 'in sales.' Sam's always been 'in sales,'" she added with a ghost of a smile. "He's one of those guys who always has a deal going, one that's going to make him rich any day now. But somehow it never quite works out, you know?"

They nodded and waited.

"I was just twenty when we got married, and things were so tight that I had to quit college and get a job—just for a while, Sam said, till he 'got on his feet.' That was another favorite expression of his. So I was waitressing at a terrible little greasy spoon, working twelve-hour shifts, waiting for Sam to get on his feet, and he was promising, promising, all the time."

She hesitated, gazing far back into her mind, her plump face drawn and distant with memories.

"God, how I loved that man," she said softly. "I've never experienced it before or since, that kind of absolute, helpless, overwhelming adoration. Just thinking about it, after all these years, can send shivers down my spine. You know?" she asked Jenny.

Charlie's face grew suddenly taut, and he gave Jenny a sharp sidelong glance, waiting for her response with intense interest, but she didn't notice his reaction. She shook her head. "Not really, Amy. I've never felt that way myself, but I can imagine."

Charlie settled back into his chair, looking strangely relieved, and Amy went on with her story. "Well, I don't have to imagine. I can remember like it was yesterday. And one day, after five years, he went out in the evening to pick up a bottle of wine for us to have with our salad and never came home. Just like that. Dropped off the face of the earth. I never saw him again and never heard a word from him until I saw that note yesterday."

Jenny and Charlie both stared at her, astounded.

"Wow," Charlie said finally with a low whistle of amazement. "I thought things like that just happened in the movies, Amy."

"So did I," she said bitterly. "But believe me, when it happens to you, it's real enough. No explanation, no reason, no way of knowing if he's alive or dead, and just missing him, missing him all the time till you feel like you're going to be ripped apart inside." Her voice broke, and Jenny gripped her hand and held it firmly, leaning over to pat her friend's broad back.

"What are you going to do, Amy?" she asked. "Are you going to see him?"

"Why should I?" Amy asked harshly. "You know why he's here, don't you? You can figure out why he's turned up right now?"

"Because," Charlie said reasonably, "he probably lost track of you, spent years looking for you and then saw you on TV and realized this was his chance to make contact again."

"Spent years looking for me!" Amy repeated bitterly. "*I* spent two years living in that flea-trap we were renting, just in case he decided to come back, so he could find me. And finally it dawned on me that he wasn't coming back, so I moved out and started trying to put my life back together. And believe me, it hasn't been easy."

Jenny looked at her with concern. "So why do *you* think he's turned up just now, Amy?"

"Hell, kid, it's as plain as the nose on your face. I'm into the big bucks, right? Over a hundred thou on Monday if I go that far. Sammy always liked the big bucks," she added grimly.

"Maybe it isn't that at all, Amy. Maybe it's like Charlie says. Maybe he had a change of heart after a few years and tried to find you and couldn't, and this has been his first chance."

Hope and despair struggled on Amy's face. She looked at the two young people in an agony of indecision. "You both think I should see him? You really think so?"

Jenny glanced over at Charlie, who shook his head. "We can't advise you, Amy," he said. "It's your life, and your business. Just don't decide anything too quickly, that's all. Keep your options open. You've got the weekend to think it over, and by Monday you should have a clearer idea of what you want."

Amy nodded thoughtfully, looking a little cheered, and grinned at them with a shadow of her old impudence. "Look, you two, no fighting on the plane, okay? People are starting to recognize Jenny everywhere she goes, and we don't want the show's image to be tarnished, do we now?"

"I'm not worried about the plane trip," Charlie said cheerfully. "It's *landing* that I'm worried about."

"And why's that, Charlie?" Amy asked.

"Because I'm afraid that Jenny's Sicilian relatives are all going to be waiting at the airport to give me a pair of cement boots and teach me to swim."

"We're not Sicilian," Jenny said with dignity. "But it's not such a bad idea, you know," she added thoughtfully. "I'll have to suggest it to Steve."

Charlie grinned. "A completely ruthless woman," he said solemnly to Amy. "How can she feel such hatred for a man who takes her roller skating, tightens her laces and everything and *then* goes out in the dark of night all the way to the wilds of the hotel lobby just to indulge her irrational craving for a candy bar?"

"Beats me," Amy said.

Jenny looked at her watch and jumped. "Charlie! The plane leaves in less than an hour. We've got to hurry! Charlie, we're going to miss the plane!"

"Don't panic, don't panic. Have I ever let you down before?" Calmly he got to his feet, held Jenny's chair for her and smiled down at Amy. "Remember what I said, kid. Give this some careful thought before you decide what color you're going to wear on Monday."

Amy gave him a shrewd glance. "Charlie, you're a real romantic, you know that? Actually, it's one of the sweetest things about you. But, to tell you the truth, I think I need more of *that* particular kind of heartache like I need another hole in the head.''

"People do change, Amy. It's been known to happen."

"Not Sam," Amy said with a smile that was almost fond. "Sam is like the mountains or the ocean or any other primitive, eternal thing. Sam Wecker will never change."

When they left the lounge, Amy was still sitting alone at the table, gazing moodily at the opposite wall and blowing thoughtful rings of smoke toward the fluorescent ceiling.

DESPITE JENNY'S PANIC they caught their flight with time to spare and ate their dinners somewhere above the lush green expanses of interior British Columbia.

"I can never understand," Jenny said, attacking her asparagus with enthusiasm, "why people always complain about airline food. I think this is wonderful."

"That's because you're pure in spirit," Charlie said. "Look, here come the Rocky Mountains. God, look at them, Jen. Aren't they magnificent?"

Jenny gazed down at the sprawling, rugged terrain and sighed in blissful anticipation. "Have you ever been to Calgary, Charlie?"

"Just once. In 1988 I came up for the Winter Olympics and had a fabulous time."

Jenny was silent as she stared down at the jagged peaks that seemed from this great height to have been modeled from Plasticine by some busy, creative child.

"Just think," Charlie mused. "I was up here watching the Olympics and you were probably at some of the same venues. Maybe you were sitting just in front of me and I never knew."

Jenny shook her head. "Not a chance."

"Why not?"

"Charlie, I couldn't afford tickets to any of the venues. I watched the games on TV like everybody else in the country."

"You're kidding." He turned in his seat and stared at her, appalled. "One of the most fabulous spectacles of the century right in your backyard and you didn't *go?*"

"Charlie..." Jenny hesitated, looking at him with her dark, level gaze. "Charlie, there are a lot of things you just don't understand. Not everybody lives the way you do, you know, or has your kind of income. I work in a bank, Charlie, as a teller. My take-home pay is about twelve hundred dollars a month. Out of that I pay rent on my apartment, make car payments, buy my food and clothes and give as much as I can to my father to help—" She broke off suddenly, as if regretting her impulsive confidences, and stared out the window again.

Charlie looked over at her, thinking about her words. "Jen, why would you have a job like that? I mean, I know it's a good job, working in a bank, and there's opportunity for advancement and all that...but with your intellect couldn't you be, I don't know, a nuclear physicist or something?"

Jenny shook her head. "Not really." She smiled. "As you and my brother are fond of pointing out at every possible opportunity, I'm not really all that bright. I just have this freaky photographic memory. I'm not any kind of genius."

Charlie grinned and raised one eyebrow, a sure sign he was about to say something to infuriate her.

"Don't," Jenny said hastily. "Whatever it is, don't say it. I don't want to have to get mad at you, not this close to home."

"Okay," he said obediently, still grinning.

"Besides," she went on, avoiding his teasing glance, "to go on into some kind of career I would have had to go to college and that would have been an expense for my parents. And that was just about the time Mama started getting sick. I certainly didn't have any desire to add to their burdens."

Charlie nodded thoughtfully.

"And furthermore," Jenny went on, "I'm a really good bank teller, Charlie. I never forget a name, face or signature. I can do most basic transactions in my head, and I could almost always tell you, to the nearest dollar, exactly what I'm carrying in my till at any point in the day."

He laughed. "I don't doubt it a bit."

The vast, sprawling city of Calgary began to materialize beneath the plane, and Jenny stared down at it hungrily, as if she had been away for years instead of less than a week. They fastened their seat belts, the plane banked and circled, and Jenny gripped Charlie's arm, her face pale, her eyes blazing with tension and excitement.

"Easy," he murmured. "Easy, Jenny. Relax."

In the terminal Jenny realized with mild surprise how accustomed she had become over the past week to letting Charlie handle all the details, like finding their luggage and booking a rental car. He was always so calm and confident, and it was such a relief just to stand back and let him look after things.

But it's not right, she thought. *I should be doing all this myself. He's going to be gone from my life in a few days, and by then I'll be completely spoiled.*

She watched him across the terminal as he dealt with the car rental agency. He wore casual slacks, loafers, and a tweed sport coat over an open-necked shirt, but his easy-fitting clothes did little to hide the athletic grace of his compact body. Even from a distance Jenny could tell that the attractive blond girl behind the desk was captivated by his bright blue gaze and his humorous, clean-cut face.

She felt a faint, surprising stirring of jealousy and then a quick stab of alarm.

My God, what's happening to me? Why am I feeling this way? He's nothing to me. Nothing but an irritation, and after next week I'll never see him again.

As if to confirm this in her mind, she wandered over to a newsstand near the arrivals board and looked longingly at the edition of *Cycle World,* brand-new and full of precious, incredibly valuable information, positioned invitingly on the shelf near her hand.

She glanced back at Charlie, still chatting to the rental agent, and observed with satisfaction that all her strange, disturbing new feelings about him were gone, wiped away by that one tantalizing glimpse of a forbidden magazine.

The only emotion she felt toward Charlie at the moment was one of deep, burning resentment.

He came back across the lobby to where Jenny waited by their luggage and gave her a cheerful smile. "All set," he announced. "Where do you want to go? Your place?"

She shook her head. "There's no point in going to my place. I live in a tiny little bachelor apartment with a studio couch, and there'd certainly be no place to put *you.* Besides," she added bitterly, "it's just full of books and magazines about motorcycles."

"You're right," he agreed calmly, ignoring the coldness of her tone. "We can't go there. How about your brother's?"

Jenny shook her head. "Their place isn't much bigger, and besides, I'm not kidding, Charlie, if I don't keep you two apart, he's going to kill you. This means a lot to Steve, this quiz show thing," Jenny said. "It was more his project than anybody's, and he spent hours mapping out a study program for me to use during my hours away from the show, to help me organize material to maximum advantage. When he finds out about you and what you're doing, I'm really afraid of what he might do to you."

"How about if you let me worry about that, Jenny? I think I can look after myself."

The planes of Charlie's face had hardened and shifted almost imperceptibly, and Jenny glanced at him, startled. From a cheerful, teasing comic he had turned suddenly grim and steely, almost frightening. This man, Jenny realized, wasn't all fun and games. He was also a person to be reckoned with. Certainly not one to be taken lightly.

"Charlie, I just don't want any trouble, okay? Let's go to my parent's place. I'll sleep in my old room and you can have Steve's, so there'll be no problems about accommodation."

"But they're not expecting us, are they?"

Jenny shook her head. "I never did manage to get hold of them. I think Mama must have spent the night in the hospital for tests, and Papa probably brought her home this afternoon. That's the way they usually do it. It'll be fine," Jenny added, seeing his hesitation. "Besides," she went on wistfully, "I could really use a day or two of wandering around the garden and the farmyard. I think that's what I need more than anything right now."

"Sounds good," Charlie said with sudden decision. "Let's go."

He followed Jenny's directions, guiding the big rental car skillfully out of the city and west toward the mountains. The late summer sun hovered just above the sweep of snow-covered peaks, raying golden fans of light through rifts in the clouds. The mountains shone like banks of jewels, glowing rose and pearl and turquoise in the wan ing light, and the clouds that swirled and obscured the peaks were pastel rainbows of mist.

A rain had fallen recently, perhaps just that afternoon, and the rolling foothills were green and fresh in the mellow twilight, smelling deliciously of fresh earth and flowers. Jenny lowered the window, sniffing in ecstasy as they swung off the main highway and down a long, tree-lined approach road.

Charlie pulled up, parked in the tidy farmyard and looked out in delight at the two-story white clapboard house with its deep, shady veranda, neatly painted and covered with vines and climbing roses. The house and outbuildings were tinted a rosy pink by the sunset glow, their windows bright gold, and seemed somehow like a place of enchantment, something dimly remembered from the fairy tales of his boyhood.

"Jenny, look! Those are grape vines! And look at all the varieties of roses and fruit trees and those tall bean poles. And those are *beehives* out there, Jen! Actual beehives!"

"I know, Charlie," she said dryly. "I've lived here all my life."

"God," he murmured, gripping the wheel and gazing blissfully at the silent farmyard. "It's like heaven. A little piece of Sorrento right here on the Canadian prairie."

"It's also heavily mortgaged," Jenny said bleakly, staring straight ahead through the windshield. "And my parents are going to lose it unless I win enough money to help them with the debts. And you're doing your best to stop me."

"That's not fair, Jenny," he said quietly. "I'm not trying to stop you from winning. I'm just doing my job for my employer as I promised I would. And you're obeying an injunction that you signed of your own free will."

"Sure, Charlie," she said wearily, getting out of the car and starting toward the house. "I want to see my parents," she called back to him. "We can get the suitcases out later."

But the house was silent and deserted. Jenny stood in the sparkling little kitchen and looked around, her face pale. She hurried through the rest of the house, ran upstairs, looked out into the back and then came slowly back to confront Charlie, who was waiting in the hall.

"They're not here." She faltered. "Charlie, I wonder if..."

Just then a vehicle drove up outside, a car door slammed and heavy footsteps sounded on the veranda. The front door opened and Frank D'Angelo stood in the entryway, gazing in bewilderment at his daughter.

"Jenny! Jenny, darling, what are you doing here? The show...you won tonight. You go back on the show Monday, no? Why are you home?"

"Just for a visit, Papa. This...this is Charlie Mitchell. I'll explain later why he's here. Papa, where is she? Where's Mama?"

At the look on her father's face Jenny stopped and put her hand over her mouth, her eyes widening in terror. Then she gave a little moan and ran forward, flinging herself into his arms.

Frank held her against his broad, sturdy chest, stroking her soft cloud of hair with his gnarled hands and patting her back while the tears ran down his weathered cheeks.

CHAPTER SEVEN

"WHAT DOES THAT MEAN, Papa, 'guarded condition'? What does it mean?"

There was a little rising note of hysteria in Jenny's voice. Charlie, sitting beside her, reached over and placed a gentle hand on her shoulder, but she appeared to be unaware of it.

"Papa?"

Frank D'Angelo got up from the kitchen table and walked heavily across to the stove, where the kettle had begun to sound a shrill whistle. He carried the kettle back to the table, poured boiling water into waiting mugs and added spoonfuls of instant coffee, measuring with careful deliberation.

"I don't know, Jenny," he said finally, his despair evident in his voice and in the unusual heaviness of his Italian accent. "Guarded, stable, critical, what do I know? Only that Mama is ... Mama is ..."

He handed a mug of coffee to Charlie, who accepted it with a quiet nod and placed it in front of Jenny, taking the second one for himself.

"I told you all of this already. They finished the surgery late last night," Frank went on, his voice more controlled. "Now she's in ICU, and we wait ... we wait to see if her body accepts the transplant, if there's no infection, if the new kidney will function, if she's strong enough to survive the shock to her system."

"I want to see her, Papa. I want to go there right now."

He shook his head. "No, Jenny. I told you, she's too weak. She needs absolute rest. I wanted to stay, but they sent me home. They gave her something to help her sleep and told me to come back in the morning. They promised to call me in the night if...if..." He fell silent, staring into the swirling brown depths of his coffee mug, lost in his sorrow.

Jenny stared at him, her dark eyes enormous in her pale face.

"Papa, I just can't believe that all this was happening, that Mama was in surgery and everybody knew about it and you didn't tell me. I can't believe it."

"It was her choice, sweetheart. She said you would be too upset to go on with your job out there and that we mustn't disturb you. She made me promise."

"Oh, God..." Jenny's voice broke, and she buried her head on her folded arms, her shoulders heaving. Charlie put his arm around her and exchanged a glance with Frank.

"Jenny's tired and wrung out, Mr. D'Angelo, and so are you. Let's sleep on it, shall we, and check with the hospital first thing in the morning?"

Frank nodded gratefully. "That's right. We'll try to sleep. Jenny, you show the young man to Steve's room." He got to his feet, paused by his daughter's bent head to caress her hair gently for a moment and then plodded out of the room and down the hall.

"Come on, Jen," Charlie whispered. "Come on, let's try to get some sleep. You'll feel better in the morning. I'll bring up our suitcases."

Obediently, almost numb in her reactions and movements, she led him through the living room and up the stairs. Charlie gazed around, enchanted by the storybook atmosphere of the house, with its gables, window seats, slanted ceilings and charming flowered wallpaper.

"This is my old room," Jenny said tonelessly, indicating a closed door, "and that one is Steve's. Was Steve's, I guess I should say," she added with a brave attempt at a smile that wrung his heart. "And the bathroom is just there, down the hall. I'll see you tomorrow, Charlie."

She vanished into her room without another word, and Charlie stood staring at the closed door with a troubled expression. Slowly he went into the other room, which was filled with boyish furnishings, battered sets of boxing gloves, posters, pennants and neat piles of motorcycle magazines.

Charlie undressed, tugged on a pair of sweatpants, went down the hall to the bathroom to brush his teeth and returned to his room. He climbed into the narrow bed and lay for a long time with the light on, listening to the wind howl and sob outside the window and staring at the pile of magazines on the bedside table with brooding concentration.

Finally, his steps leaden with reluctance, he got up again, trudged down the hall and knocked at the door to Jenny's room.

"Yes?" she said through the door.

"It's me, Charlie. May I come in for a minute?"

"All right."

Charlie opened the door, looked at her and caught his breath. Her bedside lamp was on, flooding the room with dim radiance, and she sat on the patchwork quilt, hugging her knees. She wore a dainty white nightgown with thin lace straps over her bare shoulders, half hidden by the tumbling cascades of her gloriously dark hair.

Her eyes glittered with unshed tears, and she cast him a glance of mute inquiry.

"Jenny, I . . ." He hesitated, standing at the foot of the bed, searching awkwardly for words.

Jenny looked up at him, waiting. He still wore only his jogging pants, and this was the first time, despite their week of forced intimacy, that she had seen so much of his body. His tanned shoulders were broad, flat and heavily muscled, gleaming in the moonlight. His chest and taut, lean stomach were sprinkled with a fine mat of curly hair, gilded into bright sparkles by the soft glow of the lamp.

Jenny's mouth went dry, and her heart began to pound. "What do you want, Charlie?"

"I want you to know that I'm sorry, Jenny. God, I'm so sorry. About your mother and about . . . about what I have to do now."

She watched in puzzlement and growing horror as he crossed the room to her wall of bookshelves, scanned the titles and methodically began to remove all books and magazines related to motorcycles, filling his arms with them.

Jenny huddled on the bed and stared at him, her eyes wide with disbelief and outrage. "Charlie, for God's sake," she whispered.

"Jenny, please," he interrupted. "Don't say anything. I know how this must look to you, especially at a time like this. I know what you think of me, and you don't have to tell me. But I have a job to do, Jen, and I'm going to do it, regardless of circumstances. I'm really sorry." He walked barefoot across the room, his arms loaded with books. In the doorway he paused and turned. "Jenny?" he said.

She ignored him, turning aside to gaze out the window so that all he saw was the pure, perfect curve of her cheek under a cloud of dark hair. He hesitated, gazing at her for a moment longer, and then sighed and started down the hall to the other bedroom.

JENNY STOOD by the iron-railed hospital bed, gazing down at her mother's sleeping face, so pale and transparent that Irena seemed like a ghost of a woman, barely present at all. Only the regal coronet of braids, dark against the white pillow, still bore testimony to the beautiful, strong, vital woman that Irena D'Angelo had been for almost all of her life. Her wasted body beneath the light covering was motionless, attached to a bewildering array of tubes and equipment being monitored constantly by a young nurse in a chair at the bedside.

Steve D'Angelo tiptoed into the room, gave Jenny a hug and moved over beside the slight form in the bed. "Did she wake up at all?" he whispered.

"Just for a second," Jenny whispered back. "She's too weak to talk, but she . . . she squeezed my hand."

Her voice broke, and Steve gathered her into his arms, holding her for a moment.

"You'd both better go now," the nurse whispered. "You can stop back later in the day. She might be awake then."

They nodded, looked longingly once more at the pale, beloved face against the pillows and then moved out into the busy, early-morning brightness of the corridor and began to walk together down the hall.

"All right, Jen," Steve said, shaking off the thought of his mother's pale, still body and gathering himself together with a visible effort. "Where is he?"

"Charlie, you mean?"

"Whatever the hell his name is. Your watchdog. Where is he?"

Alarmed by his tone, Jenny stopped at the entrance to the waiting room and turned to face him. "Papa told you?"

"Yeah, he told me," Steve said furiously. "And it's the biggest goddamn crock I've ever heard of. As if our family wasn't having enough bad luck already. This is just the rottenest, most—" He broke off, glowering. "I can't *wait* to get my hands on this guy," he muttered, following Jenny into the waiting room.

"Well, here I am, if it's me you're wanting," Charlie said pleasantly, getting to his feet and setting aside the magazine he had been reading. He gave Steve a calm, level glance. "Feel free to get your hands on me, Steve. It *is* Steve, isn't it?"

Steve stood glaring at the other man, a little disconcerted by Charlie's composure, his relaxed, almost amused glance and the impression he managed to give, simultaneously, of casual ease combined with a sort of dangerous, controlled power.

"Yeah," Steve said with some belligerence. "I'm Steve D'Angelo. And I want to know what the hell you think you're doing to my sister."

"I *know* what I'm doing to your sister, Steve. I'm acting as her regular escort, showing her all possible courtesy and ensuring that she follows the rules of the contest she's in, as she has contracted to do by her written signature. Now, if you have a problem with that, you just let me know."

Steve glared at him, his dark, handsome face furious, searching for a reply.

"And in the meantime," Charlie went on in that same calm, level tone, "I want to tell you that I was out this morning in the shed at your father's farm, looking at the bike motor you're designing, and I feel it's a marvel of engineering skill. It's one of the most impressive and innovative two-stroke designs I've ever seen."

"Yeah?" Steve asked, taken aback. He paused, searching for words, and gazed at the other man. "You ... you really think that?"

"Steve, I'm in charge of product supply for Forbes Motorcycles. I can tell you absolutely that we would be very interested in seeing your plans and specifications for that motor."

"Jeez," Steve breathed. "I never thought, I mean, I was just messing around, you know? It was just an idea I had, and I was trying to..." His dark face broke slowly into a delighted grin. "Hey, would you like to come down to the shop with me?"

"Steve!" Jenny hissed.

"Yeah, Jen?"

"Steve, I think you're... aren't you forgetting something?" Jenny whispered urgently. "I mean, this man is hounding me, Steve, every minute. I can't study, I'm not even allowed any of the advantages the other contestants have, I'm forced to just—"

"Do you have another model at the shop?" Charlie asked Steve, as if Jenny hadn't spoken.

"Yeah," Steve said eagerly. "I've been experimenting with a slightly different design."

All at once, it seemed, he and Charlie were in a huddle in the corner, talking bikes and motors, while Jenny sat alone on a hard vinyl bench, leafing grimly through the pages of a magazine with trembling hands and trying to control her outrage.

THE MOON WAS almost full, spilling a pale radiance across the neat rows of new garden plants and shrubs and frosting the tree branches with platinum when Steve's little car pulled up in front of the farmhouse.

The engine stopped, and the only sound in the silvery stillness was the gentle whir of insects and the occasional muted lowing of cattle in a distant field. Nighttime scents, sweet and spicy, of damp plants, early flowers and crushed sage wet with dew drifted on the soft, rustling breeze.

Steve got out from behind the wheel and walked around to open the door for Jenny, who was beside him. Charlie and Frank, jammed into the backseat, were deep in a discussion of the technicalities of winemaking and were slow to emerge and follow them across the moon-washed yard.

"I wish Sheila could have come, too," Jenny said. "I miss her. We only got a chance to talk for a few minutes today."

"I know," Steve said. "But she gets so tired these days. It's better for her to stay home and catch up on her sleep because we'll probably be awake lots of nights later on. The doctor says it could be anytime now," he added.

"But how do you determine the degree of carbonation?" Charlie was asking behind them. "I mean, is there some way of measuring it without uncapping the wine?"

"You have this special locking cap," Frank explained earnestly, "with a release valve."

"Oh, for God's sake," Jenny muttered to herself. Steve, unlocking the front door, heard her and concealed a grin.

"Well, children," Frank said, beaming as he stepped into the house and switched on the lights, flooding the rooms with brightness. "We celebrate, no? We have a sip of wine and drink to Mama's good health."

"Papa," Jenny began, "that's still a little premature, isn't it?"

"Jenny, Jenny, you heard the doctor. He said that— what did he say, Charlie?"

"That all the indicators were promising," Charlie quoted promptly. "That vital signs were stable, there was no sign of tissue rejection, and absolutely no infection or increase in white cell activity."

"Yes," Frank said, gazing at Charlie's tanned face with pure love as the younger man repeated the doctor's magical words. "That's what he said. So now we thank God and we have a little drink. Steve, fetch me some bottles."

"Okay, Papa. What do you want?" Steve paused at the doorway leading to the basement, where Frank had long since installed his own wine cellar. "Just some of the dry white wine, or are you in the mood for something really special?"

"I want Charlie to try all of them," Frank said happily, rubbing his big hands in anticipation, his broad face glowing. "The marigold and rose hip and strawberry and one bottle of the sparkling rhubarb, I think."

"Wow," Steve said with a grin. "The sparkling rhubarb, Papa? You *are* in a holiday mood, aren't you?"

Jenny leaned in the kitchen doorway, arms crossed, glaring at her father and Charlie. Charlie was busy assembling an array of glasses on the table, while Frank cut jagged slabs from a chunk of cheddar cheese and arranged them on a plate.

"I think this is awful," Jenny announced. "Sure, Mama was a lot better this afternoon, and I know that things are looking good, but it's still too early for—"

She was interrupted by Steve, who brushed past her with an armful of dusty bottles filled with sparkling liquids of exquisite color and clarity.

Charlie took one of the bottles from him and looked at it in awe, handling it with the reverence of a precious objet d'art. "Frank," he breathed, "this is beautiful. I've never seen anything so delicate. What a touch you've got."

Frank, overjoyed at the occasion and flooded with a relief and happiness that was almost too much for his big body to hold, dropped an arm around Charlie's shoulder and hugged him. "Wait, my boy. Wait till you taste it.

Steve, this is ambrosia, no? Where does Mama keep the corkscrew?"

Jenny marched from the room, head high, in an icy dignity somewhat marred by the fact that none of the three men even noticed her departure.

Corks popped, bursts of hearty male laughter issued from the kitchen, and Jenny heard the sounds of cupboard and refrigerator doors opening and closing. She settled herself in a big, soft armchair in the living room, picked up a novel and began to read, trying not to listen to the cheerful, disconnected conversation.

After a considerable time, Charlie emerged, looking a little abashed. "Sorry, Jenny," he said. "We were having so much fun, getting the strawberry wine opened without crushing the cork and testing the other two to see if they were mature enough that we didn't notice you'd disappeared. Come on in and have a drink with us."

"No, thank you," Jenny said coldly. "Personally I feel that . . ."

But Charlie had already nodded, obviously in a fever to return to the party, and vanished back into the kitchen.

Jenny curled up in the chair, staring at the blurred pages of print and trying to analyze her own reactions. She was, of course, wonderfully happy and relieved at what the doctor had told them that afternoon about her mother's condition, and his tone of cautious optimism. The idea that Irena might accept the new kidney and recover, might heal and strengthen and be able to lead a normal, active life once more was almost too marvelous for Jenny to contemplate.

But just now, she realized, apart from her mother's situation, which was admittedly wonderful, Jenny was struggling with strong feelings of treachery and betrayal. She had been so outraged back in Vancouver when she first learned that Charlie intended to accompany her to Calgary on the weekend and continue to supervise her. But then slowly, along with that realization, had come a tiny stab of malicious pleasure, a wicked little glow of anticipation at the thought of how indignant her family would be about the unfairness of Charlie's presence in her life and his restrictions on her behavior, and how they would rally around her, gather staunchly on her side and make him suffer for what he was doing to her.

She had been looking forward with considerable enjoyment to the thought of Charlie's embarrassment and discomfort in the presence of her family. It was the only revenge she was ever likely to have, and she'd been fully intending to savor it.

But it hadn't happened that way at all.

Charlie, with his remarkable charm, his deep and genuine interest in people and their lives, his easy, open manner, had won the whole family over in no time at all and with no apparent effort. Even Sheila, when they had supper with her in Steve's apartment, had blushed and glowed and chattered with unusual vivacity when Charlie talked about babies with her.

Apparently Charlie also knew a lot about babies, along with everything else, damn him.

Her thoughts were interrupted by a burst of noise that rumbled suddenly from the kitchen. She was mildly alarmed until she realized that it was Frank, singing "Santa Lucia" in Italian. Steve joined in, off-key, bellowing in English, and Charlie began to sing harmony in a surprisingly pure, sweet tenor.

"Thassa wunnerful, Charlie," Frank said as they ended the song with a flourish and much banging of glasses on the table. "Come, filla your glass. Try the marigold."

"This one?" she heard Charlie ask.

"The yellow one," Steve said. "Marigolds are yellow," he added solemnly.

"Yellow," Charlie repeated with equal solemnity "Marigolds are yellow. You're ab-absolutely right."

There was the sound of liquid bubbling into a glass and then into another one.

"Dandelions are yellow, too," Frank said after apparently giving the matter deep thought. "But the dandelion it's notta sucha nice wine as the marigold."

"Daisies," Steve said suddenly for no evident reason.

"Yes," Charlie agreed. "Daisies are yel...are yellow in the middle."

"Daisy, Daisy," Frank bellowed, "give me your answer, dooooo."

"I'm half cra-a-azy," Steve chimed in, and hiccuped loudly.

"All for the love of youuuu," Charlie sang, and the rich, lilting timbre of his voice made Jenny's throat tighten suddenly.

She set her book aside, got to her feet and marched across the room to stand in the doorway, hands on hips, glaring at them.

They lounged around the table, collars loosened, sleeves rolled up, feet resting on chair arms or cupboard ledges. The table was littered with sticky glasses containing residue of liquids of various colors, and several full bottles recently opened, were still lined up in front of them.

When Jenny appeared, they all turned and blinked at her as if her face had been a bright light suddenly aimed at them.

Charlie examined her owlishly, his eyes wide and solemn. "It's Jenny," he announced finally to the others with the air of a man making an important discovery. "Hi, Jenny. Have a drink."

"Daisy, Daisy," Frank rumbled again, keeping time in the air with a piece of cheese.

"Not Daisy, Papa," Steve said patiently, enunciating his words with great care. "It's Jenny. Jenny wants a drink."

Frank beamed. "Jenny? You wanta some wine, *cara?* Rhubarb, Jenny? Trya the rhubarb. So *good,* Jenny." He rummaged among the bottles, and then, for some reason, began to look carefully around on the floor.

"Forget it, Papa," Jenny said sharply. "I don't want a drink, and I have no intention of joining this little..." She hesitated, looking with distaste at the welter of bottles and glasses, and the cheerful, flushed faces of the three men. "This *orgy,*" she finished.

Charlie raised a wicked eyebrow, and Jenny went on hastily, anxious to forestall any suggestion he might have regarding orgies.

"I think," she said with dignity, "that I'd better drive Steve home now. Sheila shouldn't be alone too long, and he's in no condition to drive himself."

"Aw, Jen," Steve complained. "It's just a little wine. C'mon, Jen. Lighten up."

"And," Frank added in an aggrieved tone, "issa homemade."

He looked at his daughter in triumph, as if this statement clinched some vitally important argument.

"I don't care where it came from," Jenny said. "Steve's drunk, and I'm taking him home now. We'll drop your car off tomorrow morning when we go to see Mama," she told her brother. "Come on."

Still muttering in complaint, Steve got to his feet and shambled out of the room, followed closely by Charlie.

"Where are *you* going?" Jenny asked.

"With you, darling," Charlie told her solemnly, his eyes very blue. "All the time, every minute, day and night, with you. My job," he added earnestly.

"Oh, for God's sake," Jenny said.

They made the trip into the city in silence, Charlie beside Jenny in the front, Steve slumped half-asleep in the back, and delivered him to Sheila, who giggled delightedly at their story and promised to get him safely into bed.

On the way home in the moonlight Jenny drove the little car with grim, concentrated attention, trying to ignore Charlie, who leaned against the passenger door and gazed thoughtfully at her delicate profile.

"Jen-ny, Jen-ny," he sang softly, his voice barely above a whisper, "give me your answer, do."

He reached over to caress her dark hair with a gentle brown hand, and Jenny shrugged him off impatiently. "Charlie, leave me alone."

"I'm half cra-a-a-zy all for the love of you."

He let his hand drop to her shoulder, and Jenny left it there, trying to ignore his touch. But her body shivered and trembled at the warmth of his fingers, burning through the thin fabric of her blouse as they drove in silence into the moonlit farmyard.

CHARLIE AND JENNY sat in a warm square of morning sunshine in one corner of the hospital cafeteria, a cheerful room with yellow tables and chairs, banks of windows and massed foliage along one wall.

Nurses and doctors bustled in and out, coming on or off shift, greeting one another, gulping coffee and exchanging news and bursts of laughter.

A particularly noisy conversation began at a nearby table, causing Charlie to wince in pain and rub his forehead.

"Serves you right," Jenny said with satisfaction, observing his discomfort.

"Jenny, be nice." He looked over at her pleadingly and held his cup up to the waitress for a refill. "That stuff was made of *flowers,* Jen. How was I supposed to know it was about sixty-proof? It just tasted like, I don't know, nectar or something."

She relented slightly, a small grin tugging at the corners of her mouth.

"What are you thinking about?" he asked suspiciously.

"Oh, nothing," she said casually, avoiding his eyes and gazing out the window at the rainbow sprays of lawn sprinklers arching across the sunlit hospital grounds.

"Come on, Jenny. What?"

"Just what a lovely singing voice you have." Then, before he could answer, she said, "Here comes Papa."

Frank approached their table, also much subdued and walking cautiously. "She seems so much better," he reported. "The doctor says the cell something—what is it again, Charlie?"

"The white cell count," Charlie said, gulping his coffee rapidly and beginning to look somewhat more like his usual cheerful self.

"Right, the white cell count. He says it's up a little, and there could be some infection, but that's normal, he says. And they're cutting down the medication, so she's starting to feel quite a lot of pain. But she's awake and happy," Frank added, seating himself at the table, "and she wants to see you."

"Oh, good," Jenny said, getting to her feet. She wore a creamy eyelet sundress and sandals, and her face glowed with joy. She looked, Charlie thought, positively delicious. In his weakened condition, it was all he could do to keep from standing up right there in the hospital cafeteria, sweeping her into his arms and covering her face with kisses.

"Charlie, too," Frank said as Jenny turned and started toward the door.

"What?" Jenny said, pausing and looking at her father in disbelief. "What did you say, Papa?"

"She wants to see Charlie, too," Frank said, putting on his glasses and considering the menu. "I told her about him, and she wants to meet him."

Charlie smiled, got to his feet and moved over close to Jenny, taking her arm and guiding her from the room. "I won't stay long," he murmured. "I'll just say hello, and then leave you alone."

"I can't stand it," Jenny said bleakly. "Even *Mama* is going to be on your side now. I'm all alone."

"Jenny, there are no sides in this. It's not a war, you know. It's just a quiz show. A television program that will be over and forgotten by the end of the month."

"Easy for you to say," Jenny said bitterly. "You have nothing at stake."

"That's what you think," Charlie said, his voice suddenly grim. Jenny glanced over at him in surprise and then turned the corner into the intensive care unit and approached Irena's door.

Irena was partially upright, propped against the pillows, and she was a vastly different woman from the pale, ghostly shell that Jenny had seen the previous day. She still looked frail and weak, but her remarkable dark eyes, flashing with warmth and intelligence, gave life to her whole body. To the whole room, Jenny thought.

"Jenny," she said tenderly, reaching out her thin hand. "Sweetheart, I'm so happy to see you."

"Mama," Jenny said, her voice breaking. She took her mother's hand and sank into the chair beside the bed, gazing hungrily at Irena's face.

"And this must be Charlie," Irena said, smiling at the young man with the square, alert face and bright blue eyes who stood at the foot of her bed, the morning sunlight catching sparkles of gold in his hair.

"Hello, Mrs. D'Angelo," he said. "It's a pleasure to meet you."

Irena gazed at him, a long, probing, thoughtful look that Charlie returned quietly. Finally she smiled. "Hello, Charlie," she said softly.

"Mama," Jenny began, "Papa says the doctor is very optimistic."

Irena's smile faded, and she gazed silently out the window, her lovely sculpted features looking pale and remote.

"Optimistic," she repeated.

She was quiet for a moment, and they waited for her to continue.

"I keep thinking," she said finally. "I can't seem to stop thinking about it. This boy, the one whose kidney is going to keep me alive, he was just a little younger than you are, Jenny. And," she went on, turning to gaze intently at the two younger people, "he was killed in a *motorcycle* accident." She smiled without mirth. "Never, until I was almost forty years old, did I even see a real motorcycle up close. Now motorcycles seem to be all woven through the fabric of my family's life. Is this part of a plan, do you think? Some plan that we can't even begin to understand? Or is it all just coincidence?"

Jenny gazed at her mother, searching for words.

"I think there's an overall plan," Charlie said unexpectedly. "I think there has to be because the whole design of life is so intricate that it couldn't possibly happen by chance."

Irena stared at him, her eyes enormous, pondering his words. She nodded slowly. "Then, Charlie," she whispered, "was it part of a plan that a young man should die so I could live? What kind of plan is that?"

Charlie returned her look steadily. Jenny sat bewildered, gazing from one to the other. They had just met, her mother and this man who had become so strangely bound up into Jenny's life, and yet the two of them seemed to have achieved some kind of deep, instant communion that Jenny couldn't begin to fathom.

"I think," Charlie told Irena slowly, "that the negative things aren't planned. We live in a universe where free choice is possible, so accidents are also possible. But the positive things *are* planned. Good things don't come about by chance. And," he added with a gentle smile, "your recovery is a good thing."

Irena gazed at him, her face softening. "Thank you, Charlie," she murmured. "Thank you very much."

"I'll go back and have another coffee with Frank," Charlie said to Jenny, "and give you a few minutes alone with your mother."

They watched him leave, and Irena looked at the empty doorway for a long time after his departure, her face gentle and thoughtful. Then she turned to her daughter. "He loves you, Jenny."

Jenny's face went white, and she stared at her mother in shock. A rich, troubled warmth spread through her body, making her feel, all at once, shaky and weak with emotion as she struggled to compose herself. "Mama, how can you, how can you say that? He's just doing a job, Mama. They told you—Papa and Steve—they told you what he's doing to me. It's just awful."

"He loves you," Irena repeated.

"I don't know why you keep saying that," Jenny whispered. "You only saw him for two minutes and you haven't seen—"

"I saw how he looked at you when the two of you came in here. A man like that," Irena continued, "he's so honest and pure in his soul that he can't hide what he feels. Not from someone who has eyes to see."

Jenny was silent, her whole being fighting to deny her mother's words. And yet Irena was, indeed, often able to see things that were invisible to other people and to make predictions, and improbable though they seemed at the time, her predictions usually turned out to be true.

"And," Irena went on, her voice firm in spite of her obvious weakness, "you love him, Jenny."

"No!" Jenny whispered, staring at her mother in horror. "No, Mama, you're wrong!"

Irena smiled gently at her daughter. "A strange conversation, this," she mused. "We should be talking about other things maybe, but I fear for you, Jenny."

"Why?"

"Because of the way you are. When you're involved in something, it matters to you more than the whole world. You set yourself a goal, and then you're blind to everything else."

Jenny nodded, recognizing the truth of Irena's words. There was no doubt she was strongly goal-oriented and always had been.

"But sometimes," Irena went on, her voice beginning to falter a little, her frail body sagging back on the pillows, "it doesn't pay to be too single-minded, my darling. There are things in life that come along all too rarely, and we mustn't be blind to them when they happen, or we pay a terrible price to achieve our goals."

Jenny looked wordlessly at her mother's brilliant, dark eyes, trying to come to terms with what she was saying.

"Some things, Jenny," Irena said, "come to us only once. Don't lose it, darling, when you've..."

Her voice trailed off and her eyes dropped shut. Jenny sprang from the chair in alarm, bending over her mother's still form.

"It's all right," the nurse assured her, bustling in with a clipboard and jotting notations from the computer monitor above the bed. "It's just the medication. She still drops in and out of sleep all the time, but she stays awake a little longer each time."

Jenny nodded, feeling numb. "I guess...I guess I'd better go now," she murmured. "My father will be back in the afternoon."

"Sure thing," the nurse said cheerfully. "That's one classy lady, that one is," she added unexpectedly with a fond glance at Irena's calm, sleeping face. "We all love her."

"So do we," Jenny said.

She turned and started down the corridor toward the cafeteria, her mind whirling in confusion, her steps slow and hesitant.

CHAPTER EIGHT

THEY DROVE WEST with the morning sun at their backs, lost in their own thoughts. Charlie, who already knew the route to the farm by heart, worked his way skillfully through the heavy weekend traffic while Jenny gazed out the passenger window at the multicolored blur of stores and service stations, of parks and playgrounds and residential areas.

Earlier in the day they had made the trip to town in a procession of three vehicles. Frank had driven his own car, and Jenny had delivered Steve's car back to his apartment, with Charlie behind her in the rental car. Now, because Frank would be spending the day at the hospital, and other family members weren't allowed to visit until evening, Charlie and Jenny had decided to return to the farm for the rest of the day.

"So were you right?" Charlie asked suddenly.

"Pardon?" Jenny said, pulling herself out of her reverie and turning to him. "Sorry, Charlie. I was daydreaming. What did you say?"

"I asked if you were right. Did your mother succumb to my fatal charms and abandon you like everybody else?"

Jenny glared at him. "Look, this isn't a bit funny, Charlie. I don't see how you can be so smug and awful about it."

"I'm not being smug. I really want to know," he said, looking away from the road and glancing quickly at her, his blue eyes candid and serious.

"Yes," Jenny said wearily. "My mother thought you were marvelous, just like everybody else. Does that satisfy you?"

"You know, I don't think you have any idea how lucky you are," he said unexpectedly.

"Lucky? Why?"

"Because you have this wonderful family, and they all love you and support you in whatever you do and care so much about you."

"Don't you have a family, Charlie?" she asked, curious in spite of herself.

"No," he said briefly. "I've never had a family."

Jenny was silent for a moment. "So where did you come from? Were you abandoned on a church doorstep in a basket with a note pinned to your blanket, or what?"

"Nothing so civilized. It was a sleazy downtown hotel room."

His face was grim and set, his level gaze fixed on the majestic sweep of mountains rearing above the foothills. The sunlight edged his fine profile with gold and shone warmly in his hair. Jenny looked over at him in silence, waiting for him to continue.

"That's all," he said, staring at the road ahead of him with a ghost of a bitter smile. "No basket, no note, nothing. The desk clerk had no record of a pregnant woman checking into a room that night. They figured later that somebody took the room under a false name, sneaked her in there to have her baby and then left the kid behind. The chambermaid found me in the morning, wrapped in a pillowcase, screaming."

Jenny stared at him, appalled. "Charlie..." she whispered.

"They never were able to trace them," he went on calmly. "But I wasn't really available for adoption because the police were still trying to find my mother, and nobody wanted to risk taking on a kid whose mother hadn't signed formal release papers and who might turn up later and want me back. I grew up in an assortment of foster homes, and every time it started to look good for me—you know, that somebody might really want to adopt me and keep me—then they'd get sick or get divorced or be hurt in an accident or something, and I'd be back in the hands of the Social Service. So that was how I grew up."

Jenny listened, aching with sympathy, but she sensed instinctively that he needed to finish his story now that he'd started, so she kept quiet and let him talk.

"I worked my way through high school and college and made a life for myself. But I don't think you can even begin to imagine, Jenny, what it's like not to have a family. No brothers and sisters, no parents, no uncles or aunts or cousins. Do you know what I do for Christmas every year?"

"No, Charlie, I have no idea," she said softly.

"I go on holidays. Every Christmas morning since I've been an adult, I've wakened up in a hotel room. There, you don't miss it all so much, the tree and the turkey, and the little kids all excited and all the stuff other people have."

Jenny thought of her own Christmas mornings, wrapped in the glow of joy and giving and deep, warm, family happiness and felt tears prickling behind her eyelids.

"Look, I'm sorry," Charlie said briefly. "I'm not telling you all this to get your sympathy or anything. Actually I don't know why I'm telling you. Normally I never tell anybody about myself. I guess I just want you to understand how lucky you are. And," he added with an apologetic little smile, "to make you realize how good it feels to borrow your family, even just for a weekend. It feels *good* to be in your house with your family, Jen. It's just exactly what I always dreamed about when I was a kid—a family like yours."

"I didn't know," Jenny said. "I'm sorry, Charlie. You always seem so . . . so rich and cheerful and confident, and I just assumed, I think, that you must have been born with a silver spoon in your mouth."

He smiled grimly, battling his own memories, and then shook his head as if to drive them from his mind. "Anyhow," he said in his normal, cheerful voice, "that's all ancient history. Water under the bridge. What do you want to do today?"

"Well, we're on our way home, and we can't come back in till evening, and then the plane leaves tomorrow morning at nine, you said?"

Charlie nodded.

"I hate the idea of going back to Vancouver," Jenny said moodily. "I wish I could just forget the whole thing and stay here and enjoy my last week of holidays before I have to go back to work."

"Come on, Jenny. You're halfway there. Just five more days to go."

"*If* I make it that far," she said.

"None of that negative talk. Come on, let's plan the rest of the day. We'll make it your day, Jenny. We'll do whatever you want. Anything in the world."

"Then," Jenny said promptly, "I'd like to change my clothes, pack a lunch and hike back into the coulees behind the farm."

"Can I come?" Charlie asked wistfully.

She looked over at him, her face softening. "All right. The coulees always were my favorite place ever since I was a little girl," she said, smiling at the memory. "I used to play back in there for hours, pretending that Indians were about to come riding over the hill or that I was part of a wagon train, lost in the wilderness, or that I was an Indian myself, hunting for deer."

"We'll play together," Charlie told her with an answering smile. "I'm a terrific playmate, Jen. You can be the settler's daughter, lost in the woods, and I'll be the ruthless Indian brave, creeping through the darkness to scalp you."

"Do I get to stab you with a knife hidden in my petticoat?" she asked.

"Absolutely. And I'll die in agony, clutching my throat and bleeding all over the place and swearing vengeance upon you and all your people before the moon is full again."

"This," Jenny said laughing, "is going to be fun. I always wanted a playmate like that, and I could never get Steve *into* it. He was always so practical, you know? He'd say things like, 'How could she have a knife hidden in her petticoat? How come it wouldn't fall out when she was running?' You know, irritating stuff like that, just to spoil everything."

"No imagination," Charlie said sadly, shaking his head over the wheel of the car. "Imagination is totally essential to proper game playing. What shall we pack for lunch? I want egg salad sandwiches."

They wrangled cheerfully over the contents of the lunch and other details of the expedition all the way home. Once in the farmhouse, they packed their sandwiches and changed into jeans and T-shirts. Jenny found her own hiking boots in the basement and a pair of Steve's that fit Charlie.

"They look awfully heavy," he said dubiously, bending to tie the laces, the muscles of his back and shoulders knotting and flexing through the thin cotton of his T-shirt. "Couldn't we just wear sneakers?"

"Charlie, there's cactus out there, with spines two inches long. Sneakers aren't enough protection."

"All right, all right. At least we're at the same disadvantage. You're wearing them, too, so you won't be able to outrun me."

She grinned. "That remains to be seen. Here, you need a hat, too. The sun can get hot in the coulees."

She pulled on a black Harley-Davidson cap with a broad peak, bundling her hair up beneath it, and handed an identical one to him.

He tugged it on and grinned at her. The cool, handsome young executive had vanished completely, replaced by an engaging rascal with a sparkling grin beneath the shadowy peak of the cap.

He loves you, Jenny, her mother's voice whispered in her mind, and she shivered, staring at him.

"Well, how do I look?" he asked her.

"All right, I guess," she said offhandedly. "Come on, Charlie. I can hardly wait. It seems like years since I've done this."

They shouldered their backpacks, locked the house and hiked rapidly off through Frank's carefully cultivated acres. Beyond the boundaries of the D'Angelo property they crossed an open pasture filled with grazing cattle, climbed through a barbed wire fence and started into a tract of rough land crisscrossed with sharp hills and deep, brush-filled ravines.

After another mile or so, they were in a place of wilderness and isolation, a place where it would be easy to imagine wagon trains and cowboys and marauding Indian bands. Wild rosebushes massed in the coulee bottoms, along with dense thickets of brush, and occasionally they startled grazing mule deer, which gazed at them with huge liquid eyes and then bounded away up the hillsides. An eagle circled lazily overhead, so high that it looked like a dot in the sky until it swooped lower, its massive wings outspread.

The only sound was the swish of their boots through the massed sagebrush and prairie grass lining the trail along the coulee bottom, and the steady hum of insects busy in the midday sunlight.

"Hey, this is great," Charlie said looking around with pleasure. "I love this. I didn't think places like this still existed."

Jenny, ahead of him on the trail, turned to smile at him. "I've always loved this place. I used to pack a lunch like this and spend whole days in here when I was a kid. And you know something, Charlie? I've never, ever seen another single living soul in here, except for when I could talk Steve into coming with me."

He returned her smile, pausing to ease the straps on his back. "How far do you want to hike?"

"About another mile. There's a little green valley hidden among the hills up ahead, with a natural spring where you can cool your feet. It's hard to find, though," she added, frowning. "I think we have to angle north a bit, through that ravine over there."

"Okay. Lead on."

He followed her, admiring the shapely curve of her hips in the old blue jeans and the easy swing of her stride as she hiked along the rough trail.

"I think," she said, pausing, "that it must be...oh, look, Charlie! See that funny bush, all bare at the bottom with a cluster of live branches at the top?"

He peered in the direction of her outstretched hand and nodded.

"It's right beyond that in a little hollow. We're almost there."

They hiked over the lip of the hill and down into a place of pure enchantment.

The tiny green valley lay hidden and secret, as round and hollow as a bowl, rimmed by cloudless blue sky in a pure circle all around the edges. In its depths the wind stilled to a distant murmur, and the grass, heavy with golden sunshine and midday warmth, drooped lazily, starred here and there by delicate wildflowers. At the base of the hollow a natural spring bubbled out of the ground, ran over an outcrop of damp, mossy stones and vanished into a small shady cavern.

They stopped by the spring, easing their backpacks onto the ground and stretching with relief.

"My God, this is a beautiful place," Charlie breathed, taking his jacket from his pack and spreading it out on the grass.

"I know," Jenny said, looking around in pleasure. She tugged her cap from her head, shook her hair free and lifted it with her fingers to let the wind blow through it. Charlie lay back on the jacket, hands behind his head, watching her. The sun glinted in her rich hair with little fiery sparkles of bronze and glowed on the delicate oval of her face, like finely worked marble in the midday light.

"I found this place years and years ago," she told him, "when I was about ten or eleven, I guess, and I used to really believe it was magic. I always wanted to sneak out of the house and come here at midnight on a full moon to see if the fairies danced here in the moonlight, but I was too scared.''

"Of what?'' Charlie asked, rummaging through his pack for their water jug. "Your parents or the fairies?''

"Both, I think.'' She untied the laces on her hiking boots, tugged them off, stripped her socks away and dipped her bare feet in the bubbling cool spring with a little sigh of bliss. Charlie followed suit while she spread her own jacket out beside his and unwrapped the sandwiches.

"Don't forget,'' he said, wiggling his toes happily in the water, "that mine are the ones with the—''

"I *know* Charlie. Yours are the ones with the dill and pimento. You only mentioned it about fifty times already.''

"I'm very particular about my egg salad sandwiches,'' Charlie said with dignity. "Egg salad sandwiches are one of life's great pleasures and not to be taken lightly.''

"You're crazy, you know,'' Jenny observed, handing him a wrapped packet of sandwiches. "You really are.'' But her voice was tolerant, almost fond, and she smiled as she spoke.

They munched companionably on their bread and cheese, sipped the water and ate an apple each. Then they tidied the residue of the lunch back into their packs and, as if by mutual consent, lay back, side by side, caps over their faces to keep out the glare of the sun, resting placidly by the little spring.

"Don't you love this?'' she murmured drowsily. "The sun is so warm, and it's all so quiet. I feel as if everything in the whole world is a million miles away, so far away that it could never, ever find me, and nothing could ever make me feel the least bit unhappy.'' Her voice trailed off, and she stretched and flexed her legs in sleepy contentment.

Charlie lifted his cap from his face, raised himself on one elbow and glanced over at her as she lay beside him. She had her hands behind her head, cap still tipped over her eyes, with the rich hair spilling out against the soft green grass. Her long legs were drawn up, slender bare feet resting on the warm earth, stomach taut and flat in the faded blue jeans. He could see the rich curve of her breasts under the fabric of the T-shirt, even the delicate outline of her nipples through the soft fabric of her bra.

"Jenny," he whispered, his voice husky. "Hey, Jenny, are you asleep?"

"Hmm?" she murmured.

"Here he comes, Jen. Here comes the fearful savage slithering through the tall grass toward the innocent sleeping maiden."

His brown hand crept across the space between them, touched her fingers, started slowly up her arm.

She giggled and rolled toward him. "Don't forget," she murmured, still laughing, "that I have a knife in my petticoats."

Her cap fell away, and he gazed into her dark, shining eyes, just inches away from his. "Oh, Jen," he said softly, "that's not all you've got in your petticoat, girl."

Her eyes grew wide and startled as his hand reached her shoulder, inched down across the front of her T-shirt, gently cupped her breast and fondled its swelling curve.

"Charlie," she murmured. "Charlie, don't."

"The maiden is terrified," he whispered, pulling her shirt from the waistband of her jeans and sliding his hand up under it. "She tries to struggle, but she's mesmerized by the dark, hypnotic stare of his savage eyes."

His hand found the lacy cup of her bra, edged it aside, cupped her breast and thumbed the nipple. He put his other arm around her and drew her close, burying his face against the rich mass of her hair.

"She knows that it's inevitable," he murmured into her ear. "She knows that the savage is going to have his way with her."

Jenny lay there, hardly able to breathe, stunned by his nearness, by the warmth of his hand on her breast and the raging tumult of emotions that her body could scarcely contain. She wanted to resist, wanted to pull away and get up and run from this place, away from his lips and hands, from his husky, compelling voice and hard, muscular body. But she was consumed by a delicious, warm weakness, a spreading tide of urgency that swept everything aside and left only a helpless feeling of warmth and pleasure and a deep, deep yearning.

"Charlie," she whispered again, and then his lips found hers, silencing her, pressing and searching hungrily as his hand fondled her thighs, her stomach, her rounded hips and began slowly to unfasten the button on her jeans and pull down the zipper.

She drew away and gazed up at him, starting to protest again. But the sight of him, so close to her, his hair shining gold in the sunlight, his blue eyes darkened and his handsome, tanned face intent and ablaze with passion, left her weak and breathless.

Suddenly there was no resistance left in her, just a consuming desire that matched his in its intensity. She sat up, pulled her shirt over her head and turned silently for him to unfasten her bra. Then she faced him again while he knelt beside her, drew in a sharp breath and gazed raptly at her naked upper body.

Her skin was creamy and pale, her bosom full and shapely, rising gracefully from the taut flatness of her abdomen. He reached out a trembling hand to fondle her breasts, gleaming like mother-of-pearl in the bright light. Rapidly he tugged his own T-shirt off, tossed it aside and drew her close to him, holding her against the broad, muscular expanse of his chest.

"Jenny," he muttered brokenly into her hair, his voice husky. "My God, girl, you're so beautiful. No man ever held a woman so beautiful."

Slowly she drew away from him, stood up and slipped her jeans down over her hips, meeting his eyes with a gaze that was calm and steady, almost challenging. He watched in awe as her slim, rounded hips and long legs appeared, and she finally stood before him as lovely and delicately molded as a porcelain figurine in the sunlit secret valley, wearing only a pair of lacy bikini panties.

Wordlessly he stood, too, unzipped his own jeans and tossed them aside. Then he tugged off his undershorts and turned to face her, completely naked, erect and urgent with desire, the sunlight behind him gilding his body with a fiery glow.

Jenny murmured something incoherent and moved slowly toward him, melting into his arms, drowning herself in his kisses, feeling her body sinking and falling, falling through the sunlit stillness to the warm earth and the soft green grass. His body and his hands moved over her, pulling aside the flimsy panties, caressing her with indescribable tenderness, touching her and stroking her until she rose and arched and soared on an ecstasy of wanting, of need, of aching emptiness that only he could satisfy.

All of her senses were filled with him. She felt the golden texture of his skin under her hands, the hard, taut firmness of his muscular body, the rasping pleasure of his matted chest hair against her breasts. She smelled the rich, warm scent of him, of dust and shaving cream and maleness, and shivered with delight and anticipation as she tasted the light, salty flavor of his skin.

Finally, when his body merged with hers and moved within her, she felt a rich, singing excitement and a deep fulfillment that surpassed anything she had ever known. She wanted it to last forever, this feeling of completion, of fullness, of absolute, perfect harmony and satisfaction. But her body's need overwhelmed her, driving her toward climax, surging all at once against his with an urgency so powerful that both of them were drowned in it, lost in sensation, carried high on pounding waves of feeling. Finally, lost and spent and warm in each other's arms, they lay still and peaceful in the gentle sunlight.

Nearby, a meadowlark's song trilled from some hidden place, and a bee buzzed drowsily over a mass of fragrant wild roses.

Charlie raised himself on one elbow and smiled down at her lovely flushed face and tumbled hair against the grass. "My God," he whispered. "Jennifer D'Angelo, you are a remarkable woman."

"This would never have happened," she whispered back, "if I could just have gotten that damn knife out of my petticoat."

He threw his head back and laughed, his teeth very white against his tanned face, the golden column of his throat rich and strong above her. "The maiden never had a chance," he told her solemnly, rolling over beside her and cuddling her gently against him. "The wicked savage was too quick and strong."

"And maddened with lust," she added.

"And maddened with lust," he agreed. Suddenly his eyes were grave as he turned to look at her. "Do you hate me for this, Jenny?"

She gazed back at him in disbelief. "Look, Charlie," she said finally. "I'm a big girl, okay? We can joke all we like about lust-crazed savages, but you wouldn't have had a chance without my cooperation, you know. I wanted it, too."

He was silent, stroking her hair and staring moodily at the sky. "I feel as if I'd betrayed you somehow, taken advantage of the fact that you have to be in my company all the time. I feel that I've treated you badly, Jenny."

"Well, forget it," she said lightly, sitting up and reaching for her clothes. "You treated me extremely well, in fact, considering you're just a lust-crazed savage. It's been quite a long time since I've had that particular experience, Charlie, and I have to say that I really enjoyed it. So don't worry about my virtue and don't lose any sleep over the thought of taking advantage of me, okay?"

He grinned at her as they dressed. "So you enjoyed it, did you? So much for the terrified innocent maiden."

"I *am* an innocent maiden," she said with dignity. "Absolutely. And if you try to tell people anything different, I'll deny it. Who's going to pay any attention to a lust-crazed savage, anyhow? They have no credibility whatever."

He laughed, tugging his cap back down over his eyes and turning to face her. "Jenny, Jenny," he said, "you're really unbelievable, you know that? Just the most marvelous woman."

He took her arm and drew her gently toward him. His face was soft with tenderness and full of emotion as he gazed at her. Startled, she returned his look in silence.

"Jenny," he whispered huskily, "I want, I want to tell you that I . . ."

He hesitated, struggling with himself. His face was tense with feeling and his eyes were very blue, as blue as the cloudless prairie sky that soared above them. But, after a moment's silence, he turned away, his movements brisk and businesslike, his voice carefully controlled.

"Let's get this stuff packed up, shall we?" he said. "We'd better start heading back, so we have time to change and get into town before visiting hours tonight."

Jenny watched his taut, muscular body as he bent to shoulder his pack. She paused, her face concerned and thoughtful. "Charlie..." she began hesitantly.

He turned to face her, all the emotion carefully controlled, his face sparkling with its old casual, teasing grin.

Automatically she smiled back at him, knelt to pick up her own pack and started hiking slowly behind him up the hillside toward the trail.

"Papa," Jenny said, "please, don't look so worried. The doctor says this is all normal."

"Yes," Frank said. "I know he did. But they told us that a very high percentage of transplant rejections is also normal, Jenny. And I don't know if Mama has the strength to survive such a thing. I don't know if she could go through this again."

"I think," Charlie said, handing out slices of pizza from the box open in front of them on the kitchen table, "that she's a woman with enough strength of will to withstand anything. She's amazing."

"You think so, Charlie?" Frank asked, looking hopefully at the younger man. "You think she can get through this? Even if the transplant doesn't work?"

"You were there tonight, Frank. We all were. You saw what she was like, teasing and joking even though she was in pain, telling all of us funny stories about the hospital routine."

"And the doctor told us," Jenny repeated, "that an elevation of the white cell count is only to be expected, Papa. He said it's not high enough yet to indicate outright rejection."

Frank shook his head, gazing dispiritedly at his un-eaten slice of pizza. "She was in such pain," he whispered. "I could see it in her eyes, even though she'd rather die than admit it. Why can't they give her something for the pain?"

"Because," Charlie told him patiently, "the medication could mask other symptoms, Frank, and she has to be carefully monitored. She can deal with the pain. She really can. She has so much power in her mind."

He fell silent, staring at the darkened window, and Jenny glanced secretly at him.

Ever since their hour in the little enchanted valley that afternoon she had been intensely conscious of him in a disturbing new way, sensitive to every movement he made and every word he spoke. The angle of his chin, the blade of light glinting on his strong cheekbone with its shadow of golden stubble, the set of his sculpted lips, the decisive movements of his hands—all of these thrilled her, moved her in some profound and inexplicable way.

Sometimes she found it was all she could do to keep from touching him. Her hands strayed toward him of their own accord, and she had to exercise enormous self-control to keep from betraying her thoughts and feelings.

This, she thought, *is just not going to work. If I have to be in his presence every minute for another whole week, I'm going to have to get a grip on myself and take my cue from him.* He's *acting as if nothing ever happened. To him it was just a pleasant interlude and nothing more, and that's what it's going to be for me, too.*

"Shall we, Jen?" Charlie was saying.

"Hmm?" Jenny asked, startled.

"I said we'd better get to bed. It's after eleven, and we have to be up early to catch the plane, and you have to be bright and alert for the show tomorrow afternoon."

"Yes," Jenny said. "I guess you're right." She moved around the kitchen, tidying away the residue of their impromptu meal, and then paused to lay a gentle hand on her father's shoulder. "I wish I didn't have to leave, Papa. I wish I could stay with you until we know one way or the other."

"Tuesday," Frank said. "The doctor said that by Tuesday we should know what chance her body has of accepting the transplant."

"I know, Papa. You'll have to call us as soon as you know something. I won't be able to think of anything else," Jenny added wanly, "until I've heard."

"Yes, you will," Frank said, his voice unexpectedly stern. "You'll put it out of your mind and think about your job on that TV show, for your mother's sake. She was afraid of this, Jenny. She didn't even want you to know about the surgery because it might upset you. For Mama's sake you have to be brave, too, and put it out of your mind. Go ahead and do your best."

"She will, Frank," Charlie promised. "I'll see that she does. And after it's all over, when she wins the million dollars and you're all rich, I'll drop out here for a visit sometime and drink some more of that marigold wine."

"Anytime, Charlie," Frank said, beaming at the younger man with undisguised affection. "You're welcome anytime in our home. And Mama says the same thing. She likes you very much, Mama does."

He sat at the table, sipping the strong black coffee that he favored and watching in thoughtful silence as Charlie and Jenny left the kitchen and mounted the stairs to the second floor.

On the upper landing they paused awkwardly, looking at each other. "We should be up about six-thirty or so," Charlie said, "to give us lots of time. Do you want me to call you?"

She shook her head. "I brought my alarm clock, thanks."

They hesitated, standing tensely in the darkness, their faces faintly illuminated by the glow of the full moon through the long window on the landing.

"Well, good night then, Jenny," he said.

"Good night, Charlie. See you in the morning."

He turned away abruptly without touching her, went into his own room and closed the door. Slowly Jenny followed suit, moving into the warm confines of her old room, undressing, putting on her nightgown.

On her way back from the bathroom she paused silently beside his door, battling an urgent desire to knock, to go and climb into bed with him, nestle in the comforting circle of his strong arms and kiss his lips and fall asleep with her head on his chest.

But there was no sound from within, and she resisted the impulse, closing her own door behind her and slipping between the sheets.

She lay in her childhood bed, gazing out the familiar square of window at the glimmering moon beyond the gnarled crab apple tree and the broad, starry sweep of prairie sky, like a curtain of black spangled with glittering sequins. She felt a bewildering array of emotions: fear for her mother, concern for her father, worry and reluctance about her return to the quiz show the following day, all heightened by strong stirrings of sexual need and desire.

Try as she would she couldn't keep her mind from returning to the events of the afternoon, to their rich lovemaking and the overwhelming pleasure of intimacy with the man who now lay just across from the hall from her in another bed.

Just a few feet away, she thought, *but he might as well be on the moon. He won't even touch me.*

Restlessly she slipped out of bed, wandered over and curled up on the window seat, leaning her forehead against the cool glass and pondering the mystery of Charlie.

In the course of one afternoon's pleasure their positions seemed to have completely reversed. Now she was the one who longed for his touch, longed for a word of reassurance, an indication that her presence and her person were somehow pleasing to him. And he was cautious and reserved, avoiding any spark of intimacy, treating her with courteous aloofness.

She listened to the rising wind that sobbed through the trees in her father's little fruit orchard and watched the play of light and shadow as the moonlight glimmered on the swaying branches.

Charlie had enjoyed their lovemaking. She knew he had. A man couldn't disguise that kind of pleasure, not at a moment when his soul was so exposed. And some of the things he had whispered to her . . . She shivered a little and drew her knees up, hugging them and resting her chin on them, brooding.

Charlie was too honest a man, she knew, to murmur insincerities even in the throes of passion. He wasn't a man who could lie to a woman just to get what he wanted from her. And yet, after they had made love, he had immediately become distant and polite, joking in a casual, perfunctory way and trying to avoid looking at her.

Jenny sat on the window seat, thinking all the things that all women think in the same situation.

Maybe he doesn't like me after all. Maybe I was too easy, and now the challenge is gone. Maybe he was just curious and now he can file me away and forget me.

All at once she set her jaw, her lovely pale face still and resolute in the moonlight.

That's fine, she thought. *I don't have to beg him for a kind word. And after Friday, at the latest, I'll never have to see him again. There are lots of other men in the world, after all.*

But, as she returned to her bed and lay silently wakeful on her back, her dark eyes glittering in the faint light, she felt a deep, icy chill of fear. Because she knew that no matter how many men there were in the world, it would be a long, long time before she ever found another one who could thrill her in just that way.

After what seemed like hours, she finally fell asleep, toppling over the edge of consciousness into a deep night-time stillness broken only by the sighing of the wind and the melancholy cries of owls and nighthawks in the open country beyond the old farmhouse.

CHAPTER NINE

UNWELCOME THOUGH it was, Jenny's return to the quiz show still had a feeling of homecoming about it. Family groups can develop in all kinds of unlikely settings, and in many ways the game show group was a kind of family. Over the course of her week's appearance on the show Jenny had come to know all of them, along with the details of their lives. She knew that the glamorous makeup girl was hopelessly in love with a married man, that the crisp, efficient assistant producer lived with her widowed mother and a huge assortment of animals, that the wife of the handsome young second cameraman was pregnant with twins.

And then there were Amy and Eric, her partners in misery, both of whom seemed like old, old friends by now. They were already in the lounge when Jenny and Charlie hurried in, shaking the rain from their coats and brushing dampness out of their hair. Charlie took Jenny's coat politely and paused to hang the two garments on the rack, while Jenny entered the lounge, smiling, to greet her two colleagues.

To her envious eyes, Amy and Eric both seemed full to the brim, absolutely stuffed with knowledge from their arduous weekend of studying. They looked as if they were about to tip over with the weight of information, as if they had to carry themselves very, very carefully so as not to shake or dislodge any of the masses of facts that had been crammed into their brains.

Jenny, on the other hand, felt as light as a feather, distressingly empty-headed and vague, as if she would be unable even to answer the simplest question. After months and months of intensive studying and memorizing, every spare minute of her days and evenings, her week of enforced idleness had taken its toll. She could hardly remember her own name, she thought, let alone the kinds of details that Eric and Amy would certainly have mastered.

"Hello, you two," she said, seating herself across from Eric, who was trembling, as usual. "Have a nice weekend on the beach?"

Eric gave her a pallid, frightened smile while Amy beamed placidly.

"Amy!" Jenny exclaimed suddenly. "Look at you!"

"What about me?"

"You're wearing your *orange dress,* Amy."

"Well, well," Amy said, looking down at herself in mock surprise. "So I am. How about that?"

Charlie approached the table, clapped Eric cheerfully on the shoulder and grinned at Amy. "That's my girl," he said, bending to drop a cheery kiss on her plump cheek. "Go for the gusto."

"Easy for you to say, Charlie Mitchell," Amy said with mock severity. "*You've* never had the pleasure of dealing with Sam Wecker, you know. God knows what I'm letting myself in for."

But her eyes, Jenny noticed, were shining with anticipation, her whole being aglow with a sort of contained excitement.

She looks lovely, Jenny realized in surprise. *In that bright color, with her face all alight, Amy looks actually beautiful.*

Inexplicably she felt a quick stab of worry and concern for her friend, but suppressed it firmly.

Charlie appeared at her elbow and courteously handed her a cup of the vile coffee that was the specialty of the visitors' lounge. Jenny thanked him just as politely, not looking at him, and then turned aside as he seated himself next to her and began his daily mission of involving Eric in conversation in an attempt to soothe the little man's terrible nervousness.

"Excuse me," Jenny murmured. "I need to powder my nose," she added, pushing her chair back and getting to her feet.

"Me, too," Amy announced, and followed Jenny across the lounge and down the hall.

As soon as they were inside the tiled washroom, Amy slammed her handbag onto the counter and turned to the younger woman, bright-eyed and inquisitive.

"So, tell me," she whispered urgently, "how was he? Terrific, right? I'll bet he's just terrific in the sack."

Jenny stared at her friend, a flush mounting slowly on her cheeks. "Amy, how did you . . . ? What are you talking about? Did Charlie say . . . ?"

"Hell, sweetie, nobody has to *say* anything. A person just has to look at the two of you to know that something happened back home on the range, and it wasn't just hopping sagebrush. Spill it, Jen. Tell Auntie Amy all about it."

The big woman rummaged in her multicolored handbag, took out a stick of brilliant red lipstick and applied a generous layer to her already garish mouth. She caught Jenny's eye in the mirror, her lips still rounded, her plump face bright and shrewd.

"Yes," Jenny said, "something happened. Not," she added bitterly, "that you'd ever know it from the way he's behaving, Amy. Ever since he's acted like he doesn't even know me. Like I'm just somebody he met in the elevator, you know, and decided to tag along with for a while.''

Amy regarded her steadily in the mirror. ''And that reaction surprises you?'' she asked. ''You're upset about it?''

Jenny dabbed some pale pink gloss on her lips with an abrupt, impatient gesture and clicked the tube shut. ''Of course it upsets me. If he was going to regret it so much, why did he want to do it in the first place? Why not just leave me alone?''

''Jenny, Jenny,'' Amy said, shaking her head and setting her enormous silver earrings tingling merrily.

She took a hairbrush from her bag and began to brush her long blond hair, which looked brighter gold than usual and had, Jenny suspected, been touched up over the weekend.

''Girl,'' Amy went on, ''you're sweet and beautiful, and you've got a mind like a steel trap, but you've still got a whole lot to learn about men.''

''Well, tell me then, Amy,'' Jenny said. ''Tell me why he's behaving like he wishes he'd never met me. Why, Amy? God knows, I don't want a long-term relationship or anything. By the end of the week he'll be back in Chicago and I'll be in Calgary and I'll never see him again. I just want to know why he's . . . why he's acting this way,'' she finished lamely, and zipped her handbag with shaking hands.

Amy looked at her steadily for a moment, her kind, bright eyes serious for once. ''Because he's scared, Jennygirl,'' she said softly. ''Charlie Mitchell is just plain scared to death, and I suspect it's a new experience for him, poor dear.''

Jenny looked at her, startled, and opened her mouth to frame another question, but Amy took her arm and moved her firmly toward the door.

"Come on now," she said. "If we stay in here any longer, Charlie's going to suspect me of passing along contraband information, and barge in here looking for you. We'd better get back."

Jenny followed her friend's huge, swaying form into the lounge, her finely drawn face still troubled and preoccupied. Charlie, they saw, had moved around the table to lay a comforting arm across Eric's shoulders and was speaking earnestly to him in low tones. The thin little man looked much more composed, even giving them a wan smile as they approached and controlling his terror when they were summoned onstage for the preliminary round.

Jenny stood at the end, as usual, in the space reserved for the high-scoring contestant of the previous match. She was sharply conscious of Amy beside her, bright and brave in her vivid orange dress, anxiously searching the studio audience with an open, expectant look on her face, clouded at times by a painful shadow of anxiety. If Amy found the face she was searching for, she gave no sign of it, and as the house lights dimmed, she turned her attention to Jay Allen as if there were no other thoughts at all on her mind.

Eric, next to Amy, bounced and shivered and coughed in nervousness, while the fourth contestant, a placid librarian from Florida, gazed across her podium as calmly as if she were still stamping out books back in Miami.

Despite her lack of studying and her terrifying sensation of empty-headedness, Jenny sailed competently through the preliminary round, slightly ahead of both Eric and Amy. The librarian, like many of the new contestants, was hopelessly lost by the first commercial break, unable to ring in on time, incapable of answering properly, drowning in panic, and it was evident that the contest would once again be a three-way race.

Only once during the preliminary round did Jenny dare to glance down at Charlie, seated in his usual place in the front row. When she did, she met his eyes directly and was surprised to find him staring at her with a look of burning intensity and some other powerful emotion that was unfathomable to her.

Was it, as Amy had said, a look of fear? And if so, why was he afraid of her?

She returned his gaze for a long moment, trembling at the sight of his handsome, clean-cut face, finely molded lips and the depth of emotion in his blue eyes.

She could hardly believe that it had been exactly one week since she had first stood here, stared out in panic at the studio audience and seen his boyish, cheerful face smiling encouragement at her. Then she hadn't known anything about him, not even his name. And now she knew him as well as she knew anybody in her life, knew the feel of his hands, the smell of his skin, the taste of his lips and the sound of his husky voice whispering in her ears.

She shivered involuntarily and forced her attention back to Jay Allen and the question board.

Perhaps because it was the beginning of a new week, the panel apparently had decided to be merciful. The specialty questions seemed, all three of them, to be unusually easy, and each contestant answered without hesitation.

They met in the lounge after the show with a festive air of celebration, comparing notes. By now Amy had won a hundred and twenty-eight thousand dollars and had to begin considering the option of retiring with these considerable winnings or risking the whole amount in an attempt to double it. Jenny was in the same position with thirty-two thousand dollars, and even Eric now had won four thousand.

"There's no question for me," Jenny said, stirring the coffee that Charlie, with unfailing courtesy, had prepared for her by the time she'd arrived. "I'm going on. Thirty-two thousand dollars will hardly make a dent in my family's debts. I've approached this right from the beginning with an all-or-nothing attitude, and that's how I have to continue."

"Well," Eric said, "I want to quit. Four thousand dollars is more money than I've ever had in my hand at one time, you know. And I'm scared of those specialty questions. Sure, today was easy, but you know what killers they can be."

"Oh, pooh," Amy said comfortably. "You know more about classical music than anybody, son. Don't let them scare you. Hang in there. Go for some really big bucks while you have the chance, and don't be..."

But her voice trailed off and her eyes rounded in sudden panic as she looked toward the door. The other three followed the direction of her gaze as she stared, as if hypnotized, at a small man who had appeared in the entry to the lounge and was slowly making his way across the room.

If this was the fabled Sam Wecker, Jenny thought, he was hardly a figure of high romance. He was almost comical in appearance—a small, rotund man in a dapper tan suit and bright orange tie, with a huge black handlebar mustache that seemed to carry him along like the propeller of an airplane. His cheeks were round and full, his head almost completely bald.

But his eyes, Jenny saw, were bright with intelligence and sparkling with good humor as he approached their table and stood gazing intently at Amy. And all the comical element vanished from the situation when Jenny turned and saw the look on her friend's face.

Amy gazed up at the newcomer with a look of appeal, of yearning, of naked adoration that laid her soul bare and made her face seem austere and lovely.

Fifteen years of loneliness, of longing and wondering and waiting and suffering, were all distilled in that one look, a gaze that was too painful for Jenny to contemplate. She turned aside, and Charlie reached out unexpectedly to grip her fingers under the table. She held his hand, warmed and comforted by the firmness of his grasp.

"Hi, kiddo," the dapper little man said softly to Amy, "long time no see."

Amy continued to stare at him for a moment with wide-eyed wonder and finally turned to her friends. "This...this is Sam," she said in a trembling voice. "Sam Wecker."

They nodded and smiled while Amy murmured their names, and Eric began to look baffled again, lost in the crosscurrents of yet another intensely emotional situation that he didn't understand. He looked from one face to another, shrugged and finally, as usual, effected his escape by leaving for the library.

Sam Wecker sat in the younger man's vacated chair, muttering some kind of polite greeting, but the situation was almost as uncomfortable for Charlie and Jenny as it had been for poor Eric, primarily because Sam and Amy were barely conscious of them and continued to stare hungrily at each other as if nobody else existed in all the world.

"Well," Charlie said finally, "I guess we'd better get going. We're running behind time."

Amy nodded abstractedly and went on gazing at the bald little man with the big mustache, who had taken her hand across the table and was holding it with tender reverence.

"Well, goodbye, Amy," Jenny said awkwardly. "See you tomorrow."

"Hmm?" Amy said, and forced herself to look up for a moment. "Oh, right," she said. "Tomorrow. See you, Jenny." Immediately her eyes returned to the man opposite her, and Jenny was sure that neither Sam nor Amy even saw them leave.

"Wow," Charlie said in the car as they splashed through the rainy streets toward their hotel. "What did you think of *that,* Jen?"

"Well," Jenny said thoughtfully, "you could hardly call it a casual encounter, could you?"

He chuckled. "Hardly. Lots of emotion there, all right. What did you think of him? As a woman, I mean? What was your evaluation?"

"Charlie, I hardly heard him say two words. How could I form an evaluation?"

He turned to smile at her with a hint of his old teasing sparkle, and her heart beat faster. "Come on, Jenny. I know you. You're capable of forming an evaluation at the drop of a hat. You evaluate everybody."

Jenny smiled back at him. "You're right. I do. And lots of times my first impression turns out to be altogether wrong, and then I'm forced to revise it later. But," she added, staring out the windshield at the driving rain, "I think I liked him."

"I think I did, too," Charlie said. "But we don't know as much about him as Amy does, right? And it remains to be seen what *her* final evaluation is going to be."

"Charlie, if she's right, if he's just interested in her because of the money, you know..." He nodded, and Jenny continued, her voice troubled. "Charlie, you saw her face when she looked at him. If he's just planning to use her or leave her again, I wonder if she can stand it."

"It's amazing what people can stand if they have to, Jen," he said quietly. "And, in the final analysis, we have no control over other people's behavior. Just our own."

She thought about his words as they drove on to the hotel in silence, plowing through the rain-washed streets, sending huge fountains of water gushing past their tires whenever they rounded a corner.

"POPCORN, JENNY?" Charlie asked.

She nodded. "Please. Lots, Charlie. I want the biggest container."

He stared at her. "You're kidding. Look at the *size* of it, Jen. It's at least a bushel."

"I'm hungry," she said.

"How can you be hungry? We just finished eating."

"I hated that seafood casserole," Jenny confessed. "The sauce tasted funny. I covered it with my napkin so you wouldn't see and left almost all of it."

He laughed, standing in line at the concession counter, and bent impulsively to kiss her lips. Jenny stared at him, startled, but he turned aside immediately to place their order, and when he handed her the popcorn and took her arm to lead her upstairs, he was as nonchalant as ever.

Jenny walked beside him to the balcony and edged in ahead of him to the seats, wondering, as she had been all day, why he was behaving like this.

Ever since their moments of intense intimacy back in the little green glade he had been strangely withdrawn, as courteous and remote as a polite stranger. But there were these occasional brief flashes, times when he would touch her unexpectedly or say something puzzling or when she would glance at him suddenly and catch a look of hungry intensity on his face that had never been there before.

He loves you, Jenny, her mother's voice whispered in her mind. And then Amy chimed in: *He's scared of you, girl.*

"This *is* quite a generous serving of popcorn, Charlie," she said aloud. "You can share if you like."

He shook his head. "No way. You ordered it, you have to eat it. Every kernel," he added sternly, "or I won't bring you to the movies ever again."

Jenny chuckled. The house lights dimmed, and she settled back with her tub of popcorn to watch the movie.

It was a Woody Allen movie, one that Jenny had wanted to see but missed during the arduous, intense months of studying before her appearance on *Ask Me Anything.* And it was Woody Allen at his best, exploring the intricacies and absurdities of relationships of all kinds. Jenny forgot the quiz show, forgot her worries about her family, even forgot Charlie's strange and disturbing behavior and gave herself up to enjoyment.

She laughed until her sides ached, and then, at the end, she cried for happiness. She was unaware of the tears until Charlie reached over with a gentle hand and wiped them tenderly from her cheeks.

"Jenny, Jenny," he whispered, gazing down at her and cupping her face in his lean brown hand, "did anybody ever tell you that you're just the sweetest girl in the whole world?"

She stared at him, blinking in surprise as the house lights came up, but he was out of his chair and politely taking her arm, acting once more as if those words of tenderness had never escaped him.

If he's trying to drive me crazy, she thought wretchedly, *he's doing a damn good job. He really is.*

They had coffee in a little Italian restaurant and discussed the movie, arguing cheerfully over the motivations of the characters.

"I thought he was just horribly selfish," Jenny said. "He should have known how she was going to feel when he insisted on putting his mother first all the time."

"She should have had enough understanding to realize that he felt that responsibility," Charlie said. "*She* was the one being selfish, I thought. A standard womanly trait, after all."

Jenny flushed and glared at him, framing an indignant response. But, just in time, she caught the wicked sparkle in his eyes and subsided, shaking her head.

"Oh, no. You're not going to do it again," she said. "I'm wise to you, Charlie. You like to get me going, just on purpose."

He grinned. "I know," he said contritely. "It's just that you're so beautiful when you're mad. Your eyes flash and your face gets pink, even your cheekbones look more pronounced. It's a marvelous sight."

"Quit studying me, okay, Charlie?" she said. "I told you that I'm not a toy, and in a few more days I'm going to cease being a source of entertainment for you altogether. So try to get over it, all right?"

His face sobered, and he was very quiet as he paid the bill and drove back to their hotel. They passed Higgins and his mistress in the lobby, coming back from the little dog's evening walk, with Higgins nattily dressed in his plaid raincoat and matching Sherlock Holmes cap. But Charlie even refrained from drawing the heavyset woman into conversation and inquiring after Higgins's health, a notable omission.

Charlie seldom failed, when the opportunity presented itself, to enter into protracted, solemn discussions with the elegant woman. He seemed to get some kind of obscure kick out of her intense preoccupation with her nervous, irritable little poodle. And, for her part, she appeared to be convinced that Charlie was some kind of oracle on animal health, asking him anxiously about all the various digestive, circulatory and emotional problems that had plagued poor Higgins throughout his brief, overprivileged life.

Jenny glanced over at him in the elevator as they rode to their suite. He was silent and preoccupied, staring intently at the control panel, apparently deep in thought.

"Higgins looked well, didn't you think?" she ventured. "Maybe the animal psychologist is helping him with his insecurities about his real mother."

Normally this topic never failed to elicit a response from Charlie. He and Jenny had enjoyed many hilarious discussions about Higgins's emotional problems, and lively speculations as to the nature of the little poodle's sessions with his animal psychologist.

But tonight Charlie wasn't to be drawn in. He merely nodded absentmindedly, ushered Jenny out of the elevator when it stopped at their floor and walked beside her down the hall to their room. He unlocked the door, flicked all the lights on at the master panel, then hesitated, looking down at her in silence.

Suddenly Jenny was very conscious of the fact that they were really alone together, for the first time, it seemed, since their lovemaking the day before.

Last night her father had been in the house, and then there had been the rush to the airport, the flight back to Vancouver, their arrival at the game show, dinner, the movie—all of it a bewildering blur of people and activity. But now they were alone in a hotel suite behind a locked door, and she was intensely aware of him.

He had never looked so handsome, and she had never wanted so much to be close to him. She wondered if this was a genuine emotion or just a frustrated reaction to his puzzling behavior. But all she really knew was that she wanted to nestle in his arms, kiss his lips, run her fingers through his sunny hair and feel the strength of his muscular body against hers.

The intensity of his gaze was becoming uncomfortable. He seemed to be staring into the depths of her soul, reading her deepest thoughts and emotions, searching his own mind for words to express his feelings. Jenny was the first to turn aside, drawing away, shrugging out of her coat and reaching to hang it in the foyer closet.

"Should I call home, do you think?" she asked over her shoulder as she wandered into the sitting room and curled up on one of the couches. "What time is it there, anyway?"

"Eleven-thirty," Charlie said, looking at his watch.

Charlie was one of those people with a time zone chart in his head, who always seemed to know instantly what time it was anywhere in the world.

"Do you think that's too late? Papa wouldn't be asleep yet, would he?" she asked wistfully.

"No, it's not too late," Charlie said, hanging his own coat away and coming to sit opposite her. "But I don't think you should call, Jen. The hospital said they wouldn't have any definite prognosis until tomorrow, and in the meantime, if there was any bad news, he'd have called and left a message. Wait till tomorrow."

She considered, her face thoughtful. "I guess you're right," she said slowly. "It's just so hard, waiting and feeling helpless, you know?"

"I know." He grinned suddenly, changing the subject. "How do you like being a celebrity, Jenny? How does it feel to actually sign an autograph?"

"Silly," she said promptly. "I just felt ridiculous, as if I were pretending to be a movie star or something. Me, a bank teller from Calgary, signing autographs. It's just nuts, that's all."

"I thought you looked very gracious," Charlie said, still grinning. "Elegant and queenly, as if you'd been signing autographs all your life."

"Charlie, come on. Quit teasing me. It was three little girls at the movie concession, that's all. No big deal."

"It's going to become a lot bigger deal from now on, Jen," he said, sobering and looking at her intently. "People are starting to recognize you everywhere we go. The guys back at Forbes in Chicago say you're a celebrity out there, too. Things are going to start getting crazy from now on, Jen. You have to be prepared. People are going to be mobbing us everywhere, and you're going to be getting offers to do commercials and movie parts."

"Charlie, come on. Be serious."

"I am being serious, Jenny. I want you to know what to expect."

Jenny clutched one of the small velvet sofa pillows, working the fringe with nervous fingers and staring at him, her eyes wide. "You mean it, don't you?" she whispered. "You're not kidding."

He shook his head. "I'm not kidding, Jenny. It's going to be a hectic week."

"But you'll be with me," she said with childlike simplicity. "I won't be alone. You'll be with me all the time."

"Yes, Jenny," he said gently. "I'll be with you all the time."

She nodded, got up and moved across the thick carpet toward her own room. "See you in the morning, Charlie. Six o'clock."

"Jen, we can cut out the run, just this week, if you feel you need the rest. I mean, there's a lot of pressure now, and it's not going to get any easier."

"Look," she said with mock severity, "just because I set too fast a pace for you, that's no reason to try to get out of it now. This running in the morning was your idea, but I've gotten to enjoy it, and you can't wriggle out of it by pretending concern for me, Charlie Mitchell. You can just get your sneakers on and hit the bricks, the same as always."

He sighed. "You're a hard woman, Jennifer. A hard woman."

"Damn right," she said, grinning at him. But, as their eyes met, her smile faded and she stood uncertainly in the doorway, searching for words. Finally she whispered an inaudible good-night and vanished into her own room, shutting the door quietly behind her.

CHARLIE LAY in his bed, hands behind his head, staring at the ceiling and battling his own emotions. He was intensely, painfully conscious of the beautiful woman who lay just a few feet away from him, locked together with him in the privacy of this luxurious suite far up in the sky.

He had never wanted anything in his life, he realized, as much as he wanted to walk into her room right now, slip into bed beside her, brush away her filmy nightgown and hold her fragrant, curving body, kiss her beautiful face and caress her.

He groaned and rolled over, burying his face in the pillow.

You're a fool, Charlie, he told himself. *Just a damn fool. You always thought you could control everything in your life. But you're up against something that's too big for you this time. You let it go too far, and now you're into a situation you can't handle. And there's not a damn thing you can do about it.*

He tried to distract himself by thinking about motorcycles, by performing a mental exercise requiring himself to recall all the makes and models of bikes produced by the major manufacturers for the past five model years.

But before he got past the third year he remembered Jenny standing behind the podium on the set of *Ask Me Anything,* calmly giving the dry weight of the 1985 Honda Rebel.

God, what a woman. What an incredible, wonderful woman she is.

He thought of her amazing mental capacities, coupled so strangely with a childlike innocence, an unassuming, gentle concern for others and a lack of conceit that was truly amazing.

Especially when you considered how beautiful she was.

He remembered how she'd looked in the crimson silk dress, outlining the warm curve of her hips and her taut, flat abdomen, her long, slender thighs and rich, swelling bosom. And then, unbidden, the memory flashed into his mind of her creamy naked skin glowing in the sunlight, and her lovely hair spread out on the grass as she lay gazing up at him, her body rich and warm with desire.

"Oh, God," he muttered aloud through gritted teeth.

His sexual arousal was so intense that he was in actual physical pain. He rolled over again, clutched the sides of the bed and stared at the ceiling, willing himself to be strong, to endure, to overcome temptation.

He had been wrong, he knew, to make love to her. It had been an act of weakness, of spontaneous yielding to her beauty and sweetness and his own deep male yearnings.

But he couldn't let it happen again, no matter what. He was a man of integrity, and somehow he had to find the strength to resist and to carry on with his mission, doing the job he had set out to do without weakness or compromise.

Methodically he returned to his mental catalog of motorcycles, concentrating on model numbers and specifications while Jenny's eyes and lips and hair haunted his memory like sweet whispers from a world of forbidden pleasure.

CHAPTER TEN

NORMALLY CHARLIE and Jenny tended to get deeply absorbed in whatever they were doing for entertainment in the late morning and early afternoon and had to make a mad dash to reach the set of the television show on time. On Tuesday, however, Jenny was the first contestant to arrive, and she and Charlie sat together in the lounge, sipping the terrible coffee and talking quietly.

Eric arrived soon afterward, looking pale and unhappy, but brightened a little when he saw Charlie.

"I read that book," he reported, "the one you told me about on how to develop inner strength."

"Did it help?" Charlie asked.

"I thought so," Eric said. "I mean, I felt a lot better about myself back at the library. But now that I'm actually here..." He paused and studied his fingernails gloomily.

Charlie sighed. "Eric, you're a real challenge, you know that? Look, all you have to do is remember that..."

Jenny looked around for Amy, feeling an unusual pang of concern. This was the first time, she realized, that Amy hadn't been present in the lounge when they arrived, her flamboyant dress and hairstyles seeming to fill the room with vividness and good cheer.

But, Jenny thought suddenly, Amy was always alone. There was never anybody with her, no friends tagging along, no family out in the studio audience to cheer her on.

Despite her unfailing cheerfulness and warmth, she was essentially a lonely person.

Just as Jenny framed this thought, Amy swept through the door and into the lounge, but this time she definitely wasn't alone. Sam Wecker followed close behind her, laden with packages, holding her elbow with a proprietorial air. Both of them were beaming, glowing, almost iridescent with love. Amy's round face was soft and shining, and even Sam's huge mustache seemed more buoyant, more rich and luxurious.

They approached the table in a solid wall of sound, a barrage of cheery greetings that left the other three gazing silently at them, openmouthed. They had clearly been shopping and had bought gifts for everyone—tiny, beautifully detailed motorcycle replicas for Jenny and Charlie and a rabbit's foot for Eric.

Eric took his gift in solemn gratitude and immediately clutched it in his hand like a drowning man grasping at straws. "Thanks, Amy," he muttered. "Maybe this is what I need to get me through."

Amy ruffled his thin hair fondly. "What you need, sweetie," she said, "is a good kick in the rear just to get you over this silly nervousness. Charlie, kick him, would you?"

Charlie grinned and turned to Jenny, who was already deep in conversation with Sam, telling him about the movie the night before.

"You're kidding," Jenny was saying, staring at the dapper little man. "You've met Woody Allen?"

"Well, you know," Sam said with a small self-deprecating wave of his hand. "Just to have lunch with occasionally, that's all. I mean, we're not bosom buddies or anything."

"Charlie," Jenny said in disbelief, "Sam *knows* Woody Allen."

"I heard, Jen." Charlie turned solemnly to the other man. "That's nothing," he said. "*I* happen to be on a first-name basis with two well-known television stars. Maybe you've heard of them? Amy Wecker and Jennifer D'Angelo?"

Amid the general laughter Amy tugged Jenny to her feet. "Come on," she murmured. "You need to powder your nose."

"I do?" Jenny asked blankly. Then, seeing Amy's expression, she added, "Oh, you're right. I do. See you fellows in a minute."

Amy hauled her across the lounge, barely stopping to acknowledge greetings from Walker Thompson and the production crew, and hurried her into the ladies' room. Finally, with the door safely closed behind them, she turned to Jenny.

"Well?" she asked. "What do you think?"

"About what?" Jenny asked innocently.

Amy glared at her, and then, unable to sustain any negative emotion for more than a few seconds, gave her a big, booming laugh. Jenny laughed with her, delighting in her friend's exuberance.

"Oh, Amy," she said finally, "it's good to see you like this. You seem so happy. You're just shining, you know?"

Amy sobered and sank into the upholstered chair beside the vanity. "Shining, am I?" she said. "What a fool I am, eh, Jen?"

Jenny looked over at her, puzzled by Amy's sudden change in mood, and perched on the edge of the counter, swinging her legs and waiting.

"I should tell you the whole story, I guess," Amy went on. "Are you in the mood for a story?"

"Only if you want to tell me, Amy. I don't want to pry, because I know it's none of my business."

"Hell," Amy said moodily, staring at the opposite wall, "I have to tell somebody. If I don't talk this over with someone, I'm going to go crazy. And you may have noticed that there aren't a lot of people in my life, Jen. I have no family, and I guess maybe I scare other people off or something. I'm what you might call..." She hesitated and cast Jenny a rueful grin. "I'm 'larger than life,' as they say."

Jenny laughed. "You're wonderful," she said. "You're just wonderful, Amy. So tell me the story."

"Well, I'll tell you *his* story. He left the house, like I told you, fifteen years ago to buy us a bottle of wine. And at the liquor store he met a couple of old friends, guys he'd known before he met me, one of whom he still owed a lot of money to."

She glanced up at Jenny, who nodded. "I get the picture. Go on."

"Well, it's pretty straightforward. They had this little caper all planned in a town a hundred miles away. They just needed somebody to drive the car for them, assured him that nothing could go wrong, that nobody would get hurt and that all of his debts would be cleared if he'd just do it for them."

"But something did go wrong," Jenny said.

"It sure did. And somehow a security guard got shot, and they were in custody in another city. And he couldn't call me. He was too ashamed, and he knew I couldn't post bail, anyhow. So he decided to take his lumps, legally speaking, and just pretend like I'd never existed, hope I'd think he'd just run out on me so I'd be absolutely furious and forget about him and get on with my life."

Jenny stared at her friend, wide-eyed with disbelief. "My God," she murmured. "He really did it deliberately, then? Got into trouble, chose not to involve you and never once contacted you or let you know a thing about what was happening to him?"

Amy nodded. "And it worked, too. I mean, after five years or so I'd gotten to the point where I didn't think about him more than five, six hours a day."

"Oh, Amy..."

"He was sentenced, of course, charged as an accessory and served five years. While he was in jail, if I can believe anything he says, he took a degree in business administration by correspondence and spent all his time thinking about me. When he got out he came looking for me, but I was long gone, of course, with no forwarding address. I'd moved to Edmonton by then, in fact, and I lived there until just a few years ago. So Sam had no idea I was even alive until he saw me on the show last week and came right out here."

"Where does he live now?"

"Toronto. He claims to be 'into stocks.' But apparently the job isn't that pressing, since he can just set it aside and come flying out here to my side at a moment's notice."

"Amy, it's all so incredibly romantic. What a story!"

"Yeah," Amy said. "It's so romantic."

Startled by her tone, Jenny looked at her carefully. "So," she said finally, "what's the problem?"

"Oh, God, Jen, I don't know what to do. I'm all torn up inside."

"Why? Don't you have any feelings for him anymore?"

Amy stared at her. "No feelings? Now *that* would be wonderful. To wake up some morning and find that I had no feelings left for Sam Wecker, that would be a dream come true, believe me."

Jenny was growing more puzzled as the conversation progressed. "Amy," she said, "am I missing something here? If you still care about him, and he's got his life back together, and you've found each other again, why is this not a happy story? Why do you look so gloomy?"

"Because," Amy said in despair, "I don't know if I can trust him, Jenny! How can I be sure he's what he says he is? How do I know he's not out here just because he sees the chance to move on my prize winnings, and then when he's spent them he'll just be gone again, vanished into thin air, and he'll have succeeded in ruining the last half of my life, as well?"

Jenny shook her head. "If you care so much about him, Amy, you must have some understanding of who and what he is. You must know a little about his motivations, and what he's likely to do."

"No way. When you get older, kid," Amy told her sadly, "you'll learn that we hardly know a thing about anybody, not even the people we love. Everybody's a mystery."

Jenny thought about Charlie, about his strange, abrupt withdrawal from her, and the painful distance he was maintaining between them, punctuated by those occasional baffling, disturbing flashes of warmth and spontaneous affection.

"I guess you're right, Amy," she said slowly. "I guess we really don't know people as well as we think we do."

She hesitated, and both women stared moodily at their reflections in the mirrored wall opposite them.

"Do you think he really knows Woody Allen?" Jenny asked suddenly. "Does he really have lunch with him sometimes?"

Amy shrugged. "Who knows? He might be best friends with Queen Elizabeth for all we know. Or it could all just be a pack of lies. God knows, I've heard lots of them."

"And you think he's still lying to you?"

"Jenny, you should hear him. He's talking so big about all the stuff we're going to do now that we've found each other again. And half the time he sort of implies *he's* going to pay for it. That's what kills me."

"What kind of stuff?" Jenny asked.

"Oh, hell, we're going to go on cruises and fly to Australia and take in the first game of the World Series. Jenny, he's doing just what he's always done. He's pretending to be a big shot, and meanwhile he's spending my money before I've even made it...."

Amy shook her head, heaved herself to her feet and slowly left the room, with Jenny following in troubled silence.

The mood at the table, though, when they returned was far less restrained. The three men were huddled close together, and Sam was holding forth on some topic with such eloquence that Eric was struck dumb, staring at him in absolute fascination. Even Charlie appeared mesmerized by the little man's vibrant speaking voice, his dark, shining eyes and flowing hand movements.

"God," Amy muttered in deep gloom, watching this small tableau. "Nobody knows how much I love that man."

Jenny grinned in spite of herself and joined the group at the table, sitting beside Eric and settling in to listen to Sam Wecker. He was talking about opal mining in Australia, and he was so fascinating that she, too, forgot everything, lost in the images he conjured up of baking deserts and tall plumes of dust a hundred miles away, of multi-colored exotic birds and the lonely cry of wild dingoes in the dark and starlit nights.

Jenny shivered and found that it took a considerable effort of will to drag herself out of her dreamworld and return to the reality of the quiz show and the necessity to remember everything there was to know about motor-cycles.

But something served as a good luck talisman. Either it was the presence of Sam Wecker or possibly Eric's rabbit's foot. At any rate, all three of them moved easily through the preliminary round, mowing down the new contestant as they usually did, and then all of them successfully answered their specialty questions.

"Now this," Jay Allen told the audience solemnly, "puts us in a most unusual position, ladies and gentlemen. Seldom do we have a contestant who gets beyond or even chooses to attempt the third or fourth specialty question. But in Amy and Jennifer we have *two* contestants who are on the show simultaneously and who are continuing to perform at an advanced level with marvelous skill. And Eric, too," he added, giving a generous smile to the pale and terrified little man, "is doing very well."

He turned to Amy and paused for a moment of dramatic silence. Amy returned his look without expression.

"Amy," he said finally, "you have now won a total of two hundred and fifty-six thousand dollars. A quarter of a million. Will you retire with those winnings, or will you go for a final question tomorrow and either double it or lose it?"

"I'll go on," Amy said instantly. The audience cheered wildly, and only Jenny, close beside her, was aware of the tension in the big woman's body.

"How about you, Jennifer?" Jay asked, turning to Jenny, who stood lovely and composed in her vivid red dress. "You now have sixty-four thousand. Will you go on, as well?"

Jenny hesitated, thinking for a brief, wistful moment about quitting. Sixty-four thousand dollars was a lot of money. Admittedly it wouldn't buy them a motorcycle franchise, or help Steve and Sheila to escape their cramped and wretched little apartment, but it would lift the mortgage on her parents' property and pay some of the outstanding medical bills. Maybe it would even pay for a part-time nurse for her mother for a few months. And it would get her away from Charlie, whose presence was becoming more and more unsettling.

"Jennifer?" Jay Allen said.

She glanced down at Charlie in the front row, who gazed at her with fixed intensity, holding his breath.

"I'll go on," Jenny said finally in a low voice. Charlie relaxed visibly, and the audience cheered once more.

"Me, too," Eric whispered, swallowing in fright and frantically clutching his rabbit's foot. "I'll go on, too."

The closing credits rolled, the theme music sounded, and they smiled one last time for the cameras, and then escaped gratefully to the comforting familiarity of the lounge, where Charlie and Sam were waiting.

"Did I do the right thing?" Amy asked abruptly, sitting beside Sam, who put a comforting arm around her plump shoulders and drew her close to him. "Or am I just a damn fool to risk a quarter of a million dollars?"

"When you have the chance of doubling it?" Sam asked in disbelief. "And you're the smartest little cookie in the world? No way, sweetheart. You're right to go for it."

Amy glanced at him with a quizzical look that only Jenny caught. "Sure," she said, gazing moodily into the depths of her coffee cup. "Sure, Sam. I'm right to go for it."

She continued to sip her coffee in brooding silence as Sam entertained the younger people with jokes and stories, and the talk and laughter swirled around her massive, quiet form.

"ALL RIGHT," Charlie said into the telephone. "That's fine. I'll tell her, Frank. Thanks for calling." He hung up and turned to see Jenny, who had appeared in the doorway to the bathroom, wearing a yellow terry-cloth sweat suit and toweling her wet hair.

She stared at him in tense silence.

"That was your father," he told her.

Still she looked at him, her eyes full of terror, unable to speak.

"Jenny, don't look like that, darling. It's good news."

"Then why didn't he want to talk to me?" she asked in a whisper. "Why wouldn't he tell me himself?"

"Well, you know Frank. He gets kind of emotional. I think he didn't trust himself to talk to you without breaking down, so he asked me to tell you."

"Charlie . . ."

"It's really good, Jen. The white cell count is almost down to normal, she's started eating some light foods, and the new kidney is actually beginning to function a little on its own. It's . . ."

But Jenny was overcome with emotion, and she heard no more. She sank into a nearby chair, her face buried in her slender hands, her shoulders trembling.

Charlie crossed the room, picked her up as if she were a child and sat in the chair with her, holding her against his chest while she cried. The tears, it seemed, just kept coming, after being locked inside her for so long: tears of pain

and sorrow, of tension and fear and relief and thankful-
ness.

He patted her back and murmured to her, stroking her,
kissing her hair and whispering soothing words.

Gradually the storm of emotion subsided, and she grew
still in his arms, nestling against him. At last he set her
gently aside and stood up, turning away from her so that
she couldn't see his face.

"Want to go out somewhere and celebrate?" he asked
casually. "We could catch a late movie, or just go out for
a drink or something."

"Charlie," she began, standing uncertainly by the chair,
her whole body trembling. "Charlie, why are you ... why
are you acting like this?"

"Like what, Jen?" he asked lightly, prowling across the
room to look out the window. "Hey, the rain's stopped.
Let's go and—"

"You know how you're acting. Like I'm..." But she
could tell that he either wasn't listening or didn't want to
get into this particular discussion. She hesitated, looking
at his broad, tense shoulders as he stood in the dark square
of window.

"Never mind," she said finally. "I'm going to go to bed
and read a few chapters in my book."

"Okay," he said without turning. "And I'll just watch
a late movie on TV, I think. Good night, Jenny."

She stared for a moment at his lean, muscular back, but
he said nothing more, and she finally turned and went into
her own room, closing the door quietly behind her.

JENNY LAY in the darkness, staring at the muted play of
light and shadow on the ceiling, her mind crowded and
restless. She thought about the quiz show, the seven specialty questions she had already answered, and the three

more that stood between her and a million dollars. She thought about Irena in her hospital bed, and the miracle of the organ transplant that might permit her mother to live a normal life again. She thought about Amy, so much in love with her dapper little adventurer and so terrified of how vulnerable that love might make her.

But always her mind kept returning to Charlie, to her memories of the hours and hours they'd spent together, the fun they'd had and the serious conversations. She remembered her first terrible anger at him, that had gradually changed to resignation and finally to acceptance, and she remembered the way she'd felt when she lay in his arms in the sunlight.

She thought about his new coolness, his careful detachment from her and the strange, abrupt moments of tenderness. Suddenly she felt overwhelmed by everything, by loneliness and fear, homesickness and the need for human warmth and closeness.

She slipped from the bed, shrugged on her red terrycloth robe and let herself quietly out of her room, crossing the hall to tap gently on his door. There was no response. She hesitated and then pushed the door open and stepped inside.

Charlie lay in his bed with the sheets pulled down to his waist and his bare chest gleaming in the moonlight. In the dim glow of the room Jenny could see that he was wide awake, staring, just as she had been a moment earlier, at the ceiling.

"You're not asleep," she said. "Why didn't you answer when I knocked?"

He looked toward her. "I was hoping that if I didn't you'd give up and go back to bed."

She came nearer to him, her eyes gradually adjusting to the light so that she could make out his features and see the mat of curly hair, silvered by the moonlight, on his chest and forearms.

"Charlie, I'm not going away until you tell me why you're doing this."

"Jenny..."

"You spent almost all the early days flirting and telling me how great I looked, coming on to me and gazing at me as if I was wonderful. Then we made love, and now it's as if you wish you'd never met me. Why, Charlie? What did I do to offend you?"

"Come here, Jen." He reached a hand toward her, and she came reluctantly closer to sit on the edge of his bed. "What is it that you want from me, Jenny? Promises? Commitments? Declarations of undying love?"

"Of course not," she said, giving him a level glance. "How could I ask for things like that? We live different lives, Charlie, in different countries, thousands of miles apart. After Friday, if I even make it that far, I'll probably never see you again. But that doesn't change the fact that we've gotten to be good friends this past week, and I think I deserve better treatment from you." She hesitated. "I don't want promises or commitments. I just want some help to get through these last days, because it sure isn't getting any easier. I want you to hold me. I want to sleep with you."

"Jenny..." He stared at her for a long time while she returned his gaze in tense silence. "Look, what do you think?" he asked finally, his voice low and full of anguish. "You think I don't want that, too? More than anything? God, Jenny, I'm human, after all. And you're the loveliest, sweetest—"

He broke off and paused to collect his thoughts while she waited. "You have to understand, Jenny, how guilty I feel about what I did. It was wrong to use my position in your life to get so close to you. And there's no point in doing it again, because two wrongs won't make it right.''

"Why was it so wrong? It felt right to me, and I'm pretty sure you felt the same way at the time.''

"Jenny, sweetheart, there's a big difference between what we feel in our bodies and our hearts and what we know in our minds to be right.'' He took her hand, caressing it gently as he spoke, his face earnest and intense in the dim room. ''I'm supposed to be supervising you, Jen. That's why I'm here, and I'm being paid for it. To watch you every minute and prevent you from violating the rules of the quiz show. And it's not a little thing. It's a really big deal, Jenny. My company has half a million dollars at stake, as well as our corporate reputation, and it's all in my hands.''

"I know all that, Charlie. We've both known that right from the beginning. Why is it suddenly so important?''

He paused, struggling with himself, and then looked directly at her, his eyes gleaming in the shadows. ''Because, Jenny,'' he said softly, ''what happens if I fall in love with you? And God knows I'm in real danger of it. What then, Jenny? How do I enforce the rules and keep doing my job if I'm so much in love with you that I can hardly see straight? How, then, do I keep being a man of integrity? Tell me, Jen. Tell me how.''

She looked down at him with that same disconcertingly steady gaze. ''Just let me get this straight, Charlie, okay? You're afraid that if we're lovers I'll use that as leverage to sneak away and do a little studying and count on our intimacy to keep you from reporting me and getting me disqualified. Isn't that what you're saying?''

"Yes, Jenny. I guess it is.''

"So,'' she continued slowly, ''what you're really saying is that you think I'm willing to exchange intimacy for privileges, right? Or, to put it more plainly, I'm willing to use my body to give me a chance to make a lot of money."

He stared up at her, appalled. "Jenny," he whispered, "I didn't mean—"

"Sex for money," she went on relentlessly, her voice tight with pain. "That's what you're saying, basically. There's a word for that, isn't there, Charlie? And I really don't see what gives you the right to apply that word to me."

"Oh, Jen..." He sat up and drew her into his arms, holding her rigid body, stroking her hair and whispering to her. "Jenny, I never meant to—of course that's not what I think about you. I think you're wonderful and sweet and good and funny, and I want you so much." His voice broke, and he cradled her in his arms, rocking her and cuddling her with gentle tenderness.

She pulled away gently and gazed up at him, her eyes enormous, her face a pale pure oval in the moonlight. "Look, Charlie," she whispered, "how about if I make you a promise?"

"Promise what, Jen?"

"I promise you that I won't take advantage of you in the days ahead. I don't want to sleep with you in order to compromise your integrity. I just want to sleep with you because..." She hesitated and drew close to him again, burrowing against his broad chest.

"Because why, Jenny?" he murmured huskily. "Tell me why."

"Because it just feels better than anything ever felt before," she whispered back. "And I need you, Charlie. I need you to get me through the night."

He drew his breath in sharply and eased the robe from her shoulders, pulling it gently off and tossing it aside. Then, with great deliberation, he unfastened the row of tiny buttons on the front of her nightgown, opened the lacy panels and bent to kiss her breasts.

Jenny shivered, feeling the warmth and softness of his lips, the fine texture of his curly hair against her skin, the delicious sensations that began where his mouth moved slowly upon her body and spread to the very center of her being.

"Oh, God, Charlie," she whispered, "that feels so good."

"Shh," he murmured urgently. "Don't talk. Just let me..."

Slowly, carefully, he lifted her nightgown over her head and tossed it aside. Then he stood briefly to strip off his undershorts and bent to pick Jenny up and place her full length on the bed. He sat beside her again and gazed at her naked body, slender and gleaming in the moonlight. At last, still with that same slow, careful deliberation, he began to stroke and caress her, running his hands the whole length of her body, looking and touching as if he could never get enough of her.

Jenny closed her eyes and gave herself over to sensation, to waves of feeling more intense than anything she'd ever known. There was nothing, anywhere in the universe, but this bed, this man, these hands, slowly rousing her to soaring heights of need and desire.

He seemed different this time, more careful, more practiced and competent, manipulating her body and her emotions with exquisite, gentle skill. Her body was a piece of fine, pale marble, and he was a sculptor, using his warm, strong hands to shape her into something rich and fiery, aglow with feeling, shining with love.

She lost track of time and place, of everything but the emotions that were building within her. When he slipped into the bed and drew her into his arms, she didn't know if minutes had passed or hours. She only knew that she wanted him more than she had ever wanted anything in her life and that nothing, as long as she could remember, had ever felt as intensely satisfying as his lips and hands and the sense of completion that flooded her when their bodies finally joined and moved tenderly together.

He carried her far, far away, out of herself and her world, beyond the moon and stars and into a place of dreamy silence and wide, dim spaces, where soft music played and the air was warm and soft.

"Charlie," she murmured against his neck. "Oh, Charlie..."

"Shh," he whispered back. "Don't talk, Jenny. Just fall asleep now."

"Will you keep holding me?" she asked.

"Yes, darling," he said into her hair. "Yes, I'll keep holding you."

"SO, WHAT'LL IT BE? The rum and raisin or the rocky road? C'mon, Jen. We haven't got all day for this decision."

Jenny hesitated by the ice-cream stand, her face puckered with anxiety. "The problem," she explained earnestly to Charlie, who stood next to her, "is that as soon as you select one you've rejected the other. And they're both so good that I don't want to reject either."

"Look," Charlie said briskly to the bald little man behind the counter. "Two scoops, okay? One of each."

"Charlie, I can't eat two scoops! They're huge."

"I'll help," he promised.

"Oh, good."

Jenny beamed and accepted the ice-cream cone from the man, who suddenly paused and stared at her in wide-eyed amazement. "Hey, aren't you Jennifer? The girl from *Ask Me Anything?*"

Jenny flushed delicate pink and cast an appealing glance at Charlie. Although this was beginning to happen more and more frequently, she was still intensely uncomfortable with public recognition and preferred to let Charlie deal with her admirers while she stood silently by.

"Yes," Charlie said, "she is."

"Well, how about that," the ice-cream man breathed, gazing at Jenny with shining eyes. "Look," he went on shyly, "I don't want to be a bother or anything, but could I just have an autograph for the wife? She'll never believe me otherwise."

Awkwardly Jenny nodded, and he rummaged under the counter and finally handed her an old sales slip that she signed on the back.

"Could you, do you think you could just sign these other two, besides? For my two boys? They're into motorcycles now," he went on earnestly, "and they think you're just the most wonderful person on earth. They're both in there every night, right in front of the television set, waiting to hear you answer your next question."

Jenny signed the other sheets of paper, smiling at the starry-eyed little man as she handed them back.

"She's even more beautiful in real life than she is on the TV," he said to Charlie, "and I didn't think that was possible."

Jenny blushed again and became very busy with her ice-cream cone.

Charlie took her arm and started to lead her away when she heard her name being called.

"Jennifer!"

"Yes?" she said, turning to look over her shoulder.

"Good luck," the man called. "We're all behind you, you know. Everybody in the world wants to see you win that million dollars!"

Jenny smiled automatically and then shivered. As they moved away, she cast Charlie an imploring glance.

"Don't think about it," he said.

"It's impossible not to, Charlie. Whenever I think about how hard those questions are, and millions of people watching..."

"I mean it, Jen. You have to put it out of your mind until it's time to deal with it. Then you think about it, but not before. All right?"

"All right."

"Good. Come on now. Just decide what you want to eat next. We might as well have lunch in here before we take the Seabus."

"But if we're going to have lunch right away, it's silly to be eating ice cream now, Charlie."

"I don't see why," he said comfortably. "What's wrong with eating dessert first?"

"Right," Jenny agreed. "That way you can be certain you've got room for it."

They paused and turned to smile at each other, their eyes meeting and holding for a long moment. His tanned face softened, and his eyes were bluer than she'd ever seen them as he gazed down at her and reached out to touch her cheek. "Jenny," he whispered.

"Yes?"

"Eat your ice cream," he said, turning away briskly. "It's going to start dripping over your hand in a minute, and then you'll be an awful mess and I'll have to clean you up."

She grinned privately and followed him down a flight of wrought-iron spiral steps to the food stalls on the next floor.

They were in the huge Lonsdale Quay Market in North Vancouver, a fascinating multilayered glass structure overlooking the water and filled with booths and stalls selling everything from silk scarves to fresh fish. The Quay was one of their favorite places, and they often came to the market from the hotel to browse among the stalls and shops and then ride the Seabus over to Gastown.

"Have you decided what you want?"

"Fish and chips," Jenny said promptly, "and something from the salad stall."

"With alfalfa sprouts and spinach," Charlie said. "I know, I know."

"Look, do I make fun of your taste in food, weird as it is?"

"Weird!" he said indignantly. "*You're* the one who likes alfalfa!"

"Order the chips, Charlie," she said, smiling at him fondly. "And finish this ice-cream cone, would you?"

She sat at an outer table near one of the glass walls while he placed their order at the fish stall and brought her a cup of coffee.

"I have to get something," he said. "I'll be right back. Listen for our order, okay?"

She nodded and watched as he moved rapidly off, ice-cream cone in hand, his compact muscular body graceful and quick-moving. He rounded a bank of stalls and sprinted up one of the spiral staircases and out of sight while Jenny sipped her coffee and gazed thoughtfully in the direction he had gone.

These sudden excursions and impulses were normal for Charlie. At any moment he might think of something he wanted to do, vanish for a few minutes and then reappear with some wonderful and unusual thing that he had bought or seen or learned. Being with Charlie, she thought with a smile, might be a little unsettling at times, but it was never dull.

Involuntarily she thought about the night before and shivered a little, feeling the familiar sweet warmth and weakness that began at the core of her being and spread all through her body whenever she remembered how it had felt being in his arms, wrapped in his warmth, while he carried her away into worlds of pleasure beyond anything she had ever known.

She shook her head and squared her shoulders, putting all thoughts of the night before from her mind. Deliberately she turned and looked through the wall of glass at the surging expanse of salt water five floors below and the tiny shape of the Seabus far out, making its way toward the distant shore.

Jenny loved the Seabus, and Charlie humored her by finding time almost every day to schedule a ride on it as part of their entertainment.

"Imagine, Charlie," she'd say with shining eyes, gazing around at the secretaries and young executives in their crisp business clothes heading for downtown offices. "They get to ride to work on this wonderful thing across a stretch of water just like I take a city transit bus to work. Aren't they lucky?"

"They probably don't think so. The people who live here and ride the Seabus every day just think it's a boring, tedious twenty minutes out of their workday, Jen. And so would you if you had to work here."

"No, I wouldn't. I'd love it every day, looking out at the water and watching the seagulls."

"Yeah, but that's because you're just a poor, water-starved prairie girl, that's all. The largest body of water *you* ever get to see is in your bathtub."

She smiled, remembering his words and watching the Seabus dock on the far side, almost too distant to be visible, and then swing clumsily out and start across the inlet for its return trip.

Charlie materialized by the fish stall, picked up their order of fish and chips from the vendor and brought them back to her, setting Jenny's carefully in front of her along with a little gingham-wrapped parcel.

"What's this?" she asked.

"Fish and chips," he said.

"Charlie, you idiot. I mean this little parcel. What is it?"

"Why don't you open it and see?" he said casually, attacking his crispy fried fish with enthusiasm. "This is so good, Jen," he added. "I've never tasted fish like this, have you?"

But she was occupied with unwrapping the little parcel and exposing a small box. She opened it, peered inside and gave a soft cry of delight. Nestled in a mass of tissues was a tiny fabric penguin, made of many bits of glistening, multicolored silk painstakingly hand-quilted together with delicate, whimsical stitches. The penguin's eyes were bright jet beads, and his little wings were joyously tilted, as if he were about to dive and fly through the water.

"Oh, look," she breathed, lifting the bright little bird from his nest of paper and holding him in her hand. "He's lovely. Where did you find him?"

"I spotted him earlier this morning in that little gift shop two floors up," Charlie said, "and I thought you should have him. After all," he added casually, "even Eric has his rabbit's foot."

Jenny smiled over at him, her dark eyes glowing.

He smiled back at her and then turned his attention to his fish, eating with evident enjoyment.

"Charlie . . ." Jenny began.

"Hmm?"

I love you, she wanted to say. *I love you so much, Charlie, that I can hardly bear it.*

"Thank you," she said aloud. "I think he's just beautiful."

CHAPTER ELEVEN

AMY LEANED OVER during the final commercial break and tugged gently at Jenny's arm. "Jen!" she whispered.

Jenny was standing behind her podium, staring fixedly at the huge question screen and settling her mind, summoning masses and masses of information, sorting and organizing them, preparing herself mentally to deal with her specialty question. She felt the pocket of her suit jacket where Charlie's little multicolored penguin made a comforting small lump against her hand and smiled to herself.

"Jenny!" Amy hissed again.

"Pardon?" Jenny said blankly, turning to her friend. "Did you say something, Amy?"

"Not yet," Amy said dryly. "I'm still trying to get your attention."

"Sorry," Jenny said. "I'm listening now."

All at once she realized that Amy's face was pale and tense, white with fear, her lipstick a garish smear against the pallor of her plump face.

"Amy," she said, "what's wrong? Did you and Sam...?"

Involuntarily she glanced down into the studio audience where Sam and Charlie sat together. Sam beamed up at her, his face cherubic, his huge mustache shining under the house lights. Charlie, too, caught her glance and gave her a warm, significant smile that set her pulse racing and made the hair tingle on the back of her neck.

She smiled briefly in return and then turned back to Amy, who was still fidgeting behind her podium. Eric, also waiting for a specialty question, gripped his rabbit's foot and stood with his eyes closed, mouthing something under his breath.

"No, nothing like that," Amy said bitterly in answer to Jenny's questioning glance. "Sam and I, we get along just great. It's just that ..."

"What?" Jenny said. "What's the matter?"

"Jen, I don't have a good feeling about today. I feel..." Amy hesitated and cast Jenny an anguished glance.

"Come on, Amy. You've been brilliant. Why should today be any different?"

"I don't know," Amy said gloomily. "I think maybe I've been flying too high and I'm due for a fall. It seems that I've never been allowed too much happiness in my life, and maybe someone's noticed that I'm over my quota just now."

"Amy, that's ridiculous. You deserve everything you're getting. You've worked hard, and you're so happy and generous and nice to everybody else."

Amy shook her head miserably. "You're a sweet kid, Jenny, but you haven't been around long enough to learn that every time you're up life finds a way of slapping you down. And I think maybe I'm due for a slap."

"Amy, I can't stand to hear you say—"

"Look, I'm not asking for sympathy, kid. I just want a favor."

"What? I'd do anything to help you, Amy. You know that."

"Well, if I miss this question coming up and lose the bundle, I doubt that Sam Wecker will even come back-stage to say goodbye. I think he'll be gone like smoke, and

I can't stand to be left again. I want to be the one who does the leaving this time.''

Jenny stared at her, appalled, and said nothing.

"So if I lose," Amy went on in the same toneless, brittle voice, "I'm going to split. And if he does turn up, just out of politeness, then you tell him why I've gone. But don't tell him how to find me."

"Amy, I wouldn't know how to find you. Nobody knows where you live."

"Good," Amy said with satisfaction. "Let's keep it that way."

"But," Jenny began, still staring at the big woman, "but, Amy—"

"Shh," Amy said. "The cameras are rolling. Get ready, Jen. Good luck. I love you, kid."

Eric, who was first, correctly answered a complex specialty question dealing with Wagner's early operatic scores. As usual he sagged with relief afterward, his face ashen, his chest heaving.

Jenny's question was an obscure historic one this time, dealing with some little-known information about the motorcycles used by British troops during World War II. Fortunately Steve had considered the wartime history of motorcycles an important area and had drilled Jenny on it so thoroughly that she answered with little difficulty.

Then it was Amy's turn. Jenny stood digging her fingernails into her palms, feeling her friend's tension creeping into her own body and paralyzing her with fear.

"Amy," Jay Allen began in his usual dramatic fashion, "you've now won two hundred and fifty-six thousand dollars, and you're heading for one of the highest payouts in the history of our show. Are you ready for your five-hundred-thousand-dollar question in the category of international cuisine?"

"Yes," Amy murmured, her voice almost inaudible. "Yes, I am."

"Very well, then. Complete silence in the studio audience, please. I need hardly stress the importance of the question I am about to read. Now, Amy for half a million dollars, could you tell us, please, what are the three substances that can be used as the base ingredient of gnocchi?"

Amy stared at him, licking her lips nervously and clutching the sides of her podium so tightly that her knuckles were white in her plump hands with their masses of bright rings.

"Gnocchi," she began, her voice barely above a whisper, "is an...an Italian dish of dumplings served with a sauce and grated cheese. The dumplings can be made of flour or potato or..." She hesitated, her body quivering with anxiety, searching her memory. "Or..."

"The other ingredient, Amy," Jay Allen said gently. "We need three possible base ingredients, and you've given us two so far."

"Or..." Amy's face contracted with the agony of trying to remember, to draw the elusive fact from her mental stores.

The silence in the studio was so profound that Jenny could hear herself breathing, feel herself passionately willing Amy to find the answer. Jay Allen's concern, too, showed plainly as he watched the big woman.

"Amy," he prompted her quietly, "time's almost up."

"I don't...I don't know," Amy whispered, her face ghastly.

A moan of pain and sympathy rose from the audience, echoed by the host, who seemed to be genuinely suffering on Amy's behalf.

"The other base ingredient," he said finally, "is semolina."

Amy nodded, her face once more composed, a mask of stone. Jenny reached out to touch her as Jay Allen began to speak again, but Amy shrugged her hand off and turned aside, head erect, to walk quietly from the set.

Jenny watched her go and restrained herself with an effort from running after her friend. She wanted to hold the plump woman, pat her back, tell her that it didn't matter, that she still had her talents and her job offers and her friends and that she had put on a wonderful performance regardless of the outcome.

But she couldn't. She had to stay at her podium beside Eric until after the closing credits.

"Eric," Jay Allen said, "you've boosted your winning total to eight thousand dollars. What do you want to do next?"

Eric, white-faced and shocked by the brutal suddenness of Amy's fall, stared at the host in trembling silence. "I want...I want to quit," he said finally. "I'll take the money."

Jenny looked over at him unhappily, but then realized that, for Eric, this was probably the wisest choice. Despite Charlie's best efforts the little man grew more terrified with each passing day.

"And you, Jennifer?" Jay Allen was saying. "You're in a somewhat different position with a hundred and twenty-eight thousand dollars won, but the possibility, with a winning answer on the final day, of earning almost *ten times* that amount. What's your choice?"

A hundred and twenty-eight thousand dollars. Jenny stared at him, trying to think. It seemed like such an enormous sum of money. It was more than she had ever dreamed of having herself. The game show had been a joint venture right from the beginning, although she was the one answering the questions, Steve and Sheila had put hundreds of hours into this project, doing the research, cataloging the information, making up flash cards, organizing her study sessions. And, as promising as her mother's condition looked, Irena would still need a lot of expensive medical attention and supervision for some time to come.

If only, Jenny thought in anguish, *you didn't lose it* all, *just for one wrong answer.* She thought of Amy, walking bravely from the stage, stripped of all her winnings, poorer, in fact, by a quarter of a million dollars just because she couldn't remember semolina.

She glanced down at Charlie, who gazed back at her, his blue eyes warm and concerned. Just as he had on the very first day, he gave her a small thumbs-up sign. Suddenly she felt a rush of confidence that was almost reckless.

"I'll go on," she said quietly to Jay Allen.

The audience cheered wildly, Charlie smiled, the closing theme sounded, and the credits began to roll onto the monitors. Jenny stood calmly, looking into the camera for the final close-up and then turned and rushed offstage, searching for Amy.

At the entrance to the lounge she encountered Sam, who was doing the same thing.

"Jenny," he said urgently, "I can't find her. I've looked everywhere."

Jenny studied him in thoughtful silence. This was a different Sam than she had ever seen before. He had always seemed so cheerful and expansive, full of talk and big ideas, happily taking center stage and performing for any audience that happened to be nearby. But now he was pale and drawn and seemed much smaller. Even his luxuriant mustache, Jenny thought, had an uncharacteristic droop, and his dark eyes were full of pain and unhappiness.

Jenny thought of Amy's final words and wondered if the pain was for Amy or for himself.

"I'll check in the ladies' room," she said to Sam. "Maybe she wanted to freshen up a little before she faced us all, you know?"

Sam nodded and watched anxiously as Jenny entered the washroom. But it was empty, as Jenny had known it would be.

Amy was gone and she wouldn't be back.

She came out into the corridor and saw that Charlie and Eric had both joined Sam and were waiting tensely for her.

She shook her head, and Sam sagged against the wall, his little body slumped and bowed with sorrow. "The poor, poor kid," he muttered. "When I think how she must feel right now and how much she needs comforting, and yet she just took off all by herself." He turned suddenly to Jenny. "Quick, tell me what her address is. What's her phone number? How can I get in touch with her?"

Jenny returned his look cautiously. "Sam, you've been with her nonstop since Monday. You must know her address and how to reach her."

He shook his head. "We've been staying in my hotel room. She said she was living in a dump, didn't want me to see it, didn't even want me to have her phone number."

He hesitated, staring at them. "It's unlisted," he said finally. "And I have no idea where she lives. You have to tell me, Jenny. I have to find her."

"I don't know, Sam. None of us knows. She's never told any of us. The quiz show office would have her address, but they won't give it out to anybody for any reason. It's part of the contract."

"I can't believe..." He struggled for words, his face very pale, his dark eyes full of anguish. "You're saying, you're saying I've lost her again? That there's no way of finding her?"

"Not if she doesn't choose to contact you," Jenny said.

"But, but why wouldn't she ...?"

"Sam..." Jenny began, and then looked over at Charlie in despair. He slipped an arm around her and gave her a brief hug, and she went on. "Sam, it isn't easy to say this, but Amy thought, she told me she thought you were just interested in the money. And she was certain that if she lost you'd leave her again, so she wanted to be the one who left first."

The dapper little man stared at her, appalled.

"What would make her think that? Why would she?"

Jenny shook her head. "I don't know, Sam. You'd know the answer to that question better than I would, and I can't explain Amy's mental processes. I'm just telling you what she told me to say."

He stared for a moment longer, his face reflecting the bitter pain that he felt. Charlie reached toward him, but Sam turned away, trudging wearily down the corridor and out of sight.

"IS YOUR STEAK GOOD?" Charlie asked.

"I guess so. Maybe a little rare for my taste," Jenny said absently.

"You cowboys," Charlie teased. "You all like your steak burnt to a crisp. Why would you do that to a beautiful piece of meat?"

But he couldn't get an answering smile from Jenny. In fact, he hadn't been able to get any kind of response from her all through their meal. He looked in concern at her bent head as she toyed listlessly with the foil-wrapped remains of her stuffed potato.

"Look, are you going to waste those mushrooms?" he asked finally. "Because if you are, I'll take them."

Without a word she scraped the delicately browned, fragrant mushrooms onto his plate and then looked up with a polite half smile when the waiter appeared at her elbow to refill her coffee cup.

Charlie glanced over the rim of his cup to watch her lovely troubled face as she stirred sugar into her coffee. "Jen," he said, "I want to ask you a hypothetical question."

"Not now, Charlie, okay?" she said wearily. "I'm just not in the mood, you know?"

Charlie loved hypothetical questions and was always tossing them out without warning just to enjoy her reaction. Things like, "If you were going to be stranded on a desert island for life and you could take three objects for entertainment, what would they be?" Or, "If you could travel on a spaceship to other galaxies for a few years, and you knew that you were going to see all kinds of incredibly fabulous things, but by the time you returned to earth, twenty thousand years would have passed while you were gone, would you go, anyway?"

Normally Jenny enjoyed his hypothetical questions, and they often sparked lively arguments between them that lasted throughout the evening and far into the night. But tonight she just wasn't in the mood.

"This isn't that kind of question," he said. "This is a moral dilemma."

"Oh? What kind?" she asked, but without interest, still thinking about Amy's ghastly pale face and her lonely courage as she marched off the stage and out of their lives.

"If somebody told you something about themselves in strictest confidence," Charlie began slowly, avoiding her eyes and concentrating on the mushrooms, "and you promised you wouldn't repeat it, but then a situation arose where it was better for everybody's sake that another person got this information, would you break your promise and tell?"

Jenny looked over at him, suddenly alert, but he kept his head bent, carefully cutting the mushrooms into tiny pieces before eating them.

"I think," Jenny said slowly, "that the logical thing would be to discuss it with the person who gave you the information in the first place, wouldn't it, and ask permission to be released from your promise?"

Charlie looked up and met her gaze, his blue eyes troubled. "What if you tried lots of times to contact him, but he was never in his hotel room, and this was a situation where you were afraid that time was a really important factor?"

Jenny gazed at him in thoughtful silence. "Charlie," she said finally, "are you trying to say you know something about Sam Wecker? Is that it? Something you feel Amy should be told about?"

He nodded unhappily, his face shadowed by the dimness of the hotel dining room, the light from the little candle-filled globe flickering on his strong cheekbones. "I promised not to tell anybody. I hate breaking promises, Jen."

"But you still want to tell me? Why?"

"So we can talk it over and decide what to do. It's possible... it's possible that we might be able to help, if you know about it."

Jenny sipped her coffee, pondering. "I think," she said at last, "that you'd better tell me, Charlie."

He hesitated for a brief, agonized moment and then looked directly at her. "Jen, Sam's a rich man. A multi-millionaire."

Jenny smiled grimly. "I'm surprised at you, Charlie, falling for that line. Amy says he uses it on everyone. He just loves playing the big shot, she says."

"Jenny, it's not a line, at least not this time. It's the truth."

She looked at him intently. "How can you be so sure?"

"Because...because he knows what it's all about, Jenny. I mean, I'm not a total idiot myself financially, and I have some pretty good investments. And Sam's into some of the same things, but on a lot bigger scale than I am. He knows what he's talking about."

Jenny shrugged. "So he's a smart guy and he reads the paper and know how to throw a few names and numbers around. That doesn't make him rich, Charlie."

"I checked on him," Charlie said abruptly.

"Checked on him? How?"

"I called a guy I know in New York who knows every-body who's anybody in the financial world, and he con-firmed it. Sam Wecker's a very big man, financially speaking."

She looked at him, stunned into silence.

"I wouldn't have done it, checked up on him, I mean," Charlie went on earnestly. "But he told me all this in con-fidence, and I wondered if he was on the level or if he was feeding me some kind of line and maybe telling Amy the same thing. And I've gotten to care for her so much that I...I just didn't want to see her hurt. I wanted to make sure the guy wasn't a liar."

"Well," Jenny said slowly, "he sure wasn't telling Amy any stories about his wealth. She figured him for a gold digger right from the start, even though she adores the man." Jenny looked across the table. "Charlie, ten years ago he was penniless and in prison. How did he get so rich? Was it legal?"

"Absolutely. He got a stake from somewhere and bought big blocks of cheap shares in things like Chrysler just before they skyrocketed. And apparently he's got a flair for the commodities market. That's a risky business, but there are certainly fortunes to be made if you're smart and you've got nerves of steel."

"But why wouldn't he tell Amy? Why let her think that he—"

"Because he loves her, Jen. He figures he caused her so much pain for so many years, and now he comes back into her life when she's riding high, the center of attention, about to win half a million just by using her wits."

"So," Jenny said slowly, "he didn't want to minimize her achievement by bragging about his own."

"Exactly. He was being really unselfish, Jenny. A guy's first impulse under those circumstances would be to impress the woman he loves with what he's accomplished and tell her he's going to surround her with luxury for the rest of her life. It's a natural thing for a man to want to do. But Sam didn't give in to that urge because he didn't want to grab any of the limelight from her."

"Then how did you find out?" she asked, her voice barely above a whisper.

"Well, he knew I was suspicious, because I was with him one day when he took a call from his broker, so he told me about his situation and made me promise not to tell. He was going to let her know gradually after the show was over and she'd gotten all the praise and attention for her big win."

"Oh, God," Jenny said slowly, and felt a slow welling of sorrow that almost brought her to the verge of tears.

"And now she's vanished, Charlie, and we can't find her. She's broke and alone, and she's lost everything, and she'll never, ever know how much he loves her."

Charlie nodded gloomily and sipped his coffee. "You were right about the game show office. They've got her address, and I tried to get it from them, but I don't think they'd release it on a court subpoena even. They're just ridiculous."

"And there's how many people living in Vancouver?"

"Over a million in the metropolitan area. She could live anywhere within a fifty or sixty mile radius. Jen. We really have no idea."

The hopelessness of it washed over Jenny, making her feel weak and sick at heart.

Charlie watched her, his eyes cautious. "Jenny..." he began.

"Yes?"

"Look, Jenny I have a plan, but I need your help. Are you interested?"

"Of course."

"Okay. Now how about if we..."

He leaned earnestly across the table, holding her hand and talking while she listened in thoughtful silence, her dark eyes fixed on his face.

JENNY LAY IN BED, curled into a cozy ball, suspended in that dreamy, delicious state just on the edge of sleep. Charlie held her close to him, her back nestled into his chest, his hands still cupping her breasts, even though she could tell by his deep, even breathing that he had fallen asleep.

She felt richly contented, in the frame of mind where it was a pleasure to take out each separate happiness, like treasures stored in a box, unwrapping them one by one and gloating over them.

First, there was the sweet warmth of the hour that she and Charlie had just passed in a realm of bliss that seemed to grow more intense with the passage of time. His love-making was wonderful, tender, impulsive, surprising. And she knew she was falling deeper in love with him all the time, although neither of them had yet found the courage to say those momentous words.

And there was the marvelous phone call from Steve just as they came home from the concert, telling them that Irena's condition continued to improve and that she might even be going home soon.

Jenny burrowed into the covers, sighing with contentment.

And there was Charlie's ingenious plan to reunite Amy and Sam which, she thought, just might work if Jenny could play her part correctly.

At the thought of the quiz show something nagged at the back of her mind, like a tiny dark cloud drifting across the sun.

She frowned, trying to concentrate. This elusive little shadow of fear had been tugging at her for hours, a vague insecurity that she couldn't put her finger on. She had the feeling that she was vulnerable in some area, but she couldn't think what it was or what had happened to arouse her fear.

Finally she shrugged the nagging doubts away, thinking instead about the concert they had attended that evening, a Bruce Springsteen performance that Charlie had somehow been able to get tickets for, although they had been sold out for weeks.

Jenny had never been to a live rock concert, and she had been dazzled by the raw power of the music and the man's awesome physical presence onstage. He had sung many of his older favorites and some new hits that still surged in her mind.

Suddenly she sat bolt upright in bed, her whole body shaking with terror.

That was it! That was what she had been dreading, her terrible area of vulnerability.

Charlie stirred, and opened his eyes. "Jen?" he muttered sleepily. "What's the matter, sweetheart?"

"Charlie!" She clutched his shoulder frantically, her dark eyes wide with fear, gleaming in the moonlight. "Charlie, that's what it is! Charlie, I'm so scared."

He sat up, thoroughly alarmed, and looked around. "What, Jenny? What are you scared of?"

"Not here. Nothing here. I mean the quiz show. Charlie, remember this afternoon? Remember the preliminary round?"

"Sure. What about it?"

"There was a category on popular music, remember? And one of the questions was to name the song that's currently number one on the charts."

"And you missed it. So what? You're not claiming to be an expert on popular music, Jenny. It doesn't matter if one of the other contestants *occasionally* gets a question right, you know."

"Charlie," she said in despair, "you don't understand. The question was about the song that's at the top of the current charts. Current, Charlie!"

He gripped her arms, concerned by the panic in her voice, and studied her carefully. "Calm down now and tell me what you're getting at. What's the matter?"

"Charlie, I don't know any of the specs on the new bike lines. If they asked me the simplest question about the current models, I'd be hopelessly lost. I'd just have to guess."

He was silent for a moment, thinking this over, understanding at last the source of her terror.

The new motorcycle lines were introduced each year to bike fanciers by means of specification sheets delivered to dealers and articles of statistics and comparative analyses published in the major bike magazines. All of this information appeared in the spring. It was appearing, Charlie realized, right now.

"You didn't get hold of any spec sheets for the new bikes while you were preparing?" he asked.

She shook her head, fighting back tears. "Most of them weren't out yet. And neither were the magazines. They just started being distributed when I was packing, finishing things up at work and getting ready to come to Vancouver, and we just…never thought about them, I guess. We were so busy studying history and engine design and all that stuff that we never thought about the new lines. I don't know more than just a few random statistics on a couple of models. I'll bet it hasn't occurred to Steve, even yet, that this is an area where I'm totally vulnerable."

"And it wouldn't have occurred to you, either," Charlie pointed out reasonably, "if you hadn't started brooding about that one question today on popular music. There are just two questions left to go, Jen, and not one of them so far has had anything to do with the current models. Why should you be so terrified that one of these two final questions is going to be on that particular topic?"

"I just know it," she said gloomily, hugging her knees and staring into the darkness. "I feel it in my bones."

"Which bones?" he asked, running his hands over her body, tickling her and trying to distract her. "This one? How about this one over here? Ah, I bet it's *this* one."

"Quit fooling around, Charlie," she said, pulling away from him. "This is serious. It's terrible. There's over a hundred thousand dollars at stake right now. And over a quarter of a million tomorrow. And after what happened to Amy today..."

"Jen, there's nothing you can do about it. And brooding about it is just going to make you lose sleep and be less alert tomorrow. The only thing you can do is put it out of your mind and carry on. Everything will be fine. You'll see. Chances are pretty remote, after all, that they're going to toss you a question on the new bikes at this late date when they never have before."

"I guess you're right," she said without conviction.

"Of course I'm right. Come on, cuddle up and go back to sleep."

She settled in his arms, kissed him and turned over, waiting to hear his breathing deepen and grow steady and even.

But long after he was asleep she lay in his arms, staring out at the darkness of the room.

There's nothing you can do about it, Charlie had said.

But he was wrong. There was something she could do about it. She remembered with painful clarity the copy of *Cycle World* that she had gazed at so wistfully on the airport newsstand back in Calgary while Charlie was arranging for their rental car. Her photographic memory summoned up every detail of the magazine cover, including the feature article.

It was entitled, "*Cycle World* looks at the New Models," and it listed them all: Suzuki, Honda, Harley, Kawasaki, BMW, Forbes.

And inside Jenny knew there would be condensed details and specifications, set out in charts that she could study and memorize at a glance. All she'd need would be fifteen or twenty minutes of concentration and she would know all there was to know about the new motorcycles, and then this dreadful feeling of vulnerability would be gone.

But there was also Charlie.

She rolled over in bed gently so as not to disturb him and studied his quiet, composed face. Asleep, his square, clean-cut features always looked relaxed and innocent, almost boyish, and so sweet that her heart ached.

She loved him. She knew that now, knew that he mattered to her very, very much and that in spite of herself she had begun to think about a future with him, simply because the prospect of life without him was growing more and more intolerable. She was amazed when she thought about how short a time she had actually known him—less than two weeks. But in that time they'd spent more hours together and passed more time deep in conversation than many other couples did in months. She felt that she knew him through and through and that he knew and understood her just as intimately.

But Charlie was a man to whom trust and integrity were of the highest importance. If she cheated and looked at a magazine and he found her out, it was possible, just possible, that his feelings for her might prevent him from reporting her and having her disqualified. But he would still suffer terribly if she forced him to do something he believed was wrong, and his opinion of her would be damaged beyond repair.

Jenny knew this absolutely and was fully aware that she was taking a terrible risk. But she also knew that nothing was going to stop her from finding and memorizing that article as soon as she could.

CHAPTER TWELVE

JENNY STOOD behind her lectern on the set of the television show, which by now felt so familiar that she could hardly remember a time when this hadn't been part of her afternoon routine. But the set seemed different today, lonely and strange without the large, loud, comforting presence of Amy, with her garish dresses and jewelry and her warm smile.

Jenny found that she even rather missed Eric, although his tense and terrified face had actually been small comfort when he was around. It must, she decided, just be a matter of what you got used to.

Eric was in the audience, however, sitting down in the front row with Charlie and Sam and gazing up at her with adoration. He caught her eye and raised his hand, showing her his rabbit's foot. Jenny smiled at him automatically, thinking that Eric looked much better, even rather handsome in a pallid kind of way, now that he was relieved of his ghastly tension.

She couldn't however, say the same for Sam Wecker, who sat beside him. Sam looked dreadful, as if he hadn't slept all night. His face, normally round and pink with good health and cheer, was gray and sagging, his eyes heavily pouched. He slumped listlessly in his seat, rousing himself only to turn at intervals and scan the studio audience and then sink back into his chair, his whole body limp with despair.

The show began and the contestants were announced, with Jay Allen taking a brief moment to introduce each of the three new ones and say a few words about them. Two of them, Jenny had decided, were going to be interesting opponents. The third, a heavy, loud-voiced man with a bushy gray goatee, she had already written off, sensing instinctively that he somehow lacked the ability to make it very far.

But the thin, middle-aged woman beside her, whose name was Constance, seemed very sharp. Her specialty field was gunfighters of the Old West. Next to Constance was Ben, a massive, grizzled hulk of a man with kindly eyes who looked like a retired football player and who specialized, Jay Allen told the audience with a grin, in the history of dolls and dollmaking.

When he reached Jenny, he smiled at her warmly and paused. "Well, Jennifer," he said finally.

She watched him quietly, her face pale and composed and said nothing.

"Jennifer, this is the second biggest day of your life. You're going for a cash total of two hundred and fifty-six thousand dollars today. And if you make it and get through tomorrow's round, then tomorrow will be the *biggest* day of your life, won't it?"

"Yes," Jenny said. "I suppose it will."

"Now we've chatted quite a lot with you over the past eight days," Jay Allen said, "and the audience here and out there in television land knows a fair amount about you already, but it seems that they all want to know more. We've gotten thousands of calls and letters, asking about every detail of your life. Do you have any other interesting little tidbits for us today?"

"Not really," Jenny said. "As you said, I've done this so often that I don't think there's anything very interesting left to tell you about myself. But . . ." She hesitated, looking down at Charlie, who nodded and smiled, urging her on. "But," Jenny said, looking back at Jay Allen, "there is one thing I'd like to say if I could."

"Certainly, Jennifer. Anything you want."

Jenny glanced up at the indicator lights to see which camera was filming at the moment and turned to face it, looking earnestly into the lens. "I'd like to say hello to Amy, who left the show yesterday. Amy, I know you'll be watching, and I want you to call me at my hotel right after the show because I have something very important to tell you. Please, Amy," she concluded, and then relaxed. She smiled at Jay Allen, who looked a little confused, but quickly recovered himself.

"Well, folks, there you go. *Ask Me Anything,* your friendly neighborhood messenger service. Now, Amy," he went on, turning to face the camera himself with an engaging grin, "you heard the girl. Amy, *call home!* You hear?" A wave of laughter rocked the studio audience, and Jay smiled, waiting skillfully for the mirth to subside. "And now," he said finally, "let's get on with the show."

Jenny looked down at Charlie again, who grinned and nodded his approval. But he was distracted by Sam beside him, who began to shake his arm and whisper in his ear in sudden, wild excitement, his face alive with a desperate hope.

As Jenny had expected, the loud overbearing type was knocked out in the preliminary round, leaving Ben, Constance and herself to answer questions in their specialty fields. Both of the new contestants were successful and departed triumphantly for the lounge while Jenny waited.

The show host paused in front of her, holding her question card in his hand and allowing the dramatic tension to build to almost painful heights. Jenny stared at the card as if mesmerized, knowing, just *knowing,* that it contained a question on the specifications of the new bike models and that she was going to miss it and lose over a hundred thousand dollars.

Her stomach churned with terror.

Get on with it, she urged Jay silently. *Just get on with it, would you? And if this question isn't about the new bikes, I swear to God I'm going to get hold of a magazine tonight somehow, no matter what, and memorize that article, because I'll die if I have to go through this again tomorrow.*

"Jennifer, your specialty question for today is in three parts. You understand the rules. You must answer all three parts correctly or none of your answer will be valid."

Jenny nodded, her heart thundering in her chest, her throat dry, remembering grimly what had happened to Amy on her three-part question the previous day.

"All right, then. Silence in the audience, please. Jennifer, for two hundred and fifty-six thousand dollars, please tell us, first, the name of the only production motorcycle that uses an actual automobile engine, second, its country of manufacture and, finally, the make of automobile engine that powers this particular motorcycle. Remember that you have thirty seconds in which to answer."

Jenny felt such an overwhelming surge of relief that she was almost light-headed, even a little faint. She sagged against the podium, struggling to compose her voice.

"It's called…the motorcycle is called the Amazonus," she said finally, "and it's manufactured in Brazil. The automobile engine that it uses is a 1600 cc Volkswagen engine."

Charlie forgot himself completely and leaped to his feet down in the front row, clapping and shouting. He was not, however, at all conspicuous, because almost everyone in the studio was doing the same thing.

Jenny smiled and let the roar of applause wash over her, feeling wonderful. She was as light as a feather, soaring and rich with relief and happiness.

But despite her triumph of the moment she was also more than ever determined to get her hands on a copy of *Cycle World* just as soon as she could.

"WHY DOESN'T she call, damn it?"

Jenny paced restlessly around the sitting room of their suite and paused occasionally to frown at the telephone.

"Charlie, what if she doesn't call? What if it doesn't work? What if she thinks it's a trap of some kind, or she didn't even bother to watch or..."

Charlie sat on the couch, his arms spread casually along the back, and watched Jenny in troubled silence. She wore faded jeans and a cherry-red Calgary Stampeders football shirt, and her dark hair was caught back in a long, heavy braid. Her cheeks were flushed, her eyes bright with fear and tension. She looked, he thought, heartbreakingly lovely and, as always, he had to fight to keep from rushing to her and gathering her into his arms.

But he restrained himself, knowing instinctively that she didn't want to be touched just now. In fact, she had seemed remote and distant all day, wrapped in her own thoughts.

"She'll call," he said. "Don't forget about the tape delay, Jen. The show just finished airing a few minutes ago. She'll think it over and then she'll call. I don't believe she could resist a direct appeal from you, not like that."

"What if she wasn't even watching?" Jenny threw herself into a chair beside the telephone, picked up a small sofa cushion and began tossing it nervously in her hands.

"She'd be watching," Charlie said. "She wouldn't come to the studio, for fear of running into Sam, but she wouldn't have missed seeing how you did. She really loves you, Jen."

"I love her, too," Jenny said. "I don't know what I'll do if she doesn't call. I'm so hungry," she added plaintively. "I always get hungry when I'm tense. My stomach is just in a knot."

"Let's order something up from room service, then," Charlie said, still looking at her with love and sympathy. "We don't have to go over to the Spaghetti Factory to eat, you know. We could just call down and—"

"No!" Jenny said sharply.

Charlie raised his eyebrows in surprise at her vehemence.

"I mean," Jenny said, a little abashed, "that I really need to go out tonight, Charlie. I can't stand sitting around doing nothing. I just have to get through this awful evening somehow."

She cast him a quick, cautious glance, hoping he hadn't caught anything from her tone. It really was essential to her plans that they go out to eat and to that particular restaurant too.

"Jen, what is it? It's not just Amy, right? You're upset about the show? Worried about tomorrow?"

"Well, of course I am. Who wouldn't be? It's a million dollars, you know. All or nothing. God, Charlie, I'm so scared."

She glared at the silent telephone again and then sank back into the chair, clutching the small pillow and looking moodily at the ceiling.

"But you're not still worried about the new bike lines, are you? I told you the final question wouldn't be on the new line, Jen. Look at today's question, an obscure old dinosaur like the Amazonus. That's what they were interested in. And questions like that, you just eat them up."

"I know. You're right, Charlie. I'm not all that worried. That was just...just the middle-of-the-night terrors, I guess."

Her voice was light and casual. He glanced over at her, still concerned, but she gave him a bright smile and got up to prowl aimlessly around the room again.

"I just need for it to be over, that's all," she said over her shoulder. "And I wish Any would call."

"Jen what about after it's over?"

"What about it?"

She turned to face him, and looked back at her, his blue eyes clear and direct in his tanned face.

"Well, I just think maybe you and I should discuss the future a little bit, don't you? I mean, one way or the other tomorrow is our last day together. But I know absolutely that I can't bear to see you leave my life, Jenny. Not now."

She trembled under his vivid blue gaze, his eyes so pure and penetrating that they seemed to look right into her soul.

But if he could really see into her soul, she thought, he wouldn't want to have anything more to do with her. Because she was planning to betray him, possibly even to shame him, to break her own promise to a man who took promises so very seriously.

"Not right now, Charlie, okay?" she said abruptly. "Let's not discuss the future now. Let's wait until after tomorrow, because I'm just so..."

I'm so scared, she finished silently, *I'm scared my plan won't work, and you'll catch me, and then you're going to hate me, Charlie, and you'll be gone for good. Oh, God...*

"Look, Jenny," he began, "I don't think you understand what I..."

But whatever he was going to say was left unfinished, because at that moment the telephone rang, shrilling unnaturally loud in the quiet room.

Jenny and Charlie stared at each other, and then Jenny moved over, picked up the receiver and whispered, "Yes? Hello?"

"Okay, kid," Amy's voice boomed through the receiver. "What's up?"

"Amy!" Jenny sank into the nearest chair, limp with relief. She caught Charlie's quick, warning glance and gathered herself together, sitting erect and thinking rapidly.

This was going to take skill, timing and good instincts if she was going to be able to pull it off, knowing how deeply suspicious and frightened Amy was.

But Amy helped her considerably by plunging right into the topic.

"Don't tell me, Jen. Let me guess. Sam got you to do that, didn't he? He wants to get in touch with me and he can't find me, so he decided to use you right?"

Jenny was silent, trying to remember how she had planned to organize this conversation.

"After all," Amy went on, her voice tight with pain, "Why not? Sam Wecker's always been willing to use anybody to get what he wanted."

"Why should it have to be Sam's idea?" Jenny asked. "Why couldn't I just decide, all on my own, that I didn't want someone as nice as you to drop out of my life, so I used the only method I could think of to get in touch with you?"

"Jen, if you're going to ask for my address or my phone number or anything like that, forget it. I know he's still hanging around, and I'm not giving that man any chance to get close to me ever again."

"But why would he want to?" Jenny said. "If you're right about him, I mean? I thought the whole idea of your disappearing trick was to be the first to leave. If you're so certain he wants to dump you, why would he be devising ways to get in touch with you?"

"You don't know him," Amy said darkly. "I've been thinking. He probably doesn't have two nickels to rub together, likely used borrowed money to rent that nice hotel room just to impress me with how well he's doing. And I made the mistake of telling him that I'd been offered a job doing a dining column. He knows that it pays fairly well, so he figures he'll just find me and move in and live off me again as long as I'm earning money."

Jenny was silent, struggling to order her thoughts, knowing how terribly important it was that she handle this properly. Because if Amy didn't believe her or got angry and hung up, they would have lost their last chance ever to contact her. A public plea wouldn't work a second time, not with someone like Amy.

"Amy, it wasn't Sam's idea for me to ask you to call. He didn't even know I was going to do it." Jenny hesitated and took a deep breath, meeting Charlie's eyes and nodding in response to his urgent glance.

Amy waited in silence on the other end of the line.

"Actually," Jenny went, "this was Charlie's idea."

"Charlie! What's he got to do with it?" Amy asked. Then, in a fonder tone, she said, "How is the cute little devil, anyhow?"

"Charlie? He's just fine. He really misses you."

"So you went on national television to ask me to call you so you could tell me that Charlie misses me?"

"Not just that. There's something else that Charlie wants you to know. Something about Sam that he found out by accident."

"Yeah?" Amy asked, her voice guarded and cold. "And what's that, Jenny?"

"It's kind of hard to believe, Amy. I know you're going to have trouble accepting it, but we really needed to let you know, anyhow."

"Why don't you try me, kid? You'd be surprised what I'd believe about Sam Wecker."

Jenny remembered how it felt as a child, standing on the high diving board at the pool, and the terrifying, heart-stopping moment when you knew you were going to jump and nothing could save you.

"Amy, Sam's not a gold digger like you thought. He's a very rich man, Amy. I mean, super-rich. Millions."

There was a long, long silence, and Jenny stared in dismay at the telephone receiver, terrified that Amy might have hung up. "Amy?" she said finally. "Amy, are you there?"

"I'm here," Amy said grimly.

"Well, say something."

"Okay, Jen. How about goodbye?"

"No! Amy, you've got to believe me! Please, just let me talk, just for a minute."

"One minute, Jenny. That's about as much of the rest of my life as I want to be wasted with Sam Wecker's lies. I mean it, Jen. Talk. You've got one minute."

So, knowing that Amy meant every word she said, Jenny began to talk rapidly, recounting what Charlie had discovered, how he checked on his findings, and how his friend in New York had verified Sam's financial status.

She finished at last and paused, out of breath, while the silence on the telephone once again stretched to unbearable lengths.

"Amy?" she said again.

"My God," Amy said in a hoarse whisper.

Jenny waited, looking over at Charlie in silent pleading.

"And Charlie really believes this is on the level?" Amy said. "*Charlie* believes this story?"

"He's right here, Amy. Do you want to talk with him?"

"No, please, Jen, don't put him on. It's okay. I couldn't . . . couldn't talk to anyone right now."

Amy's voice broke, and Jenny waited in sympathetic silence while her friend struggled to compose herself.

"Why, Jenny?" she whispered at last. "If this is really the truth, why didn't he tell me himself? Why make such a big thing about how great I was doing on the show and all the money I was going to win and how wonderful it was going to be?"

"Don't you see, Amy? It was out of love for you. He really loves you. We're absolutely convinced of that, Charlie and I. You should see him now that he thinks he's lost you again. He's just a broken man."

"I don't understand."

"Oh, Amy, look at it from his point of view. He used you, left you, hurt you terribly, lost you and then made a success of his life and found you again. And when he found you, *you* were about to become a huge success, doing something fantastic. So he . . . he didn't want to upstage you. He—"

There was a sudden harsh sound on the other end of the line, and then an abrupt click. Jenny stared at Charlie, her eyes wide and frightened. "She hung up, Charlie. She just started crying and hung up."

He returned her gaze in silence while she set the receiver carefully back in place. "Well, what do you think?" he asked finally. "Will she call him?"

"I just don't know. She's so suspicious and so terribly hurt and self-protective. And I know, of all people, how much it must have hurt to lose out like that when she was so close to winning all that money. I don't know if she can trust herself or anyone else right now or even believe any of this." Jenny gazed into the distance, brooding.

"Regardless, we have to try to put it out of our minds now. You did your best, Jen."

"Did I?" She cast him an appealing glance. "Did I handle it all right, Charlie? I felt so awkward and scared, having two people's lives in my hands like that and not really knowing what I was doing."

"You did great. You handled it just right. From now on the ball's in Amy's court. She has to think it over and make her final decision. We've done all we can do."

He crossed the room, drew Jenny into his arms and kissed her with tender thoroughness. She clung to him, her whole body thrilling at the feel of his lips, the texture of his lightly stubbled cheek, the warmth and strength and sweetness of him.

But then, remembering what she was planning to do within the next couple of hours, she pulled aside, gave him a bright, forced smile and reached for her jacket.

"Well, like you said, we can't do anything more. Let's head over to the Spaghetti Factory and order their biggest plate of meatballs. I'm starved."

"You're still sure you want to go all the way over there when you're so hungry? We could eat right here in the dining room, you know."

"I know, but I'm just really in the mood for pasta, and theirs is the best in the world."

"Okay. I can't argue with that."

He followed her out the door and down the corridor to the elevator, his eyes resting thoughtfully on her slender back.

ONCE THEY WERE at the restaurant, though, and Jenny's plate of spaghetti and meatballs was set in front of her, she was too tense and excited to have much appetite, and she had to force herself to choke down enough of her food to keep Charlie from getting suspicious.

So much of the success of her plan depended on timing and luck, and Charlie's own habits. At this particular restaurant he always ordered a double helping of the Spaghetti Factory's homemade spumoni ice cream for dessert and ate it slowly along with a rich liqueur. It was a taste delight that Jenny, too, had found wonderful after he first introduced her to it, but she had no intention of enjoying the treat today. She only prayed that he would.

"Dessert?" he asked finally, looking at the remains on her plate. "Or are you going to finish that?"

She pretended to hesitate. "I don't know. I think maybe, Charlie, I'm just nervous about tomorrow, I guess. My appetite isn't what it should be, it seems."

"We won't bother with dessert, then." He swiveled in his chair, looking for their waiter.

"No, no, you go ahead," she said, trying not to sound too eager. "I know how much you love that ice cream. I don't mind waiting."

He wavered and looked across at her. "But you'd just have to sit here, then, watching me eat. You know how I like to savor my dessert."

Jenny smiled. "I don't mind. I'll have another cup of coffee and enjoy your enjoyment."

He smiled back at her and reached across the table to touch her cheek lovingly.

"I know what I'll do," she said casually, as if she had just thought of it. "While you're eating I can just run out to a shop down the street and pick up a couple of things

and be back before you're done, so we can head straight
for the Aquarium afterward."

"What do you want to buy?"

"Oh, you know," she said, deliberately avoiding his eyes
as if she were embarrassed. "Just some . . . some sanitary
supplies that I need that I forgot to pick up earlier."

"Sure," he said, instantly considerate. "That's a good
idea. Is there a drugstore nearby?"

"I think," she said, looking into his clear blue eyes and
hating herself for her duplicity, "that we passed one just
a couple of blocks down, toward the train terminal. I can
run out, buy my stuff while you're eating dessert and be
back in just a few minutes. That way we won't have to be
late for the killer whale show."

"Okay, sweetheart," he said, and the warmth and love
in his smile made her feel even more wretched. "Hurry
back."

She returned his smile, flushing a little, gathered up her
handbag and walked quickly out of the restaurant. Once
she was safely on the street, she heaved a deep sigh of relief, looked around to get her bearings and began to run.

Her plan was simple.

She was going to find a drugstore. That much of her
story had been true. But not the one she had mentioned,
in case she took too long getting back and Charlie came in
search of her. She was heading a couple of blocks in the
other direction, hoping to find a little convenience store
where she could buy a copy of *Cycle World*. Then she
planned to curl up on a park bench, a curb, a doorway—
anywhere—and read the article on the new bikes. If she
concentrated hard, it shouldn't take her more than twenty
minutes or half an hour to memorize all the important
points and feel fully prepared for the final question.

After that she would dispose of the magazine and rush back to the restaurant, hopefully arriving soon after Charlie had finished his dessert and coffee and was just starting to get really worried. She would laugh and tell him that she'd taken a wrong turn, become disoriented and wandered several blocks through Gastown before she'd been able to find her way back to the restaurant. The kind of thing, in fact, that had happened to her often enough in the past two weeks that there was no reason he shouldn't believe her.

It could all work, she told herself, and then she'd get a chance to memorize the new specifications, and Charlie would never have to know. So far her plan was functioning perfectly, but she had to hurry.

She ran faster along the deserted, dirty streets, hardly noticing that her flight was carrying her deeper and deeper into the desolated slum area at the heart of the city, wretched and silent in the misty spring twilight. Behind these blackened windows people lived dreadful lives of poverty and violence, lives that Jenny could barely imagine.

At last she came to a gritty little convenience store and felt a flood of relief. She rushed inside, tense and breathless, and with an enormous surge of gratitude, saw that there was a copy of the bike magazine on the rack. At the last moment she remembered to pick up a box of sanitary napkins, as well, and stood restlessly at the till in the musty, untidy store, waiting with barely concealed impatience for the elderly proprietor to ring up the sale.

He paused, his fingers poised over the change in his till and stared at her through thick glasses so smeared and grimy that she could hardly see his eyes. Jenny turned away, feeling hot and awkward.

"Please," she murmured, "I'm in kind of a hurry. Could you . . . ?"

"Well, I'll be damned. You're Jennifer, from the TV show. Ain't you?"

"Yes," she whispered. "And I have to get back to—"

"Could you...could you sign this here picture for me?"

Jenny stared, amazed, at a large pulpy sheet of paper with her own face smiling back at her.

"This . . . this is me," she said stupidly.

"It sure is, Jennifer."

"Where did it come from?"

"There's a guy sellin' them all over town. Makin' a fortune. He gave me a pile of them at wholesale, an' I'm gettin' a buck each for them."

"But nobody asked me. I didn't give permission."

"He says he was in the studio audience with a telephoto lens an' caught this the other night. Hell of an idea. Guy's makin' a fortune."

Jenny shivered with distaste and outrage at the idea of someone selling her picture, but she didn't have time to make an issue of it. And besides, this elderly store owner had nothing to do with the production of them. He was just using the chance to make a little money.

Amy warned me, she thought. *Amy said things like this would be happening all the time.*

Automatically she signed her name on the picture and reached for her change.

"Could you make it say, Love, Jennifer?" the little gray man asked wistfully.

Jenny drew in her breath in, picked the pen up again and did as he asked.

Finally, in a fever of impatience, she completed the transaction and escaped from the store, running as fast as she could down the street leading away from the restaurant and looking for a place to hide and study her precious magazine.

Almost at once she found what she was searching for, an empty doorway, deeply recessed, just off the street. The building was boarded up and deserted, but there was still a forgotten entry light burning overhead, and if she crept fully into the lighted space, she would be almost invisible from the street.

She settled herself in the alcove, spread her jacket on the cool concrete and sat down, opening the magazine with trembling hands. Pictures of gleaming new motorcycles sprang out at her, and the printing swam in front of her eyes. She hesitated, breathing hard, frowning at the bright pages. Then, very slowly, she closed the magazine.

She couldn't do it.

Over everything, the bikes, the articles, the charts and graphs, she saw the image of Charlie's clear blue eyes, his warm, trusting smile, his handsome, honest face alight with laughter.

He believed in her, and she knew he loved her. And she realized she couldn't do this to him, no matter what it cost her.

Staggered by her sudden insight, by the knowledge of how much she cared for him and what he had come to mean to her, she got slowly to her feet, wandered back out onto the street and found a brimming wire trash barrel. She tossed the magazine into it, pushed it firmly down out of sight and stood for a moment longer, looking at the mountain of garbage with a brooding expression.

Then, feeling all at once strangely light and joyous, as buoyant as if she were walking on air, she turned and began to retrace her steps.

She was nearing the outer fringes of the squalid downtown slums again, just a few blocks short of the commercial district, when she glanced at her wristwatch and saw with amazement that less than fifteen minutes had passed. Charlie would still be eating his ice cream, barely even beginning to get concerned.

And she could sit down opposite him again and look directly into his dear face, feeling clean and honest, and tell him that she loved him.

She could hardly wait.

Oddly enough nothing else really seemed to matter any more, not the game show or the questions or the money. None of it. All that mattered was getting back to Charlie and kissing him and telling him how she felt. Once more she started to run, her face breaking into a joyous smile of anticipation.

In her haste she was unaware of the motorcycles until they were all around her, swirling everywhere, a mass of large, powerful bikes, filling the quiet evening with the harsh roar of their choppy V-twin engines. She realized in confusion that she was halfway across a deserted intersection, and the motorcycles surrounded her completely, enclosing her in a small, tight circle from which there was no escape.

She looked up in growing alarm at the riders on the big motorcycles. They were a frightening sight, covered with tattoos and scars, many of them wearing only skimpy black leather vests that exposed hairy naked chests. They rested on their bikes, booted feet extended, greasy hands gripping handlebars, their bearded, evil faces circling her with raucous laughter.

"Hot damn, you were right, Slash! It's really her!"

"Hey, Jennifer, give me a kiss."

"Come to Poppa, baby, you're the lady I been lookin' for all my life."

Jenny froze, her whole body gripped with numbing, sickening terror. She forced herself to stay calm and tried not to look directly into any of the hairy, grinning faces. Instead, she glanced rapidly around at the mass of bikes that encircled her, searching for an opening of some kind that she could dart through and make her escape.

Charlie, she thought frantically. *Charlie, where are you? Oh, God, Charlie, I'm so scared. I've never been so scared in my life.*

One of the riders shifted sideways to get a better look at her, and Jenny saw a small sliver of daylight beyond his body. She gathered herself together and made a dash in that direction, but the man just laughed, reached out a long, brawny arm and caught her as she passed.

She was vaguely conscious of a paralyzing fear and of a confused mixture of sensations. She smelled the rank, stale smell of the man's body, felt the painful scrapes of a chain across his vest that rubbed on her cheek, heard the harsh laughter of the men and the unmistakable sound of their massive bike engines revving.

Then she was tossed onto the back of one of the motorcycles, and they all swept away, with Jenny clinging to the side rails on the passenger seat to keep from being thrown off.

Although she was almost sick with terror, her brain worked as methodically as ever, analyzing and assessing her situation. She couldn't jump off, not at this speed. Her body would never survive the impact with the pavement. And she couldn't shout to passing cars for help, because she was being carried in the middle of the pack, where any human voice would be inaudible over the roar of the motors.

She realized, as well, that even if she could capture the attention of some bystander, nobody was likely to have much desire to get involved, not considering the size and appearance of the group that held her captive. And in the squalid neighborhood that they were entering, people weren't likely to have the slightest concern what happened to her, anyway. She was just one more lonely victim, caught up and helpless in a world of violence.

The bikes swirled around a corner, their engines pounding, roared into a grimy parking lot and pulled up under a sagging canopy behind a large, smoke-covered brick building. Jenny was lifted from the bike, pushed into the middle of the group and bundled quickly into the building and up several flights of a narrow, musty stairwell.

She was realistic enough to have some idea what awaited her and to know that she wasn't likely to escape from it alive. By now her terror was beginning to recede and be replaced by a great, aching sadness. She felt sorrow for herself, for her family and friends, for all the suffering this was going to cause.

But more than anything else she felt a deep regret that she wouldn't be seeing Charlie again, and she had never told him that she loved him.

CHAPTER THIRTEEN

CHARLIE LINGERED over the last of his ice cream, sipped his liqueur and glanced at his watch with growing uneasiness. Jenny had been gone more than twenty minutes. It shouldn't have taken that long to walk a couple of blocks, make one purchase and come right back.

But he knew any number of things could have happened. People recognized her now everywhere she went and tried to draw her into conversation, and she was too shy and polite to be rude and brush them off. And she had such a terrible sense of direction. She was entirely capable anytime of turning right instead of left and finding herself hopelessly lost within a few minutes if the area wasn't familiar to her.

At the thought of her wandering around the downtown core by herself, Charlie's fine, handsome face contracted with worry. He nodded absently at the waitress as she refilled his coffee cup and debated what to do.

If he left now and set off looking for her, she might come back any moment, miss him and panic. But if she was out there, lost and growing frightened...

He loved her so much that he could hardly bear the thought of it. He got to his feet with sudden decision, carried the bill to the front and paid it.

"Do you remember the girl who came in with me?" he asked the hostess at the till. "Dark hair in a braid, red football shirt?"

"Jennifer? Of course."

"Right," Charlie said, startled once more by how famous Jenny had become. "Well, when she comes in, could you tell her I said to wait for me here and I'll be back in a few minutes?"

"Sure thing," the girl said cheerfully.

Charlie paused, anxious and hesitant. "You're certain you'll be here the whole time? There's no chance that you'll miss her?"

"I'll be right here," the girl said wearily, "until ten o'clock tonight."

"Thanks," Charlie said, smiling at her and tipping her five more dollars.

She accepted it with a startled grin and watched his compact, athletic figure wistfully as he hurried out the door.

He started off down the street toward the train terminal and located the drugstore with no problem. But when he questioned the lone clerk at the front desk, he found that nobody of Jenny's description had been in the store that evening.

"You're absolutely positive?" Charlie asked the bored young man, who was watching rock videos on a small television set behind the counter. "It would have been just a few minutes ago. She's tall and pretty, with—"

"Look, mister," the boy interrupted, "you already told me all that. This is the most boring job in the world. If somebody who looked like *that* came in here, you think I wouldn't remember?"

"Yes," Charlie said. "I guess you would. Thanks, anyway." He started for the door and then turned. "Are there any other drugstores or convenience stores in the neighborhood?"

"Define neighborhood."

Charlie controlled his impatience with an effort. "Five-block radius," he said coldly.

"Yeah, about four. There's..." The boy's spotty face briefly puckered with concentration, and then he gave directions to several other locations.

Charlie thanked him again, stepped out into the twilit streets and pondered the situation. His mind was haunted by two equally disturbing fears. One was that Jenny had become lost and gotten into some kind of trouble, a terrifying picture. The other was that she had decided to give him the slip and betray him, after all, by sneaking away to steal some forbidden information.

He could hardly decide which thought was most upsetting to him.

On the other hand, he told himself, she could have gotten lost, just as he'd first suspected, taken a circuitous route and even now would be back at the restaurant, waiting for him. He quickened his steps and was almost running by the time he reentered the lobby.

The hostess, when she saw him, just shook her head, and he rushed out again, growing more and more alarmed.

Doggedly he began to make the rounds of the store addresses the boy had given him, inquiring at each of them if anybody answering Jenny's description had been in within the past half hour, always getting the same answer.

Finally he reached the last place, a seamy, messy store manned by a disreputable little man wearing smeared eyeglasses.

"Yeah, sure," the man said. "Must have been about half an hour ago, I guess. Jennifer, it was. The girl from *Ask Me Anything*. She was standing right where you are."

"Are you sure?" Charlie asked him urgently. "You're absolutely certain?"

"Look," the man said proudly, and held up his auto-graphed picture.

Charlie stared at it, his throat tightening with dread. "Could you," he began casually, "tell me what she bought?"

"Sure. Some sanitary napkins."

Charlie felt a great surge of relief and love and turned to go, rushing toward the door in a fever to find her.

"And," the man's voice said behind him, "a copy of *Cycle World.*"

Charlie's stomach churned, and a cold chill ran down his spine. He turned slowly to face the proprietor.

"What did you say?"

"I said she bought a copy of *Cycle World,* too."

Charlie stared for a stricken moment at the man's round, ingenuous face, half obscured by the dirty glasses and then nodded blindly and left the store.

Out in the street he blinked in the waning light and fought a ridiculous and unmanly urge to burst into tears.

Numb with pain, he remembered Jenny, warm and lovely, lying in his arms and promising not to betray him. He had loved her so much, grown to trust and adore her, actually begun to plan a life with her because she had become so dear to him. Even now, though he knew she had deliberately lied to him and used him, he longed to see her, to hold her in his arms, to hear her voice and her warm laughter, to tease her and kiss her and watch her childlike enjoyment of the pleasures of life.

"Oh, Jenny," he muttered brokenly. "Jenny, how could you do this to me?"

He wandered aimlessly down the street and sank onto the bench by a bus stop, his head in his hands, remembering images of Jenny as bright and scattered as broken bits of rainbow.

He saw her on the game show set behind her lectern, composed and lovely, and at the opera, laughing at the comic attics of the buffoon. He saw her in Stanley Park, her hair full of sunlight, watching the sidewalk artists in fascination and sharing her popcorn with a nearby child. He saw her in the little enchanted valley near her home in Calgary, her magnificent naked body gleaming in the sunlight, her eyes warm with desire. And again he heard her whispering to him, *I promise I won't betray you.*

His heart ached with longing and sorrow, but at last his mind was clear.

He understood everything now, her urgent desire to eat at the Spaghetti Factory, her insistence that he have dessert even though she didn't want any, her casual intention to "run out and pick up a few things."

This was no sudden impulse on her part. It had been carefully, deliberately planned, the whole thing, and he had been so blindly in love with her that he had been completely taken in. Now he knew, she would be hidden somewhere, devouring the current bike specifications, committing them instantly to memory. And then her plan would be to get rid of the magazine, run back to the restaurant and tell him laughingly that she'd gotten lost again and taken all this time finding her way back.

It almost worked, he thought. *If I hadn't come looking for her and found this store, I'd have believed her.*

His sorrow changed gradually to a kind of sick wretchedness and finally hardened into cold, bitter anger. He sat erect on the bench, thinking.

She'd had the magazine in her possession now for over half an hour. That was all the time it would take for her incredible, computerlike mind to catalog and memorize the facts. She had probably finished her research and was back at the restaurant by now, waiting for him, all her lies ready.

At least, he decided, he would spare himself the misery of that particular encounter, and also give *her* something to worry about. He would go back to the hotel and let her wait for him at the restaurant until she gradually realized he wasn't coming back.

In spite of his disappointment and anger he still felt a brief, anxious pang at the thought of leaving her alone in this neighborhood. But then his mouth tightened coldly.

The hell with it, he decided. *She's obviously tough enough to look after herself. She'll be safe inside the restaurant, and she's got money and credit cards. She can call a cab from there when it dawns on her that I'm not coming back, and once she gets to the hotel, I'll be waiting for her.*

Grimly he got to his feet, stuffed his hands deep into his jacket pockets and trudged back down the street to the lot where he'd left the rental car. The fading sunlight washed over the littered streets with a sad, pale glow, and a few sea gulls in the corner of the parking lot squabbled drearily over some scraps of garbage. Charlie unlocked the door of the car and got in slowly, so heavy with loneliness and misery that it was all he could do to turn the key in the ignition and drive off toward the hotel.

JENNY WAS CROWDED and pushed into a large, rectangular room, which must at one time have been the drawing room of an elegant apartment with graceful ten-foot, stamped metal ceilings and elegant scrollwork on the ornate wall moldings

Too terrified at first to look around, she concentrated on the ceilings and moldings above her head. They were the last remnants of the room's former splendor, and they probably still existed, she thought, only because they were too high up to damage. The rest of the place was unbelievably squalid, reeking of dirt and garbage and other smells less easily defined, many of them emanating from a filthy little kitchen that was visible through an archway at one side of the room. This room was presided over by a man who had been alone in the apartment when they arrived. He had a bald head encircled by a flowing fringe of long gray hair, and was so elderly that he looked incongruous in his jeans, motorcycle boots and leather vest.

The big main room was furnished with greasy couches, scarred wooden tables and chairs, a huge old television set and sagging shelves containing a frightening array of weapons, including chains, guns and knives of all descriptions, from tiny, deadly switchblades to machetes. On one wall was a huge, crude banner, reading, Satan's Warriors. Other walls held big, lurid charts, listing the names of members and adorned with the colors they had earned.

Anyone who knew anything about motorcycles also knew at least a little about bike gangs, and Jenny had a vague idea of the kind of hideous, savage feats each gang member had to perform to earn his various "colors."

She shuddered and felt herself being pushed onto a large, high-backed wooden armchair that had been dragged into the center of the room.

The men encircled her, more like a pack of slavering wolves than human beings. She closed her eyes, bracing herself for the inevitable, praying for strength and courage.

After a few moments of breathless terror, she became aware that someone was very near her, standing over her, pressing something against her.

Not a weapon, she thought in confusion. Not a knife or a gun.

The object that was being shoved now into her face seemed to crackle like paper. She tried to slow her breathing, to calm her terrified mind, to compose herself and think rationally.

Slowly she opened her eyes and saw a fierce, bearded face just a few inches away from her. Although they had all looked the same at first, she was beginning to be able to distinguish a few of the bikers. This one, she knew, was the grinning giant who had caught her when she tried to escape from the circle in the intersection and had tossed her with brutal, triumphant laughter onto the back of a motorcycle.

His eyes were a cold gray, and a purplish scar ran down his face from his left eyebrow to the corner of his mouth. He wore a greasy red bandanna wrapped around his head, and a black leather vest that hung open over his matted chest. His bare arms were huge and menacing, with biceps that rippled and bulged with every movement.

He was staring at her, his scarred face passionately intent, and continuing to shove a piece of paper at her. Along with the paper, she realized in growing bewilderment, there was a ballpoint pen and something that appeared to be a photograph.

Her mind raced. Were they going to make her write some kind of false statement to be attached to her body when they dumped it? Or a suicide note or some other cruel mockery?

He was whispering something, hissing in her ear, but she couldn't make out what he was saying. Gradually her natural instinct for self-preservation began to assert itself. She forced herself to calm her mind and concentrate on what he was saying.

"Just right here on the back, okay?" he was whispering, his battered face so close to hers that she could almost feel the scrape of his coarse beard against her cheek.

She stared up at him, uncomprehending, and he pushed the photograph at her. She braced herself to withstand whatever horror it contained and looked at it.

The image in the photograph was a little old lady, smiling and gray-haired, standing in a flowered apron among the near rows of a vegetable garden. She appeared to be clutching a hoe.

Jenny blinked in astonishment and looked up again at the savage face so close to hers.

"My grandma," he hissed. "She watches them TV shows all the time. She thinks you're great. If you could just put it on the back of this here picture . . ."

He pushed the pen and the sheet of paper at her again. The other paper, she realized, was one of the photographs of herself, identical to the ones being sold in the sleazy little convenience store and apparently others just like it all over the city.

She stared at the hulking biker and licked her dry lips. "You want an autograph?" she whispered.

He beamed, a fierce smile that split his hairy face and showed cracked, yellowed teeth.

"Yeah, for my grandma. Could you . . . d'you think you could put her name on it, too? She'd really like that."

Jenny's head spun, but she nodded dumbly. "What's your grandmother's name?"

"Gracie. Her name's Gracie."

Jenny nodded again, looked at the sweet, wrinkled face in the little snapshot and obediently began to write on the back of her own large photograph, holding it against the broad wooden chair arm to give her a firm surface. Her hands were shaking so badly that it was difficult to form the letters, but she bit her lip and persevered.

"Best wishes to Gracie from Jennifer D'Angelo," she wrote.

The circle of bikers pressed closer, with a surging, threatening rumble. The huge man crouching near her, who was clearly the leader, turned and snarled at them and they slunk back like animals, watching avidly.

The man beside her bent nearer, his breath hot on her cheek, and whispered again. "Could you put something about me on there, too?"

Jenny fought off a growing sense of nightmarish unreality. "About you? What do you mean?"

He glanced over his shoulder, scowled horribly at his filthy, grinning colleagues and then turned back to her. "My grandma," he murmured, "she's a real nice lady. An' she worries about me all the time that maybe I'm gonna get in trouble or get in with a bad group of friends. Stuff like that, you know?"

Jenny nodded and glanced involuntarily at the dirty room, the banks of weapons, the charts of evil accomplishments, the group of dangerous and violent men who surrounded her and wondered how Gracie's grandson could possibly find a worse group of friends.

"So," he continued earnestly, "if you could just put something about me on there to make her feel better, so she don't worry, you know?"

"I see," Jenny whispered. She took the pen again and began to write beneath her autograph. "Your grandson . . ." She paused and looked up at the biker. "What's your name?" she murmured. "So I can write it here," she added.

He leaned even closer until his lips were almost touching her face and his foul, nicotine-laden breath made her head swim. "It's Francis," he breathed into her ear.

"Really?" Jenny said, feeling a warm glimmer of comfort at the familiar name. "That's my father's—"

"Shh!" he hissed violently. He glanced quickly over his shoulders again, and then looked earnestly at Jenny. "Them guys, they don't know my name's Francis," he whispered. "They call me Mad Dog. I wouldn't want them guys to know my real name."

Jenny peeped out at the raucous circle of men and got his point. "Your grandson, Francis," she wrote hesitantly, "seems to be a very nice person."

He took the paper when she finished, held it in his callused, greasy hands and read it carefully, his bearded face breaking into a slow smile. "Now that's nice," he said. "That's real nice." He turned to the others. "Okay. You guys can take turns with her, but no crowdin' an' no pushin', you hear? Slash, you're next."

Jenny tensed in horror, but her sense of reality deepened as the men began to file slowly into her presence, closely and savagely supervised by Mad Dog, who remained at her elbow in scowling vigilance.

Each of them had a picture they wanted signed or a page from a bike magazine or photographs of themselves posing with their motorcycles. Some of them wanted to lean close to her with whispered questions, mostly about different bike models, sometimes about herself, and Jenny, her mind numbed with astonishment, did her best to answer them.

One man reached out a gnarled, mutilated hand with several fingers missing and tried to touch her hair. Mad Dog tensed and looked menacing, and the man hesitated, scowling. Jenny glanced up at him in alarm, but the others just shoved him aside and continued their slow procession past her chair with their endless stream of crumpled pictures and whispered questions.

All at once the place filled with tension, emanating from the far side of the room near the kitchen. Two men stood close together, glaring at each other, clearly locked in some kind of conflict. Their eyes were furious, their shoulders tense beneath their ragged vests, while the room grew suddenly quiet.

Jenny shivered at the almost palpable aura of violence that surrounded all these men, wondering what had roused the two by the kitchen to such anger. One of them, she saw, was the poor wretch who had tried to touch her hair, while the other combatant was the strange elderly man who presided over the kitchen.

Mad Dog, too, became aware of this disorderly conduct in his small empire and turned to study the action.

"Stand back," he said finally to the group who still waited by Jenny's chair. "Don't anybody go near her, less you want to get killed. I'll be right back."

He strode across the room, grasped the two antagonists by their vest collars and drew them close together for a furious but muffled three-way conference. At last he let them go, dusted his big hands on his filthy jeans and returned to Jenny's chair. "They was havin' an argument," he reported.

"Oh," Jenny said faintly.

"They was fightin' about what to serve you for, you know, refreshments. Snake, he wanted to go out an' buy some champagne an' caviar or something classy like that, an' the Old Man, he wants to make scones an' tea."

Jenny felt more and more like Alice stumbling onto the Mad Hatter's party. Craziness, she thought, was beginning to seem almost normal, and she could hardly remember a different, saner world.

"Who...what did they decide?"

"We decided that the Old Man, he runs the kitchen, so he should have the final say."

At that moment the Old Man himself appeared by her chair, his wrinkled face creased in a beatific smile, his cloud of thin white hair floating behind him. "Miss D'Angelo," he asked, "do you prefer your scones with raisins or without?"

Jenny stared at him, wondering how many more shocks her mind could absorb. His eyes glowed with bright intelligence, and his voice was cultivated and exquisitely modulated, with the unmistakable accents of an upper-class British education.

"Somerset Ellison," he said by way of introduction, extending his hand. "It is truly a pleasure to meet you, Miss D'Angelo. You are a remarkable person."

"You're, you're English?" Jenny asked.

"Quite so. As a matter of fact, I was once an instructor of comparative religions at Oxford."

Jenny looked around the squalid room and back at him, searching for words.

"I find this life-style rather more interesting than the academic milieu," he told her. "We all must make our own choices, mustn't we?"

"I suppose we must," Jenny said. "I feel like Alice," she told him, "at the tea party. Maybe this is all a dream. Or am I crazy? I can't seem to get a grip on reality."

"We seem to spend our lives, all of us," the Old Man told her gently, "trying to get a grip on reality. Perhaps *that,* in itself, is the impossible dream, don't you think?"

"Perhaps," Jenny agreed numbly.

"Now about the raisins...?"

"Oh. I guess raisins would be nice," Jenny said, and watched as he hurried away in his stained black leathers and heavy motorcycle boots back to the dirty little kitchen to prepare their tea.

While Jenny finished with her procession of admirers, feverish activity began to take place in the main room, accompanied by muffled curses, horribly violent threats and close supervision from Mad Dog.

They were clearing off all the tables in the room, tossing weapons, pornographic magazines, bike parts and chains into various corners to clear the surfaces. One table contained numerous packets of crisp bills, neatly labeled. These were handled with somewhat more respect and transferred carefully to one of the shelves.

Then the tables were hauled together in a long, continuous row and set with an assortment of cracked crockery mugs, tin cups and teacups without saucers. One cup, of fine bone china with matching saucer, exquisitely delicate and incongruous in these dreadful surroundings, was carried out and placed reverently at the head of the table.

"My grandma give me that cup," Mad Dog murmured to Jenny. "She always says tea tastes better from a nice cup, an' she give it to me one year for Christmas. She'll be proud to know you used it."

"Mad Dog, he put a guy in the hospital once just for usin' his grandma's cup without permission," Slash told Jenny in a conversational tone.

"Oh," she said again.

When the furnishings and appointments were finally arranged to the Old Man's satisfaction, Mad Dog called the party to order. Fierce conflicts erupted immediately over the seating because everybody wanted to be placed near Jenny. These men, she realized, lived so close to the edge of violence that they would fight anytime, about anything. But Mad Dog apparently had them well controlled, and the coveted seats at Jenny's end of the table were assigned arbitrarily by their leader, according to his own system of patronage.

The men filed in and sat down with much scuffling of boots and jostling of elbows. They were, however, relatively quiet and orderly, and Jenny noted in amazement that there had even been some rudimentary attempts at grooming. Hands had been washed, at least as far as the wrists, and some of the rough heads of hair had actually been slicked back with dampened combs.

Mad Dog sat at the end of the table opposite Jenny, his face still fierce and alert, watching over the long rows of men like the headmaster at a boys' school.

Gradually she began to be fully convinced that these men meant her no harm, that in fact they regarded her with an awe and reverence that bordered on worship just because of her incredible knowledge of motorcycles. Actually, she realized in astonishment, she was probably safer among this group of rough men than she would be anywhere else in the world, because they would, without hesitation or regret, kill anyone who tried to harm her.

With that realization her terrible, soul-numbing dread ebbed away, leaving her feeling limp and hollow, almost light-headed. As if in a dream, she watched the Old Man approach the table, carrying a heaping platter of scones that steamed lightly and gave off a delicious fragrance. He set the platter ceremoniously in front of Jenny, hurried back into the kitchen and returned with two teapots, one of which he set before Jenny and the other in front of Mad Dog.

"It's a rather nice Earl Grey," he murmured to Jenny, passing her on the way to his own chair and picking up his paper napkin. "I've been saving it for a special occasion."

Jenny nodded, still feeling numb and began to pour. Hands reached for scones, sugar was stirred into tea, and the milk jug was passed. A murmur of conversation began, carefully adjusted to her presence. Curses were choked off abruptly while other breaches of manners or speech were sharply disciplined by Mad Dog, by the simple expedient of leaning across the table and rapping the offender's knuckles smartly with his butter knife.

Once she realized that she was in no danger, Jenny began to relax, almost to enjoy herself. These men certainly were knowledgeable about motorcycles, and it was undeniably flattering to converse with people who hung on her every word and who discussed at length topics that weren't even within the scope of comprehension of the average person, but on which she was an expert.

A good portion of the conversation, for instance, centered on the relative merits of shaft and belt drives on bikes as opposed to chain drives, a topic on which Jenny had very decided opinions. Every time she opened her mouth to say something the table grew instantly silent, and fifteen pairs of eyes—fourteen *pairs,* she corrected herself, the fifteenth man wore a black eye patch—all turned to her in deference as she spoke.

I just can't wait, she thought in delight, *to tell Charlie about this. He's going to laugh for a week when I tell him this story.*

At the thought of Charlie her face contracted a little with concern. He was going to be so worried about her. But soon the gang would take her back to the hotel, and she'd tell him the whole story and they'd laugh about it together.

And then, she thought, smiling to herself, her face suddenly glowing with joy, she'd tell him how she bought the magazine and then threw it away, realizing that she couldn't betray him because she loved him.

She smiled again and turned to the Old Man. "These are just lovely scones, Mr. Ellison. The best I ever tasted."

"Thank you," he said. "I used to spend a great deal of time in the kitchen, watching Cook. Amazing how much I learned down there and how it has stayed with me all these years."

"The Old Man, he's a real classy guy. Lived in one of them big castles over there in England," Snake told Jenny.

"Where did you grow up?" Jenny asked Snake.

"Here an' there," he said briefly, and she didn't pursue the topic.

She became aware of a harsh, whispered discussion down at the other end of the table between Mad Dog and a group of the men near him. Finally Mad Dog made an abrupt gesture with his hand, silencing them and looked down the table.

"Jennifer," he inquired politely, as if she had just dropped in to pay a social call, "how long do you think you can stay?"

She stared at him. "Well," she said hesitantly, "I really should be getting back. My friend will be getting worried about me, and I'd like to get a lot of rest tonight because tomorrow is..."

The shaggy heads up and down the table nodded in unison. They all knew what was happening tomorrow.

Jenny was touched, thinking of this rough circle of men, sitting each evening in front of their television set, cheering her on.

"The reason I ask," Mad Dog went on, "is because some of the boys here would like to call the Devil's Disciples an' invite them over to meet you."

Jenny's stomach churned with sudden terror. She looked at the eager faces all around the table and realized what a coup it was for this group to have her right here in their clubhouse and what status it would give them among the other bike groups. But she was also aware that, with the addition of another violent group, possibly in rivalry with this one, her position would grow much less secure.

And she knew, absolutely, that she had no desire to become the center of attention at a rally of bike gangs.

"Please," she whispered, licking her lips and looking pleadingly at Mad Dog. "I don't think so. I really have to get back very soon. Right away, in fact."

"Sure thing. Let's just finish our tea and then we'll take you wherever you want."

She relaxed and ate the last crumbs of her scone, sternly forbidding herself to think about the condition of the kitchen, clearly visible from where she sat, in which this food had been prepared.

Teacups were drained, and the Old Man got up to clear the table, enlisting help from a couple of the younger members, while Mad Dog proudly showed Jenny around the clubhouse. She noticed, however, that he discreetly bypassed the labeled bundles of money stacked on the shelf.

Finally the group massed and filed out of the building, clattering down the steps once more with Jenny in their midst. This time she rode on the back of Mad Dog's bike, and he sat erect, almost quivering with pride as she mounted the passenger seat behind him.

Other bikes idled and then revved noisily, pulling out and circling in formation in the parking lot behind the shabby tenement. Even the Old Man, Jenny saw, was on a motorcycle, a strange apparition with his gray hair streaming from beneath his little leather helmet.

They formed an honor guard with Mad Dog and Jenny at the head, flanked by outriders and backed up by the rest of the group, and sailed out of the parking lot.

"Where to?" Mad Dog shouted over his shoulder, an
Jenny told him, her voice barely distinguishable over th
din of the motors.

He nodded, swerved into the street and roared off acros
town in the direction of her hotel. Jenny clung to his waist
delighting in the ride, marveling at the skill with whic
these men handled their powerful bikes. They rode in clos
formation, banking and turning in perfect unison, a pei
formance as synchronized and graceful as a motorize
ballet.

Before long they were in the elegant area of town wher
the luxury hotels were situated and where other drivers an
pedestrians watched their passage in horrified fascina
tion. They surged up under the canopy of the hotel, thei
bike motors deafening in the enclosed space. Jenny coul
see the doorman, wide-eyed with terror, ducking back int
the building to reach for the security phone.

She got off and shook Mad Dog's hand as he sat, bootee
feet extended, grinning at her.

"Thank you," Jenny said politely. "I had a lovel
time."

He beamed and leaned closer. "That was real nice," h
said, "what you wrote for my grandma. I surely do ap
preciate it."

Then, as suddenly as they had come, they were gone
sweeping out to the entry and off down the street with
howl of tires, leaving a stench of burning rubber in thei
wake.

Jenny watched them go, listening to a chorus of "Goo
Luck!" calls that drifted back on the evening breeze. Th
tightly packed group of machines rounded a corner an
vanished, and the night was still.

She turned and walked slowly into the hotel. The doo
man, still shaking with fear, stared at her wordlessly

"Hello, Max," she said pleasantly, passing him on her way into the lobby.

"Miss D'Angelo!"

"Yes, Max?"

"Are you . . . are you all right?"

"Certainly. It's a lovely evening, isn't it? It's nice to see the stars for once instead of all that rain."

He nodded dumbly and watched in stunned silence as she walked gracefully across the lobby toward the elevators.

On the way up to the suite Jenny shivered with anticipation, wondering how Charlie was going to react, thrilling at the knowledge that she was, at last, going to tell him how much she loved him.

Oh, God, I hope he's here. I hope he's not waiting down at the restaurant or out looking for me. He's going to be so worried.

She got off at her floor, ran down the hall, fumbled in her handbag for her key and unlocked the door with trembling hands. When she let herself into the foyer and hurried through to the living room, she saw with an enormous rush of gratitude that he was there, sitting in the glow of light cast by one of the lamps, reading a book.

"Charlie, thank God!" she said. "I was so afraid that you might not be here. I can't tell you how . . ."

He glanced up and looked at her quietly.

At the expression on his face Jenny's breathless voice trailed off and she watched him, puzzled, as he got to his feet and moved silently around the room, switching on the rest of the lights. Then he turned to face her.

"Charlie," she began again, "you just aren't going to believe—"

"Probably not," he said coldly. "But you can tell me your story, anyway, Jenny, for what it's worth."

She stared at him. "You're mad at me," she said "Charlie, don't be mad at me. I didn't do anything wrong I have to tell you what it was like, what happened. It's s incredible, Charlie..." Her voice faltered, and she stoo silently, looking in unhappy dismay at his remote shut tered face.

CHAPTER FOURTEEN

JENNY'S THROAT TIGHTENED, and her heart began to thud painfully in her chest. His face was so cold and angry, his body so taut and controlled. There was no relief at seeing her safely back, no joyful welcome, no warmth in his eyes.

The tender, happy feelings that had blossomed within her began to wither and die. She had felt such joy ever since she'd thrown the magazine away out of love for him and an overwhelming desire to share her emotions, to tell him how she felt and confess her love.

But there was no way to say tender things to a man who stared at her with this kind of icy distaste.

"Charlie," she whispered, "you don't understand. I know how it looks, but it wasn't that way at all. You have to let me explain."

He indicated a chair opposite him with formal politeness and waited while she sat down. Then he seated himself across from her, regarding her silently. "Okay, Jenny. How about if you tell me how it was?"

Her mind raced, wondering how much to tell him. Maybe, considering how angry he was, it would be best not to mention buying the magazine at all.

"I went out, like I told you, to buy the things I needed," she began hesitantly, unnerved by his cool, measuring stare and then began to talk rapidly, the words tumbling over one another in her eagerness to tell her story. "And then on the way back to the restaurant, this bike gang rode up, and they recognized me from the show. I guess they all watch it every day. And they sort of kidnapped me and took me away to their clubhouse, and I was so scared, Charlie. I thought they were going to kill me or, you know, but they just..." She paused, out of breath, and cast him an appealing glance.

He shook his head, his handsome face twisted in a sad, bitter smile. "Jenny, you're a smart girl. Surely you could come up with a more plausible story than that."

"It's the truth!" she said, beginning to feel a small stirring of indignation.

"I see. And what drugstore did you buy your supplies at? The one you told me you were going to?"

She looked at him cautiously, wondering suddenly how much he knew. "No."

"Why not, Jenny? Did you get lost again?"

"No," she said once more.

"So why didn't you go to that store?"

She thought rapidly, stalling for time. "You knew before you asked that I didn't go there. How did you know?"

"I knew," he said patiently, "because I was sitting at the restaurant waiting for you. When you didn't come back, I went down to the store and asked the clerk if you'd been in, and he said he hadn't seen you. So where were you, Jenny? And why did you lie to me?"

She bit her lip, looking down at her hands twisted together in her lap. "Because," she said in a low voice, "I was planning to buy a magazine and memorize the new bike lines and not tell you."

"So, did you?"

She looked at him, meeting his eyes steadily. "No," she said "I didn't."

A quick spasm of pain clouded his face, to be replaced by that same remote, withdrawn look once more. "Why not?"

"Because..." She hesitated and looked up at him with a pleading glance. "Charlie," she whispered, "you're making this awfully hard for me, you know."

"Well, it's been awfully hard for me, Jenny. Please answer my question. Why didn't you buy the magazine?"

"I decided not to because I realized that I...I cared too much about you to do that to you. I just couldn't betray you like that."

His expression didn't change, although a cold glint of disappointment and pain flared briefly once more in the depths of his blue eyes. "Jenny, quit lying to me."

"I'm not lying! It's all true! I was on my way back to the restaurant and this bike gang—"

"Forget it with the bike gang, okay, Jenny? It's just so damn ridiculous." He paused, his voice suddenly weary and drained of emotion. "I was at the convenience store, Jenny. The clerk told me you bought the magazine. He even showed me your autograph."

Jenny stared at him, fighting back tears of sorrow and humiliation. "Okay," she said. "I did buy the magazine. But I wasn't lying to you, Charlie. I just wasn't telling the complete truth, that's all. I did plan the whole thing deliberately and bought the magazine and was about to read it. I admit all that. And then, when I opened it, I couldn't do it. I realized that I..."

She paused again, longing to tell him how she had felt at that moment, of the swelling, overwhelming floods of love she had experienced that had made her unable to betray him, even in private. But she couldn't form the words, not while he was looking at her so coldly.

He got up and moved over to the telephone. His jaw was set and determined, though his steps dragged with reluctance. "What are you doing?" she asked in alarm.

"I'm calling Walker Thompson," he said tonelessly. "I have to tell him that Forbes is withdrawing its prize, and I have to tell him why."

Jenny stared at him, stunned and disbelieving. "You can't do that!"

"Why not? Because we slept together?" he asked bitterly. "Because I allowed myself to develop feelings for you that I should have kept under control?"

"No! Don't *say* that!" she shouted, feeling a sudden hot, searing outrage that swept through her body and left her shaky and weak.

"Then why not, Jenny? Tell me why I shouldn't report you and have you disqualified for cheating."

She stood up and confronted him, her face white, her eyes blazing. "Because I didn't cheat."

"Oh, for God's sake, Jenny. Let's just stop this right now, okay? No more lies. You don't know how much it hurts me to have you lie to me after the way I felt about you. Jenny, I was so—" His voice broke, and he tightened his lips, picking up the receiver of the telephone.

Her control snapped. She rushed across the room, grabbed the receiver from his hand and slammed it back into the cradle. Then she faced him, taut and quivering with fury. Her cheeks were flushed and her eyes burned.

"Look," she began in a low, tightly controlled voice, "you may be the world's most upright man, but it just so happens that you don't own a worldwide franchise on honesty, you know. Other people do tell the truth, too, just occasionally. You're not the only one. And I'm telling you the truth now. *I didn't read that magazine.* Not one word.

If you call Walker Thompson and say that I did, then *you'll* be the one telling lies."

He looked at her in silence.

"I didn't read it, Charlie," she repeated. "I didn't read it because..." She paused and then continued. "The reason I didn't, well, that's not important anymore. It seemed important at the time, but I guess it isn't any longer. The fact remains that I didn't cheat, and that's the absolute truth."

Their glances locked, blue eyes meeting dark brown in a steady, defiant challenge.

Jenny whirled, marched into her room and reappeared almost at once, carrying the hotel's Bible from her bedside stand. "See this, Charlie? It's a Bible. Hold it for me, please."

He took the book from her, continuing to stare at her in puzzled silence, and she placed her slim hand on it and looked directly at him. "I swear on this Bible and on my mother's life that I didn't read anything in that magazine or in anything else," she said. "May God strike my mother dead if I'm lying."

His eyes widened in stunned amazement while he continued to study her face. Finally, hesitantly, he handed the book back to her. Then, slowly, he turned away, walked into his own room and shut the door.

JENNY LAY in her bed hours later, gazing at the dim, moonlit shadows on the ceiling and feeling more miserable than she ever had in her life.

She had won, she realized, but it was a hollow victory. He wasn't going to report her. He was going to allow her to take the final question, and he would award her a half-million dollar check if she answered it correctly.

But he despised her for what she had done, and that was never going to change.

She bit her lip, wishing she could cry and perhaps relieve some of the agony that seemed to be wrapped around her heart, choking the life from her. But her eyes were dry and hot and no tears would come.

She twisted and rolled over in the wide bed, burying her face in the pillow, wondering what he really thought and why he had decided not to report her purchase of the magazine. Did she truly believe she was cold and greedy enough to tell a lie while swearing on her mother's life? Or had he just been sufficiently shocked by her actions to feel a small glimmer of doubt?

What was he thinking right now?

She moaned softly and rolled over onto her back to stare at the ceiling again.

She had known when she planned to buy the magazine that she was taking a terrible risk. She was fully aware of Charlie's views on trust and integrity. But their relationship had been so warm and sweet, and she had felt so serenely confident of getting away with it, of being able to read the articles, memorize them and return to him as if nothing had happened. She hadn't felt that it was cheating, not really, because everyone else was doing the same thing.

What she hadn't reckoned on was the full weight of his reaction, of the terrible depth of his hurt and betrayal. She suspected it wasn't just because she had bought the magazine. He would probably have forgiven her that, knowing the pressures she was under. His pain sprang from the fact that somewhere deep down in spite of the way he had backed off from his threat to report her, he still believed she was lying, and there was nothing she could do that would convince him otherwise. He believed she had read the magazine and was continuing to lie to him and the thought of her betrayal was more than he could bear.

Over all her disappointment and pain and anger, over all her indignation at his refusal to believe her, she felt more than anything else a dreadful, hopeless remorse for having hurt him so badly.

"Oh, Charlie," she whispered aloud in the darkness, her eyes wide with misery. "Charlie, I'm sorry. I didn't want to hurt you, darling. I love you, Charlie...I love you so much."

But there was nothing to answer her, just the muted hum of the air conditioner and the ghostly beams of moonlight playing across the walls and ceiling.

AFTER A FEW HOURS of fitful sleep, Jenny awoke in the morning and found that Charlie had left to go jogging without her. She was puzzled briefly, and then she understood.

He doesn't feel the need to supervise me anymore, she thought. *He believes I've already cheated and that he's compromised himself by not reporting it, so there's no point in watching me anymore.*

A heavy, crushing wave of pain and loneliness washed over her, threatening to drag her down into terrible depression. She fought against it and tried to busy herself with small tasks, washing her hair, trimming her nails, putting on her makeup. Finally, sadly, she began to pack her clothes, knowing that this part of her life was over and that, regardless of what happened during the afternoon on the quiz show, she would be on a plane in the early evening, flying back home, all alone.

She heard the outer door open and close while she was packing and slow footsteps approached her room. She tensed and looked around.

Charlie appeared in the open doorway, still wearing his gray sweat suit. His curly hair was damp from his run, his handsome face flushed.

Jenny looked at him and felt a rush of compassion. Normally he didn't look so worn-out after their morning jog, and she realized he must have pushed himself hard today, running at top speed to hold his unhappy thoughts at bay.

Her throat tightened and she swallowed painfully, waiting for him to speak.

"Good morning," he said politely.

"Good morning, Charlie. Did you have a nice run?"

"It was okay. Have you eaten?"

"Not yet," she said, flinching at the cool, withdrawn courtesy in his voice and manner. Nobody, listening to their conversation, would ever suspect they had laughed together, kissed passionately, lain naked in each other's arms, quivering with ecstasy.

"Well, don't wait for me, then," he said. "I'm going to have a shower and go out for a while. You might as well go down and eat now."

"All right," she said, biting her lip and turning away to hide her pain. "I'll just finish packing and then go on down and see you later."

"Sure." He hesitated, as if about to say more, and then turned aside and disappeared into his own room.

Jenny moved slowly around laying out her pink wool dress to wear that afternoon on the show and packing the remainder of her sparse wardrobe. When she was done, she left her room, looked for a moment at his closed door and then slowly left the suite and went down to the coffee shop alone for breakfast.

Not until she was seated at the table, sipping coffee and waiting for her cinnamon roll, did she fully realize how much she missed him, and how she had come to depend on the warmth and fun of his company. It was hard to believe there had been a time, not so very long ago, when she had resented his presence desperately, when she would have given anything to be free and alone like this.

Now all she could think of was the happy breakfasts they had enjoyed in this very room, joking and teasing, visiting with Estelle, the voluble mistress of the poodle Higgins, chatting with the pert little waitress and talking, talking together about everything under the sun.

Her breakfast came, and she thanked the waitress automatically, looking without appetite at the warm, fragrant sweet roll. Through the etched glass windows, far off across the lobby, she saw Charlie's familiar athletic figure, wearing casual cotton slacks and a crisp sport shirt, coming out of the elevator, and her heart leaped. But he didn't enter the coffee shop, he just passed on through the lobby and out the massive front doors into the morning sunlight.

She fought back the miserable loneliness that surged through her once again, squared her shoulders and forced herself to choke down her breakfast, taking a long time over her meal to postpone the moment when she would have to return to the silent, deserted suite.

At last she paid her bill and departed, riding up in the elevator and letting herself into the hushed stillness of their rooms. The maids had already cleaned, and Charlie, courteous as always, had left her a note, saying that he would be back in time to take her to the game show studio in the early afternoon. Jenny walked across the sitting room, switched on the TV and settled herself to pass the long hours that stretched ahead until then.

But she couldn't seem to focus on any of the daytime offerings. Her mind kept wandering aimlessly about, reliving the events of the past twenty-four hours, probing at the pain and hopelessness of her situation.

She thought in passing about Amy and wondered what had happened to her friend. It was incredible to realize that less than twenty-four hours ago she and Charlie had sat together in this room, waiting tensely for Amy to call so that they could tell her the truth about Sam. So many terrible things had happened since then that it might have been a lifetime ago. The events of the previous day, before her fateful dinner with Charlie and her aborted escape attempt, all seemed small and misty, lost in the distance and strangely unreal.

I wonder what happened to the two of them, Jenny thought. *I wonder if she called him and gave him a chance to tell his story.*

Just as she framed the thought a knock sounded on the door. Her heart thudded, and she flushed with excitement, hoping that it was Charlie coming back to talk to her, to sort things out and make everything better again.

She ran to the door, threw it open and blinked. Amy stood there, massive and beaming, bouncing with good cheer. Sam was hidden behind her, equally cheerful, the bristling ends of his mustache just visible in the dim hallway.

"So what do you think of *this* kid?" Amy asked, thrusting her pudgy hand toward Jenny.

"What?" Jenny asked, bewildered.

"This," Amy repeated, waving her hand.

Jenny studied the hand, which seemed different somehow. She pondered and realized that all the glittering rings were gone from Amy's left hand, all but one on her third finger.

"Oh!" she said, drawing her breath in suddenly.

On Amy's plump finger was a diamond so large that its blazing light seemed to fill the whole room with rainbows.

"We're engaged," Sam said proudly, coming into the room beside Amy and seating himself comfortably on the sofa. He radiated happiness, his face shining with pure joy.

"Well, congratulations," Jenny said, smiling at both of them. "I'm so glad things are working out for you. I think you both really deserve to be happy."

"You know," Amy said, her voice suddenly rough with emotion, "we owe a lot of it to you, kid. If it was all up to us, we'd probably be messing up the rest of our lives, too, just like we did the first part." She paused and looked at Jenny with warm sincerity. "Thanks, Jenny," she said softly. "Thank you so much."

Jenny blushed and smiled. "It was nothing. Just a little meddling, that's all. And, anyway, most of it was..." Her voice caught suddenly. "Most of it was Charlie's idea."

"Where is he, anyhow?" Amy asked, looking curiously around the suite. "Where is that cute little devil? I wanted to see him. I'm going to give him a big hug."

"He just...he had to go out for a minute," Jenny said, avoiding her friend's eyes. "He should be back soon."

"He left you all alone without tying you to the sofa? Isn't he afraid you'll sneak down to the lobby and do some illegal research?"

"I guess...I guess he isn't," Jenny faltered.

Amy gazed at her shrewdly. "Jen, is anything wrong?"

Jenny stared at Amy's plump, kind face and came close to breaking down. She had an almost overwhelming urge to throw herself on that soft massive bosom, tell Amy the whole story and be comforted and reassured.

But she restrained herself, knowing how selfish her impulse was. This was the happiest day of Amy's life, and it would be terrible to intrude her own grief on it and cloud Amy's joy.

So she smiled and shook her head. "I'm just a little tense about this afternoon," she said. "I'll be fine."

"Sure you will."

Amy smiled at her and then looked over at Sam sitting quietly in the opposite chair. Their eyes met and held with a look of pure love that flowed between them, as warm and palpable as a beam of sunlight. Jenny watched them, her eyes misting briefly. "So you two are engaged," she said. "When are you getting married?"

"We're already married," Sam told her cheerfully.

Jenny stared at him blankly. "You are? Since *yesterday?*"

Amy chuckled. "Since fifteen years ago," she said. "You see, I never bothered to file for divorce all those years because there was nobody else I wanted to marry, I guess."

"And I certainly didn't," Sam chimed in, "because I've never loved anyone but this girl, ever."

"So you're actually still married," Jenny said slowly, looking from one beaming face to the other.

"You bet," Amy said.

"Then why the diamond?"

"We're married," Sam said, "but we were never really engaged. I couldn't afford to buy her a ring back in those days. So I thought I'd just do it now and make twice as certain that she's really mine."

"I'm so happy for you both," Jenny said. "I really am. I think it's a wonderful story."

"So do I," Sam said softly, smiling at his bride.

Amy smiled back as starry-eyed as a young girl in love for the first time.

"What happens now?" Jenny asked.

"Well," Amy said, glancing over at Sam, "we're going to Sam's place in Toronto first, I guess. God knows, I've got nothing holding me here. But before that," she added, "we'll go over this afternoon to watch you win your million dollars. Neither of us would want to miss that. And then we'll beat it, because you and Charlie are going to want a little time alone. When does your plane leave?"

"Eight o'clock," Jenny murmured, looking down suddenly at her hands. "I have to board at seven-thirty."

Amy nodded, mistaking the cause of Jenny's sudden agitation. "Don't worry, kid," she said softly. "You'll be seeing him again soon. Charlie Mitchell isn't going to let you slip away that easily. Not if I know him and how he feels about you."

Jenny swallowed hard once again and saw with relief that Amy and Sam were getting ready to leave, announcing the need to do a great deal more shopping. She escorted them to the door, smiling bravely.

"Well, good luck, sweetie," Amy said, pausing to squeeze her hand. "We'll be there this afternoon, and we're all pulling for you, all the way."

"Thanks, Amy. That helps a lot. It really does." She leaned over, kissed Amy's plump cheek, shook Sam's hand and closed the door gratefully behind them, glad to be alone with her shaky emotions.

She thought about the game show and her final question, now only a few hours away, and realized in amazement that it didn't really matter at all. Just yesterday that question had seemed like the most important thing in the world, but today it meant nothing to her.

She had lost Charlie, and that was what mattered. Money could be earned, and if you didn't have it, you could finds ways to manage without. But the kind of love that came once in a lifetime was something so rare and

precious that if you squandered your chance, you could
never repair the damage.

All at once she understood her mother's words to her
that first morning in the hospital about the danger of getting so obsessed with her own goals that she would pay far
too great a price.

She sank into a chair, covering her face with her hands
and was still and silent for a long, long time, sitting alone
in the quiet hotel suite while the morning sunlight played
gently over the rich draperies and furnishings.

FOR THE TENTH and final time Charlie sat in the studio
audience, gazing up at Jenny as she stood under the lights
behind her podium.

The cameras weren't rolling yet, and people swarmed
everywhere, running around on the set, making last-
minute adjustments to the mikes and the lighting, shouting incoherent directions from the wings, pulling at the
contestants' clothes and touching up their hair. The studio was filled to overflowing and seething with tension,
jammed with onlookers waiting to see the beautiful dark-
haired girl make television history. Charlie was crowded
into a seat with Eric on one side, still grasping his rabbit's
foot, and Amy and Sam on the other, exuding love and
encouragement.

On the stage three other contestants stood in their places
along with Jenny, but Charlie could hardly see them. His
whole being was fixed on the pale, still face, the dark eyes
and lovely, slender body that had captivated him so much
just two weeks earlier. She was even wearing the same high-
necked pink wool dress, the one she'd worn the very first
time he ever saw her.

He shifted awkwardly in his chair, and Amy, mistaking
the cause of his unease, reached over and patted his knee

lovingly. "Don't worry, sweetie," she murmured. "The kid will come through. She'll be great."

He murmured something in return and looked hungrily back up at the woman on the stage, astounded by his own reactions.

Charlie had always been a rational, controlled, intelligent man, priding himself on his sensible and disciplined approach to life. But now he discovered to his dismay, his mind was no match for his emotions. Intellectually he knew that this woman had betrayed his trust and compromised his integrity, that he had been drawn in by her charm and beauty and fallen helplessly into a trap.

He knew that.

But the knowledge couldn't seem to change the way he felt. He didn't know if he could trust her, but he still ached for her with every fiber of his being. Even though his mind grasped and regretted what she had done, his heart and soul continued to yearn for her, and his body thrilled to the very sight of her, to the curve of her cheek and the lift of her bosom and the proud carriage of her head.

He loved her. He would love her for the rest of his life. And still, in spite of everything, he wanted more than anything in the world to walk up on that stage, gather her into his arms and kiss her, take her and carry her off with him to some sweet secret place where there was no pain, no betrayal, no anger, just the warm, rich love and happiness that they had known together.

After all, what had she done that was so terrible? She had looked at a magazine after promising not to. But she had been motivated by love for her family and a crushing sense of responsibility. Could he even be certain that under such pressure he wouldn't do the same thing?

He ached to tell her how he was feeling, to beg her forgiveness and feel close to her again. But it was impossible, he knew. For one thing his wounded pride had caused him to be so harsh and brutal to her that she was unlikely to forgive him. And the rare, sweet love and trust that had grown between them was so damaged and blighted that in spite of his customary buoyant optimism, Charlie didn't see how they could retrace their steps.

He knew she would be leaving and that he wouldn't try to hold her. He would probably just give her a polite farewell, he thought wearily, and watch her walk out of his life. Then he'd spend the rest of his days searching for a woman who could somehow compare with her.

The show began, and the people massed in the studio watched with barely controlled impatience as the formality of the preliminary round proceeded. Every time Jenny gave a correct answer they cheered wildly, all of them anxious to see her get into the final round and receive her last, momentous, million-dollar question.

Charlie sensed the charged atmosphere in the room and thought of it multiplied by thousands all across the country, where the whole continent in just a couple of hours would be watching Jenny on their TV screens and urging her on to success.

She was very pale and quiet, never once looking down into the studio audience, not even at Amy, showing no emotion whatever. But she was more brilliant than she had ever been, answering almost every question in the preliminary round, sweeping all three of the other contestants aside as if they didn't exist. In spite of himself Charlie marveled at the scope and depth of her knowledge and the incredible functioning of her brain. There was, he thought in despair, nobody in the world like her. Nobody at all.

A deafening roar of applause swept the studio audience as Jenny stood alone behind her podium, the only winner in the preliminary round, waiting through the commercial break for her final question. The room rocked with excited, barely controlled tension, and security guards were busy near the stage, trying to contain the crowds of people surging forward to get a better look.

Jenny waited in taut stillness throughout the commercial run, her face cold and expressionless, staring fixedly at the huge question board across from her.

Finally the cameras whirred once more, and one of the wheeled dollies rolled silently in to get a close-up of Jenny's face while Jay Allen strode forward and earnestly addressed the studio audience.

"Ladies and gentlemen, and all of you millions watching in your homes, this is it. Today Jennifer D'Angelo will answer the final specialty question in the field of motorcycles, and if she's correct, she'll receive five hundred and twelve thousand dollars from the producers of *Ask Me Anything,* one of the largest payouts we've ever made in our history."

He paused, gazing into the camera lens. Jenny waited silently, not looking at him, her eyes still fixed on the opposite wall, her face unreadable.

"And, in addition to that prize money, Mr. Charles Mitchell of Forbes Motorcycles is in the studio audience right now with an additional check for five hundred and twelve thousand dollars to supplement our own prize money."

The audience murmured and stirred while another camera panned the front row and picked up Charlie's face on the monitors.

"So," Jay Allen went on, "it seems very fitting that Jennifer's final question should deal with the Forbes line of motorcycles. I am about to read the question, which is, once again, in three parts. Jennifer, after I finish reading the question, you may begin to frame your answer. Because of the tremendous importance of this final question, and relative complexity of the question itself, you will be allowed sixty seconds instead of the customary thirty to give your answer. Are you ready?''

Jenny looked at him finally and nodded. "Yes, I'm ready."

"All right." He gave her a warm, sincere smile of encouragement, and she looked back at him quietly. Then he glanced down at his card and began to read. "Name the three..."

A brief, noisy scuffle broke out at one side of the room, where a few members of the audience were trampling others massed along the aisle in their eagerness to press forward for a better view.

Jay Allen paused and frowned in the direction of the small altercation, quickly being hushed by the security guards.

Dorothy, the assistant producer, rushed onto the set carrying her ever-present clipboard. "Start again, Jay," she called to the show host. "We'll edit that bit. Tape's rolling."

He nodded, waited for the cameras to catch his face once more and lifted the card. "Name the three models of Forbes motorcycles *in the current model year* that have made significant changes to their engine size or configuration and briefly describe those modifications."

Jenny looked at him, her face strained, her dark eyes enormous in the creamy oval of her face.

Charlie, in the front row, stiffened and clutched the sides of his chair. He remembered the article in the magazine she had bought, the one that he knew she had read only the previous evening. The three major changes in the Forbes bike engines had been the lead item in that article. There was absolutely no way Jenny couldn't answer this question correctly.

She had won a million dollars.

But for some reason she was taking a long time to answer. She continued to stare at Jay Allen with that same unfathomable expression on her face and a distant look in her dark eyes.

The studio audience was so hushed now that the tiny breathings and rustlings of the packed crowd were clearly audible. A sudden cough from the middle of the room sounded as loud and startling as a gunshot in the strained silence.

Finally Jenny opened her mouth to speak, her eyes still fixed on the suave show host, who watched her tensely. "I'm sorry. I don't know."

Then, in the midst of a stunned, disbelieving silence, she turned quietly and walked off the set.

CHAPTER FIFTEEN

CHARLIE SAT in the shocked stillness of the audience, hardly even breathing, staring in bewilderment at Jenny's vacant podium. His mind was a battleground of warring ideas and conflicting emotions, and he struggled rapidly to sort out his thoughts, trying to adjust himself, trying to think what to do.

Gradually he became aware that Amy was shaking his arm. He turned in confusion, focusing on her plump features. Tears ran down her cheeks, and her face was twisted with pain.

"Charlie," she whispered huskily. "Oh, Charlie, the poor kid. Go back there and find her, Charlie. She needs you."

He continued to gaze at her in blank silence. Then, all at once, a smile spread across his face and his blue eyes sparkled with pure, delighted happiness.

"She didn't know the answer, Amy," he said slowly. "She didn't know it! God, isn't that wonderful?"

He hugged the big woman, kissed her with resounding thoroughness and leaped from his chair while Amy watched him in amazement, turning to exchanged a bewildered look with Sam.

Charlie stepped forward, vaulted lightly onto the stage and strode past Jay Allen, who was delivering a sad, solemn little closing speech to the main camera.

"Stop the cameras," Charlie said to the startled crew. "And stay in position, everybody. The ending will have to be shot again."

"Mr. Mitchell," Dorothy protested, rushing forward. "Please, get off the—"

But Charlie didn't even hear her. He disappeared through the metal acoustic wings at the edge of the set and bounded up the steps to Walker Thompson's office. The producer, who was behind his desk watching the action on a bank of television monitors, turned to face the door as Charlie entered.

"Look, Mitchell," he began angrily, "I don't know what you think you're doing, but—"

Charlie stepped into the office, closing the door quietly behind him.

"Give her another question, Walker," he said. "Right now. Call her out, give her another question and film a new ending."

The producer's jaw dropped, and he stared at Charlie in genuine astonishment.

"You're crazy," he said finally.

Charlie faced the other man, his tanned, handsome face set in rigid lines, his eyes glinting dangerously. "Oh, no," he said softly. "I'm not crazy. And you're going to give her another chance."

"Why would we do that?"

"Because," Charlie said, "that wasn't a valid question."

"Look," the dapper little executive began, "do you want me to call the security guards?"

"That information wasn't released in the media until last Tuesday, the day after Jennifer's first appearance on the show," Charlie said calmly. "There's no way she could have acquired those facts without violating your own rule against studying while performing as a contestant.''

Walker Thompson stared at him for a moment, his jowly face slowly turning ashen. Then he pressed a button on his intercom and spoke into it. ''Get Myron in here, would you?''

Almost instantly, Myron Lenz opened the door and stepped into the office, and both men turned to look at him.

Myron was a graduate student at UCLA, who supplemented the costs of his seemingly endless education by heading up the research team that developed the questions for *Ask Me Anything*. He was an emotionless, scholarly type, so mechanical and robotlike, Charlie sometimes thought, that if Myron got a really short haircut, you'd be able to see the glint of wires and computer chips just under his skin.

''Myron,'' the producer began, ''Mr. Mitchell here is claiming that D'Angelo's last question wasn't valid because the information was too recent.''

''The specification sheets for the current model year have been in the hands of the dealers for almost a month,'' Myron said tonelessly.

''Jennifer D'Angelo lives in Calgary,'' Charlie said. ''In *Calgary,* gentlemen,'' he repeated, leaning over Walker Thompson's desk, his blue eyes blazing. ''And there are, as yet, no Forbes dealers west of Thunder Bay, Ontario. Even if she had written to a dealer, requesting copies of the spec sheets, it's not feasible to expect that they could have been in her possession in time for her to memorize the details before her first appearance on this show.''

''Specifications have also...'' For the first time in Charlie's memory Myron faltered a little, and then collected himself. ''They have also appeared in the major bike magazines this spring and been readily available to the public."

"That's where you're wrong, kid," Charlie said softly. "Details on those three specific models of Forbes motorcycles have appeared *only* in the current issue of *Cycle World,* which, as I said, hit the newsstands last Tuesday, the day after Jennifer's first appearance on the show."

Myron stared at Charlie, his face openly distressed behind his heavy horn-rimmed glasses. "I'm sure," he began, "that other magazines have also—"

"You can be as sure as you want to, Myron," Charlie said. "But I'm in charge of product supply to Forbes, and no specifications or information on the new product line are *ever* released to the media without my approval. Do you understand me?"

Myron nodded slowly.

"And," Charlie went on, "you can look for a month, but you won't find any press releases on these bikes except in that one issue of that particular magazine. And Jennifer—"

His voice broke suddenly, and his eyes softened, with a brief, faraway look of deep tenderness, while the other two men looked at him in surprise.

"Jennifer," he went on, composing himself again, "couldn't have read that article because she was obeying the show's injunction not to acquire new information while appearing as a contestant. In addition, I have personally spent two weeks of my time supervising her, and I can confirm," Charlie concluded, looking at them, his eyes shining with warmth and conviction, "that she hasn't broken any of the rules."

Myron glanced at Walker Thompson, who shook his head. "Sorry, Mitchell," he said. "It was a nice try, but we can always point to the fact that the spec sheets were delivered to the dealers well before the start of the show. The question will stand.''

"No, Walker,'' Charlie said gently. "I'm afraid you're wrong. You're going to do it my way.''

"And why,'' Walker Thompson asked with detached interest, "would I choose to do that?''

"You see this face, Walker?'' Charlie asked in that same gentle voice, pointing at his own clean-cut features. "Look very, very carefully at this face. Because, unless you decide to call that girl back and give her a fair question, you're going to see this face tonight on every evening news program in the country, telling the world the truth about your television show and the hypocrisy of these rules that are made but not enforced and how a contestant lost a million dollars just because she followed your rules.''

The producer stared at him, aghast. "Why would you want to do a thing like that?'' he whispered. "You company's already had all the publicity benefits, and this way you're saved the necessity of paying the prize money....''

"I'm just interested in fairness, Walker,'' Charlie said. "It seems to me that far too often in this world integrity goes unnoticed while dishonesty is rewarded. And, if I have any say in the matter, that's not going to happen here. And,'' Charlie concluded with a sudden steely edge to his voice, "it just so happens that I have quite a bit to say about this particular situation. So I'd advise you to play it fair, or you're going to suffer the consequences.''

The two men stood in tense silence, their eyes locked, while Myron fidgeted restlessly in the doorway.

Walker Thompson was the first to look away, reaching for his intercom and pressing the button. "Get Dorothy up here, please,'' he said. "We're going to have to shoot a new ending.''

JENNY SAT ALONE in the visitors' lounge, sipping her last cup of awful coffee. She noticed that people seemed reluctant to approach her, maintaining a respectful, awkward distance, as if she had been recently bereaved, and they were unsure how to express their sympathy.

She supposed that she had in fact, been bereaved: she had, after all, lost a sure quarter of a million dollars and the possibility of four times that much. But she didn't really feel the loss of the money, because it was nothing to her compared with the far greater loss she had already suffered, that of Charlie's love and respect.

She knew that these feelings of calm detachment about the prize money weren't likely to last. Probably, very soon, the full reality of what she had lost would sink in, and she would feel terrible, for herself as well as her family. But just now the money truly didn't seem to matter all that much.

She looked up when Dorothy hurried over to her, and smiled wanly. "Hi, Dorothy. I'm so glad it's all over."

"Well, it's not quite over, Jenny. That's what I came to tell you. They're giving you another question, and we're shooting the ending over again."

Jenny gazed up at her, bewildered. "But why? Why would they do that?"

Dorothy shrugged. "Don't ask me, sweetie. I just work here."

"But . . . but does that mean . . . ?"

"Jay just explained it to the studio audience. It has something to do with the timing of the particular question they asked," Dorothy said, and then grinned warmly at her. "All I know is that the top brass decided it wasn't a valid question, and I got the word from Walker to get you out there onstage for a different final question. So here we go."

Still confused, Jenny followed the bustling little assistant back out onto the stage, blinking in the lights and wincing at the sudden deafening roar of applause from the studio audience.

She felt uncomfortable and disoriented, as if she had stumbled into a place where she didn't belong and was horribly exposed and conspicuous. This feeling, she realized, was because she had been so sure that it was all over, and with great relief she had already begun to take her place in the world once again as an ordinary citizen. It seemed so strange to be thrust suddenly back into the limelight.

Trembling, she took her place behind her podium and tried to compose herself. She glanced down at her friends in the front row and caught a swift impression of Eric's face, taut and pale with tension, and Amy's broad, beaming smile and the crisp, curling ends of Sam's mustache. From the corner of her eye she saw Charlie's fine tanned features, his face quiet and austere. Her heart lurched and then stilled. She turned away and looked at Jay Allen.

"Hey, Dorothy," he called. "Do you need a new intro, or what?"

"No, we can edit the other one in," she called from the wings. "Just give us a few seconds lead-in on camera four and then read the question."

He nodded, winked at Jenny, faced the camera and held up a card. "Jennifer, this is your final question for over a million dollars in total prize money. It deals with certain design details of a particular motorcycle, and your responses must be absolutely precise. Do you understand?"

She nodded.

"The motorcycle in question," he went on, "is the 1981 Yamaha XV920." He cast Jenny a quick, questioning glance, and she nodded quietly once again. "For that specific motorcycle," Jay Allen said, "we want you to give us the statistics on engine bore and stroke, and on horsepower."

Jenny continued to gaze at him with that same serene feeling of detached calm, almost smiling at the ludicrous difficulty of the question. It was unlikely, she thought, that anybody, anywhere in North America, could answer that question from memory.

Carefully avoiding the familiar faces in the front row, she allowed her gaze to drift out over the audience over the sea of hushed, expectant faces, the hundreds of eyes fixed avidly upon her, while her mind ran through masses of complex bike specifications.

"Jennifer?" Jay Allen urged her anxiously. "Your time's almost up."

She turned to face him and began to speak, her expression still faraway, almost dreamy. "The bore and stroke on the 1981 Yamaha XV920," she said, "was 92 by 69.2 millimeters. The horsepower it delivered was 67.0 at 7,000 rpms."

His mouth dropped open, and he glanced down once more at the card in his hand and then back at her. Slowly he turned to face the camera and the studio audience.

"That," he said in a voice hushed and choked with uncharacteristic emotion, "is absolutely...*correct!* And Jennifer D'Angelo has just won over *one million dollars!*"

Bedlam broke out in the studio audience, sustained and uncontrolled. The big amphitheater rocked with noise, hundreds of flashbulbs popped, and the crowd surged forward. A few people tried to leap onto the stage and had to be restrained by the security guards and members of the production crew.

Jenny stood quietly through it all, dazed and disbelieving. In her mind she was still back in the lounge, drinking her coffee, alone with her defeat, and this sudden turnaround was too rapid and incredible for her to encompass.

She tried to smile as Walker Thompson presented her with a check and murmured something indistinguishable over the roar of the crowd.

"Okay," she heard Dorothy shout above the uproar. "Now the Forbes check! Get Charlie up here! This is running so damn long that I guess we'll just have to edit out some of the earlier bits to make time for the presentations."

Then Charlie was in front of her onstage, holding out a check, shaking her hand. Jenny trembled and felt almost faint, here in front of these hundreds of staring faces, at the feeling of his lean brown hand as it pressed hers warmly. She knew his eyes were fixed on her, but she couldn't bring herself to look up at him. It was all she could do, in fact, to keep from breaking down completely.

Just the touch of his hand was almost more than she could bear.

At last, mercifully, the theme music sounded, the closing credits began to roll up on the monitors, and the audience, still wildly excited, settled into a dull roar of applause.

"Mr. Mitchell," Walker Thompson said to Charlie, "could you come up to my office for a moment, please? Your managing director has advised me that he intended—in the event Jennifer correctly answered her final question—to set up a tentative schedule of television commercials using footage from *Ask Me Anything,* and we need to look into the matter of residuals."

"All right," Charlie said in a distracted voice. "Okay. I'll be up there in—could you just give me a second, please? I want to—"

But when he turned, Jenny was already gone, escaping gratefully to the relative quiet of the wings and the back-stage lounge.

Once she was there she gathered her scattered faculties and began to think rapidly. What she wanted more than anything was to avoid another encounter with Charlie. Being near him was just too painful, and she couldn't bear to see him for a last time or say goodbye to him or ex-change some awkward, strained pleasantries after his ter-rible anger of the past day. She just wanted to leave it like this with no farewells or discussions, because she knew absolutely that she couldn't endure any more emotion.

He'll be in Walker's office for at least half an hour, she thought. *And my things are all packed. I just have to change, grab my suitcase and I can leave.*

If she found a ride right away and rushed over to the hotel, she could pick up her belongings and head straight for the airport. She wouldn't have to board for several hours, but she could have a meal at the terminal and fill in her time there, and it would spare her the agony of having to see Charlie again, would spare her looking into those deep blue eyes, so full of anger and hurt, so certain that she had betrayed him and mocked his love and trust.

She moaned silently, took her coat from the rack and shook off the group of well-wishers and media people who crowded around her.

"Please," she murmured, "I don't feel well. I just need a little time to myself. I'll talk to all of you later."

Escorted by one of the brawny young cameramen, she rushed out through the back of the studio and into a wait-ing limousine. Safely inside, she leaned back against the rich leather seat, eyes closed, exhaling a great sigh of relief and luxuriating in the peace and silence.

When finally she opened her eyes, she met the gaze of the driver in the rearview mirror. He was an older man, with gray hair and a blunt, strong face, and his eyes looked into hers with steady compassion. He seemed vaguely familiar, and she realized at last that he was the same driver who had met her at the airport the very first day she had arrived in Vancouver before her appearance on *Ask Me Anything,* the one who had driven her to her hotel.

That day seemed like a century ago.

"Congratulations, Miss D'Angelo," he said quietly. "You did a wonderful job."

"Thank you," she murmured, smiling automatically.

His gentle kindness was almost too much for her overwrought emotions, and she looked away quickly, gazing out the side window at the rain-washed streets and biting her lip.

When they reached the hotel, she asked him to wait, then ran through the lobby, standing in a fever of impatience as the elevator descended and slowly climbed again. Finally, up in the silent suite of rooms, she looked around one last time, her heart aching, thinking of all that she and Charlie had enjoyed here, the silly games and the long, serious talks, the squabbles and teasing and the hours of deep, deep tenderness and passion.

Her throat tightened, and she set her jaw with sudden resolution. In her room she tore off the pink wool dress and hurried into a pair of jeans and a soft white fleece top, pulling on socks and sneakers.

Then she packed the last of her things away, made a final check of the bedroom and the two bathrooms to be sure she hadn't left anything behind and returned to her own room to fasten the straps on her suitcase.

"What's this?" a voice said in the doorway. "Leaving without saying goodbye?"

She whirled, her heart hammering painfully in her chest.

Charlie stood there, drops of rain glittering on his shoulders and in his hair, his eyes intensely blue. His face was controlled and calm, with a strange, unreadable expression.

"I...I guess so," she murmured. After that first glance, she couldn't bear to look at him, and she dropped her gaze, avoiding his eyes. "I don't like goodbyes," she finished lamely, her cheeks flaming.

"Jenny, look at me."

She forced herself finally to look up at him, meeting his steady gaze in silence. The planes of his sculpted face gleamed in the dim half-light of the rainy afternoon, and he had never looked so handsome. She loved him so much that the sight of him was almost more than she could bear, but she kept her eyes fixed on him bravely, longing for this moment to be over so that she could make her escape.

"Jenny, you weren't lying to me, after all. You really didn't read the magazine."

Her lips parted in wonder, and her eyes widened. She stared at him in stunned astonishment. "How did you know? What changed your mind?"

"Oh, sweetheart..." A spasm of pain crossed his face, and he struggled to compose himself. "Jenny, the details on the new Forbes bikes were the lead item in that article in *Cycle World*. There's no way with your memory that you couldn't have answered that first question if you'd actually read the magazine."

"No, I didn't read it, Charlie. I told you I didn't, and it was the truth."

He clenched his hands into fists, fighting for control, gazing at her with such intensity that his eyes seemed to be burning. "Then why did it take you so long to get back here last night, Jenny? What were you really doing all that time?"

"I told you. A bike gang came along when I was on my way back to the restaurant, and they—"

"Jenny!" he interrupted her, his face a mask of horror. "You mean that actually happened? You were really kidnapped by a motorcycle gang?"

She nodded. "They were a group of Satan's Warriors. And they took me to their clubhouse."

He made a strangled sound and moved slowly across the room toward her. His face was white beneath his tan, his eyes dark with emotion.

"Sweetheart," he whispered, "I'm so sorry. I was such an arrogant, overbearing idiot, all because I was so terribly hurt when I thought that you . . ." He shook his head, trying to find his voice.

She watched him in silence, waiting for him to continue.

"Never mind that," he said finally. "I didn't believe you, but now I can see that you're telling the truth. Oh, Jen, darling, I can't stand the thought of . . ."

He hesitated, standing close to her, and struggled once more to collect himself while she went on looking at him quietly. "Did they? They didn't . . . ?"

"No," she said with a little half smile. "They didn't. I was so scared at first, Charlie, I thought I was going to die, I mean literally, and it was such an awful place, just horrible." Her words tumbled over each other, and she drew a deep breath to compose herself. "But they just wanted my autograph and stuff. They acted as if I were a goddess or visiting royalty or something because my specialty field was motorcycles. They served me tea."

"Tea!" he interrupted, staring at her in amazement.

She nodded. "And scones. With raisins," she added.

His eyes crinkled briefly. "My God. No wonder I didn't believe you, Jenny. You have to admit that you *do* strain a man's credulity sometimes."

She felt such joy that she could hardly contain herself. The situation was difficult for her weary mind to grasp all at once, but she knew he was telling her he believed her, and he was smiling at her again, and she could hear the warmth in his voice. Seeing his tender smile, after the coldness he had shown earlier, made her body surge all at once with overwhelming love and happiness, and she looked away in confusion.

"Later, Jenny," he went on, "you can tell about tea and scones with the Satan's Warriors. Right now I want to know why you didn't read the magazine. I know that you bought it and that you didn't read it, but I need you to tell me why."

She looked up at him, meeting his eyes steadily, all her emotions under control at last.

"Because I love you."

He gazed at her in intent silence.

"I had the magazine right in my hand, and I knew that I had all kinds of time to get it memorized and get back to you without making you suspicious. But then I realized that I couldn't do it. I'd promised you I wouldn't, and you trusted me, and I loved you too much to betray you and—" Her voice broke.

"Oh, my darling," he said. "My sweet darling. I love you, too. I love you so much."

He gathered her tenderly into his arms, kissing her eyelids, her cheeks, her lips and throat, murmuring husky, broken endearments.

Jenny gave herself up to the joy of his touch, hungering for more, glorying in the kisses and the warmth that meant the whole world to her.

But he drew away finally and looked at her. "Jen, you never would let me talk about the future. But I think now it's time we did."

She hesitated and then remembered something. "Charlie, the limousine. The driver's waiting downstairs."

"No, he isn't. I sent him away when I got here. Jenny, we have to talk about what happens next."

She shook her head, her eyes clouding with pain. "I don't want to."

"Why not?"

"Because next," she said, "I'm getting on a plane to Calgary, and you're going back to Chicago, and I can't stand it."

He grinned, with a little of his old teasing sparkle. "Not even now that you're a millionaire? You still feel some interest in having me around, even though you have all that money?"

She looked up at him, her eyes level and serious. "It doesn't make the slightest difference, Charlie," she said. "When I thought I'd lost everything, after the first question, you know?"

She cast him a brief, inquiring glance, and he nodded.

"Well, I was sitting back in the lounge, all by myself, drinking a cup of coffee, and I realized that it didn't really matter at all. All that mattered was that I'd lost you, not the money. And after they gave me the second question and I won, I still felt exactly the same."

He thought this over and smiled at her. "Well, I'm not that easy to lose, Jenny. Not when I'm so much in love that I can hardly stand it. And I may not be a millionaire, like you, but I'm still a pretty good catch, you know. I just got a promotion."

She looked at him in surprise. "A promotion? Really?"

He nodded, his face solemn, his eyes sparkling. "I've been talking to my boss about it for the past week on the phone. I've been offered the position of junior vice president in charge of Canadian operations."

She stared at him, still confused, trying to understand what he was saying.

"It's a really good job," Charlie said. "And the office will be located in Calgary. They want to penetrate the western market, and they feel that the eastern Canadian market can be serviced well enough from Chicago."

"Calgary!" she exclaimed, gazing at him, her dark eyes enormous.

He nodded. "I'll be able to see Irena out working in her garden in the fall and play with Sheila's baby and help Steve perfect the design on that bike engine and get Frank to teach me to make wine from flowers."

He sobered, looking down at her with an intent, serious expression while she stared back at him, speechless with wonder. "If that's okay with you, Jenny," he said softly. "Do you want me in your world, part of your family, for the rest of your life?"

"Oh, Charlie . . ." She burrowed into his arms, kissing him with rapturous delight.

"Jenny . . . ?" he whispered.

"Hmm?"

"Jen, why are you leaving so early? Your plane doesn't lift off for hours yet."

"I know. I just didn't want to have to see you again when I thought you were so mad at me."

"Don't go yet, Jenny. We have to go out for a nice meal and order champagne to celebrate your victory. At least let me have these last few hours to spend with you and try to make it up to you for being such a fool."

She looked up and smiled tenderly, covering his lips with her fingers. "Don't say that, Charlie," she whispered. "I love you."

"Oh, Jenny, sweetheart." He kissed her with rising passion and then hesitated.

"What, Charlie?" she murmured against his chest, smiling to herself.

"I want so much to... God, darling, after the way I've behaved, I don't even know if I have the right to ask."

He was holding her tightly, his taut, muscular body straining against hers, and she could hardly be unaware of what it was that he wanted.

She smiled again and leaned back in his arms to look at him. "Charlie..." she whispered.

"Yes, sweetheart?" He gazed down at her and caught his breath. Her lovely face glowed with warmth and desire, and her dark eyes were shining.

"Charlie, don't you know by now that you can ask me anything?"

THIS JULY, HARLEQUIN OFFERS YOU THE PERFECT SUMMER READ!

**EMMA DARCY
EMMA GOLDRICK
PENNY JORDAN
CAROLE MORTIMER**

From top authors of Harlequin Presents comes
HARLEQUIN SUNSATIONAL, a four-stories-in-one
book with 768 pages of romantic reading.

Written by such prolific Harlequin authors as Emma Darcy,
Emma Goldrick, Penny Jordan and Carole Mortimer,
HARLEQUIN SUNSATIONAL is the perfect summer
companion to take along to the beach, cottage, on your
dream destination or just for reading at home in the warm
sunshine!

Don't miss this unique reading opportunity.

Available wherever Harlequin books are sold.

HARLEQUIN

Romance

**This June, travel to Turkey
with Harlequin Romance's**

**THE JEWELS OF HELEN
by Jane Donnelly**

She was a spoiled brat who liked her own way.

Eight years ago Max Torba thought Anni was self-centered—
and that she didn't care if her demands made life impossible
for those who loved her.

Now, meeting again at Max's home in Turkey, it was clear he
still held the same opinion, no matter how hard she tried to
make a good impression. "You haven't changed much, have
you?" he said. "You still don't give a damn for the trouble you
cause."

But did Max's opinion really matter? After all, Anni had no
intention of adding herself to his admiring band of female
followers....

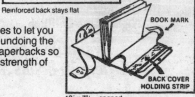